Katie Kincaid Lieutenant

By Andrew van Aardvark

Katie Kincaid Lieutenant

Author: Andrew van Aardvark

Editor: Margaret Ball

Copyright © 2021, 2022 NapoleonSims Publishing

www.NapoleonSims.com/publishing

Cover image copyrights:

Space Station: Illustration 77255756 © 3000ad | Dreamstime.com

Space Ship: Illustration 39388070 © Algol | Dreamstime.com

Mars: Illustration 112951438 © Ivanmollov | Dreamstime.com

Figure created From LaFemme model in Poser | www.posersoftware.com

Red hair: Photo 93331466 / Female © Mykola Kravchenko | Dreamstime.com

Space ship interior: 127380755 @ SDecoret | Dreamstime.com

Starry background: © Brandon Siu | Unsplash.com

All rights reserved.

Paperback   ISBN: 979-8-49256-492-6

Hardcover   ISBN: 979-8-49256-694-4

Table of Contents

1: LTSG Kincaid's Night Out	1
2: LTSG Kincaid Takes a Trip	21
3: LTSG Kincaid is XO	37
4: A Rocky Start, Kincaid	63
5: Settle In, Kincaid	77
6: Do Your Job, Kincaid	93
7: A Warm Reception for Katie	107
8: A Pause for Katie to Think	121
9: A Chance for Katie to Help Some	135
10: Katie On Patrol	153
11: Katie Does E-mail	165
12: Katie Never Quits	177
13: Katie Commits	189
14: Katie Fights	199
15: Katie Cleans Up	213
River Class Corvette Fact Sheet	223

Prologue

So, dear, deeply encrypted diary, my old friend, my tim[e] on the *Susquehanna* was probably the happiest of my life.

It was a revelation. It's amazing how good it is to be pa[rt] of a group of people who trust each other. People who n[ot] only trust each other, but are competent. People who agree o[n] their goals and the means to achieve them.

She was a happy ship. I have never seen a happier on[e.] My time on her probably kept me from becoming a bitter an[d] cynical old woman.

The *Susquehanna* was an existence proof for me.

My time on her was educational as well as pleasant.

Sadly, that time was cut short.

I was promoted prematurely to the XO's slot on the Humber.

The Humber, another river class corvette, was a siste[r] ship to the Susquehanna. That aside, she was entirel[y] different. She was a learning experience of an entirel[y] different sort.

I didn't know anyone on the Humber. Her reputation wa[s] mixed, and I didn't know who to trust. I wanted to trus[t] everyone, but found them distant, disengaged, and no[t] interested in indulging young hotshots who wanted to chang[e] things they were perfectly happy with.

Didn't help that I took an immediate and visceral dislike t[o] my bosun. Frankly, without any objective justification at firs[t.]

It's a long story.

It follows below.

I hope you find it educational.

Maybe you'll even find it amusing and inspiring as storie[s] of other people's troubles overcome can be.

1: LTSG Kincaid's Night Out

The evening was old. The air was stale. It was slightly oppressive, smelling faintly of bodies and beer. The earlier din of too many people in too small a space had died down. The party had broken down into small groups of individuals murmuring to each other. The conversations were desultory, though young Lieutenant Creighton seemed to be having a fairly intense one with the even younger Ensign Lee. The entire crew had been wondering when James and Lillian would finally act on their obvious attraction to each other.

Katie's feelings were mixed. Her head was fuzzy. Her mouth felt muzzy. More like she'd been chewing on too much cloth or eaten too many crackers than she'd had too much beer.

Katie lightly rubbed the dark wood of the table in front of her. It had a distinct, worn grain. It was slightly sticky, with decades of spilled drinks at a minimum. Large slabs of old wood filling utilitarian purposes weren't something you saw much of out in the Belt, but this was old Mother Earth herself. There were places like this where you found things like this big old table.

The party had been for Katie. Still was she guessed. A double-barreled party. It was her birthday (her 23rd), and she'd just been promoted both. Lieutenant (Senior Grade) Katie Kincaid, that was her. Young for the rank and on the fast track, apparently.

Katie looked around the dark, dimly lit and still crowded room. People had started to make their excuses and slip off, but not many yet. What lighting there was, was yellowish and flickering and limited in its reach. Not candle light, they weren't that old-fashioned here, but a good simulation of it.

Katie would have said it was the faux British pub you found throughout human space only given their location this place might really have been here for a thousand years or more and not have looked too different on its first night of operation. Also, they were in Ireland and the locals would have likely not appreciated being mistaken for English or Scots or even Welsh.

Katie had been studying up on the tribes of Earth. Her life was becoming increasingly political. She had no doubt the trend would continue.

Katie looked around at her crew mates. They were, all of them, off of the SFS *Susquehanna*. A Space Force corvette assigned to the Earth station and the finest ship in the fleet. Just ask any of them. The *Susquehanna* had superb morale. They were a happy lot.

Content now after a long evening of good food, good drink and better company. Faces flushed, still animated mostly, but slowing down now. More of them slumping back to just relax a little before finally accepting the night might be done. Many of them had gone off to the heads to deal with the inevitable results of a little bit too much drink.

Katie had been with them barely two years and she knew they were just as happy on duty if nowhere near so relaxed. They were sharp when on duty. They were a good crew.

Better than most. Just how that had come about was still something of a mystery to Katie, and the stars above knew she'd been trying hard to crack that puzzle. Just how the captain and XO of the *Susquehanna*, along with the rest of their senior officers, had managed to bring that about was a matter of some immediate concern to her.

Because, once again, Katie had a choice to make. A potential task that she might not be up to.

She reflected on that. Choices were a good thing, right? Katie snorted. Took a small sip of her remaining beer. Three-quarters gone, it was. It was Kronenbourg, a light French-German beer with quite a history. Perhaps a Guinness would have suited the setting better, but the XO had thought that the lighter beer would be more to Katie's taste for what had been a predictably long evening. Katie was usually a wine drinker when she drank at all. A single glass of red wine, a Cotes de Bordeaux usually, with the occasional special meal, was her normal speed.

Perhaps that was part of the secret behind the XO's success. He wasn't too familiar with his charges. He was always careful to be entirely proper. Kept a certain cool distance if truth be told. But he did pay attention to his people. He made it clear in all sorts of ways, many of them admittedly small, that he cared about them. That he could be counted on to be conscientious in seeing to their welfare.

Katie had mixed feelings.

Katie had grown up an only child with busy parents. She was by nature a loner with her own interests and agenda. She was not naturally a people person.

It might be her job to be more like the XO. It was definitely on her current agenda. It was not at all something that came easily to her.

"You're supposed to be pie-faced happy, not sunk pensively into hard thought," came a voice. That of the XO himself.

"Sorry, sir."

"For tonight, call me Jerry," that worthy said, sitting himself down next to Katie and turning his chair a quarter to face her. "It's a big choice we've dumped on you, I know. It's irregular, but losing officers before their term is up and having to replace them on short notice is not normal and has SFHQ scrambling. The Martian Queen departs in less than two days. We don't have any couriers to spare and the optics would be bad anyhow. We need a body to send to her. We don't have a lot that are suitable. No offense, but you are very junior for an XO's slot. If SFHQ Personnel didn't need to know pronto if you, me, and the captain think you're up to it, I would have held off telling you about it. Hate to spoil this for you."

"Yes." Katie had to stop and force herself not to say "sir". "Jerry," she said. "I've been happy on the Hanna. I wouldn't have expected to have been asked about my next posting for a couple of years yet, anyways. Just starting to get a good handle on being Weapons Officer. Yeah, this is pretty unexpected, and I wasn't prepared for it. Caught me on the wrong foot, sir."

The XO nodded. "And the Humber being out on the Mars station, you can't even ask around quietly to see what you'll be getting into."

"She's been out there by herself for years now, and she's gone through Executive Officers rather quickly, hasn't she?"

Jerry frowned. "And been entirely without for long periods because of the time it takes to get replacements out there, too. captain and crew seemed to have managed despite that. We've no reason to believe there's anything wrong. Most likely it's just a run of bad luck. It's not perfect, but this is an incredible opportunity for you, Katie."

"And you know I'm ambitious."

"It's no secret," the XO said. "In fact, likely part of the reason SFHQ is offering it to you is that they think you'll take it because of that. Fact is not only are most other possible candidates older, they're settling into life here in the vicinity of Earth and not likely to be eager to drop everything to go off to the Mars Station for several years."

"Bit of a problem, isn't it?"

"It is, but an opportunity for you."

"I wonder about what happened to Lieutenant van Eych."

"He was mugged after a late night out on Mars Station. He was in a bad part of the place for some reason."

"That's what the police said."

"Yes, and true as far as it goes. Look, fact is Katie, is that if there was foul play, they don't dare be too obvious again, and, though you don't look it, you're tougher than Dirk ever was."

"You knew him?"

"A friend, not a close one, but a friend. A real nice guy, but more a go along to get along sort. Not at all a hard case."

"And I'm a hard case?"

"Katie, when the going gets tough, you're the hardest case around. I make a point of checking out the background of all my reports. Tried not to be obvious about it, but I've been watching you. You're not hard-nosed for its own sake, and you seemed to have learned some circumspection. Also, nobody expects a rather pretty young woman who's only medium sized to be a tough guy. But in any fight, or just a tough place, I'm placing my bets on you."

Katie blinked. "Ah, thank you, sir."

"Jerry," the XO sighed. "We both know it's not entirely a good thing. You do what's needed. But there's always a cost, isn't there?"

Katie smiled sadly and nodded. Heavens, she was maudlin tonight. Even not at full speed, she'd thought she had better control than this. The XO wasn't wrong, though. "God's own truth, sir."

The XO smiled. It wasn't a pretty smile for all the sympathy it held. "So, it's not just about your feelings or what's best for you and your career. I think you're the best person for this job. I think it's your duty to take it."

Katie surveyed the room and all her happy shipmates. She felt a twinge of jealousy. "Yes, sir."

"Anyhow, I'm hoping you'll say yes. I'll see you at 1145 hours in my office. I'll need your decision then. Right now, I'm done for the evening. I suggest you finish up soon too." With that, the XO got up, gave her shoulder a clasp, and left the room.

Katie finished her beer, and saying a few goodbyes on the way, did the same.

***

Katie wasn't woken by the alarm she'd set. Set because she'd known she was a few sheets to the wind and could only afford a few hours of rest before having to wake up and go to breakfast. Breakfast with friends not off of the *Susquehanna*.

Katie was woken by one of those friends. Her boyfriend, in fact, Lars, Lars Thorson. He gently shook her by the shoulder until she came to from a dreamless sleep.

Her head stuffy. Her mouth dryly full of fur, it seemed. Her muscles and bones all aching. Katie could have felt much worse. She knew that. She mightn't be much of a drinker, but she had been to these social events before and tried to match the more experienced partiers out of misguided politeness, and paid the price for it. All the same, she'd have liked to have rolled over and gone back to sleep.

"Katie, Katie, you need to wake up," Lars was softly saying.

"Aren't you in Sweden, Lars?"

"No. I took the red eye from Stockholm."

"Just a minute. Water?"

Lars went for water while Katie lay there trying to gather her wits. She was in a dim room, kitted out in faux Victorian. Fancy furniture made of dark wood and wallpaper with floral designs. It all had a faintly musty smell, but the air was nevertheless fresh, slightly moist and cool. It smelled like no spaceship that had ever existed. Like no contained environment in space ever did. It was disconcerting and thrilling all at once to be on Mother Earth. Katie doubted she'd ever get completely used to it. If four years at the Academy, and regular trips down the last few, hadn't done it, likely it wasn't going to happen. She wondered what Mars would smell like.

Formally, she hadn't decided yet to go to Mars, but she knew which way she was leaning. Lars wasn't going to like it. Katie pulled herself up to a sitting position. She pulled he sheets and blankets up to keep warm. Part of them were cool, part of them were warm from her lying in them, they all had a high thread count she could feel with her hands. Natural fibers, she guessed, nothing like the synthetics she'd grown up with.

Katie wondered if she could have, maybe, in an alternative time line, been an historian studying the different ways different classes slept throughout history. "And feather-beds were a 16th century innovation in England", she could hear herself lecturing. It would have been as interesting and less awkward than being a Space Force officer. She could have settled down with someone like Lars easily, if she'd been such a person.

"Here you are," Lars said, looming over her. Gangly with a shock of blond hair. Bright blue eyes she'd grown altogether too fond of.

"Thanks," she said, taking the glass of water he was offering her. She sipped. It was cool and flat. It felt very good indeed. "I didn't expect to see you here. I didn't give you much notice."

"That's true, but you could be gone tomorrow, couldn't you?"

Katie nodded, took a sip of water, and didn't look at him. "We knew something like this could happen. I warned you when we first got together."

"Neither of us wanted to make a permanent commitment then. Only I did think we'd have at least another year or two."

"Me too." Katie looked directly at Lars. Handed him the now empty glass. "I've become more than just fond of you too, Lars." Katie swung herself out of bed and went to look out the window. The ever so cute and historic street of the market town they were in was empty in the dim but brightening morning light. An idyllic scene that did not match Katie's mood.

Behind her, Lars spoke. "We fit together. We're a good team. We complement each other. You're a visionary, but I'm good at knowing how to get things done. And, Katie, I've come to love you."

Katie shook her head and continued to look out the window. Her eyes stung. The heavens knew it was nice to be doted upon. Nice to not always have to be taking care of oneself, because there was someone who could be counted on to be thinking of you without expecting anything obvious in immediate return. Could be she'd taken unfair advantage of Lars. Only as much as she liked him, as affectionate as she felt towards him, she did not love him. And even if she had, it would not have changed what she considered her duty to be. "I won't say it hurts me as much as it does you, Lars. It does hurt. I am fond of you. I do regret it, but the Space Force is more than just a career to me."

"You've got to balance your life and your work or you're likely to burn out. Even if you don't, you won't be young forever. Do you want to be old and have nothing to show for it except for some ships' crests and a certificate of appreciation for good service to hang on the wall? Your grandmother, the Admiral, might be famous, but is she really happy?"

Katie shook her head. She turned to look at Lars. It was hard to believe you could be so close to someone and still misunderstand them so thoroughly. "My life is my work and I'm not doing it to be happy," she said.

Lars stared back at her as if he couldn't quite believe what she was saying.

Katie busied herself dressing. Very efficiently. Years of drills, knowing seconds could mean life or death, saw to that. "Haven't made my mind up quite yet," she said as she pulled a top on and started to quickly pack. Katie was always organized to be able to move on in minimal time and with minimal fuss. "But that's not going to change. Let's get down to breakfast, and we can talk about it some more on the way out to the spaceport. Okay?"

"Okay," Lars said.

Katie knew by the flat way he said it that things were never going to be the same between them again. "Let's go," she said. Katie had other friends. Ones she'd not given much warning to that either. Ones she had to say goodbye to in the little time she had remaining.

Together, they left.

* * *

Pat was grinning. Pat, Master Chief Petty Officer Patrick Joseph O'Conal the Humber's bosun was always grinning, or at least smiling. It was his vocation to work with people, getting them organized to achieve the results he desired, and to that end, he employed both carrot and stick. He preferred to make the carrot the more visible part of the incentives he provided. Also, a spoonful of sugar helps the medicine go down as the old children's song went.

So no matter what, Pat was always grinning or at least smiling.

Another thing Pat made a point of was staying well informed. Better informed than any of the other actors in his sphere. His sphere being not just the Humber itself, but Mars Station and various useful contacts down on the surface of the planet itself. Also, the Space Force in general. To that end, he had made a point of cultivating the Humber's lead communicator, Petty Officer Adnan Awad. He had his hooks deep into him. And so, Awad didn't just keep him informed on what messages came and went from the Humber, he made a point of monitoring all the traffic the Humber's quite advanced communications suite could manage to overhear.

Awad quite legitimately had the keys to decrypt most of that traffic, too. In fact, he even had the keys to some encryptions that he technically shouldn't have had, such as those for messages that passed between SFHQ and the marine detachment on the local Mars Station.

"So, we're getting a new XO," Pat said, leaning over Awad in the tiny comms room. Security being an issue, it wasn designed to hold many people and room was always an issue on any spaceship, but more on a corvette than most.

The communicator hunched over in his seat, half turned and smiled wanly at Pat. "It's not formalized yet," Awad said. "This isn't a formal administrative notice. It's more a situation report. They actually call it a SITREP, from a marine that was consulted in SFHQ to his friend leading the detachment on Mars Station."

"Captain von Luck?"

"That's right."

"So what's he say?"

"They had a hard time finding anyone suitable and willing to take the job both."

"A long trip out to a short posting with no glory to be found and not under the eyes of possibly appreciative senior brass either."

"Above my pay grade, Bosun."

Pat grinned a little wider and patted the communicator on the back. "Too true, too true, buddy, but it behooves us to keep tabs on what our superiors are up to. To better anticipate their needs, you understand?"

Awad nodded without enthusiasm. "Yes, Bosun." Awad was sweating.

Pat could smell it as well as see it. Maybe he was pushing the man a little hard, but this was vital information. "So, are they going to leave us on our own for the next year before we finally get recalled to Earth space then?"

"Probably not," Awad answered. "Look, I can print off a hardcopy and you can read it yourself."

"Nope, discretion is the better part of valor. Best you never make any copies of any sort. Delete all record of our even seeing it if you can do that without leaving traces."

Awad paled. Pat figured that most of the time he was in denial about the shadiness of what they were doing. Technically, monitoring all signals traffic locally was part of his job. Decrypting and reading it when it was between known, ostensibly friendly parties, was not. Awad had still not figured out it wasn't possible to follow all the Space Force's regulations and remain effective. "An abundance of caution, you understand. Are we getting a new XO or not?"

"Probably."

"Who? Any info on them?"

"A newly made Senior Lieutenant. Katherine Kincaid. I think I've heard of her."

Pat nodded, and unable to grin more widely, crinkled his eyes a little. "Me too. Young Belter girl. First Belter to make it into the Academy, let alone through it. Put the panties of all the little old ladies of both sexes at SFHQ in a bit of a twist I'm guessing."

Awad bit his lip. From his expression, you'd think he'd bit a lemon. Speaking of upset old ladies. "Seems to have made a splash wherever she's gone, Bosun."

"An energetic young woman, by all accounts," Pat said. "But, maybe, a little naïve and inclined to flailing about." He showed Awad a painful array of teeth. "Guessing that's how some apple carts got upset."

Awad glanced about furtively. Looking for what? A spy? A clue? An escape, maybe? Who knew? The communicator hawked and swallowed. Disgusting. "What about our apples and our carts?"

Pat converted his wide grin into a confident smile. He decided to have a little fun. What was life without some fun? What were magic tricks without a little distracting patter? He'd switch metaphors and twist the subject, and leave Awad a bit confused and uncertain. Then he'd throw him the lifeline of something he'd want to believe garnished with tasty certitude and confidence. Awad, like most of the sheep that made up the bulk of humanity, would swallow it hook, line, and sinker. An old trick, but a good one. "Our ducks are all lined up in a row, copacetic like. Yeah, we've had to improvise a lot, but that just gives us a good general-purpose excuse for everything non-standard."

"It's true, isn't it? They stuck us out here and none of the usual routines and protocols applied. We had to improvise everything to keep the ship running and the crew from all disappearing. We didn't have any of the support you get in Earth space. We had to reach out, right?"

There you go. People think what they want to. "Exactly. They sent us out here for what was supposed to be a year and then forgot about us. It's a minor miracle we managed to keep it all going. We can be proud of that. They should be giving us medals, not getting all picky." A little resentment easily converts to self-justification. Also, nobody minds doing a little finger pointing when things go wrong.

Awad nodded to him. Heavens, the man was even flushing a little with anger. It wasn't completely appropriate, but Pat couldn't help smiling wider. "They make a mess and we clean it up, and then they pick on us because we're a little dirty. It's not fair," Awad said with sudden outraged heat.

Pat figured he'd stoke the fire a little. "That's right, but they're all politicians before anything else and they care more about how things look than the reality of them. Fortunately, I know how to handle those sorts of people. They're very predictable once you realize what their true priorities are."

Awad frowned, thinking of it. "This Lieutenant Kincaid, is she like that? She's a Belter and they say she's smart."

Pat let his smile thin and tried to look thoughtful. Not something his usually very useful bluff appearance was that well adapted to. "The Admiral's granddaughter who managed to get through the Academy as one of their youngest ever candidates. The one that it seems they're fast tracking." He shook his head, trying to give the impression the thought discomforted him. "I've got to guess she knows her politics. Figure she's not clueless about managing optics. She'd have to be as dumb as a post not to have a few clues. To be a bit politically sensitive. Only you know, Adnan, the Belt's not Mars, the Belters really think everyone ought to be equal. The

Founders and Homesteaders on Mars, well, you know what they're like."

"They think they're better than everyone else. They think of us as Earth trash, and they treat the migrant workers like something between livestock and vermin. Calling them assholes would be an insult to assholes everywhere." Awad grinned nastily when he said that. Normally he was a politely mild man, and it seemed to be a great relief to him to be able to express his opinion of Mars' ruling classes. They were fiercely ideological Libertarians who fervently believed that in a dog-eat-dog world, being top dog proved your superiority. They had no respect for those who quietly tried to be good cogs in a larger organization. That description fitted most of the Humber's crew. The crew, in general, not just Awad, bitterly resented the disrespect.

"Just so and I think the class divisions here are going to be a shock to our young Belter girl," Pat said. "Between a mess that could derail a promising career,that we're handling, and that, I don't think it'll be hard to get her on our side. Trust me."

"Yes, Bosun."

"That's my man," Pat said before leaving.

***

In spite of feeling tired out and out of sorts because of too little sleep and a bit too much beer last night, and the irritation with Lars, Katie found herself feeling happy as she sat down to a large English-style breakfast. The food looked good: piles of mashed potato, home fries, beans, eggs, steak, bacon, ham, sausage, pancakes and even some melon and other fruit. The strawberries and cream looked particularly good. Not a lot of fresh cream out in the Belt.

But it was seeing her friends gathered, not the food so much, that was cheering her up. She didn't get to see anywhere near enough of them, let alone all of them together. They were all just too busy.

"You sure you didn't order too much?" Colleen was saying to Susan next to her, as Katie made herself comfortable. "We're not teenaged calorie-burning machines anymore."

Susan was her usual cool self. She gave Colleen a small sphinx-like smile. "Colleen, you worry and fret so much that you're burning extra calories just sitting there." Susan's eyes twinkled. She was in an uncommonly good mood. Katie was glad to see it. Normally Susan leaned into gloomy Nordic fatalism a bit too much. "It's good to see you haven't changed."

Colleen snorted and ducked her head. Looking up at her old friend, she didn't seem able to keep a twisted grin from appearing on her freckled features. "You haven't changed much either, Lieutenant, soon to be senior, Fritzsen. Not so sure that's a good thing."

Susan grinned. As well, she might. Katie wasn't the only one on the fast track. "The Space Force, in its infinite wisdom, appears to approve of me."

Katie turned and grinned at her old friend not just from the Academy, but from the modern biathlon team that they'd led to two back-to-back gold medals in the Worlds. "That's because they don't know you the way we do."

Susan's eyes glinted. "They know who gets results without excessive angst and trouble."

"Down girls. Down," Stephen Lee chipped in from the other side of Susan. His tone was full of an exaggerated faux tiredness he didn't quite manage to keep a note of amusement out of.

Katie glanced over at Lars, who was trying not to look miserable and left out. As a one-time competitor in the biathlon, which was where Katie had met him, he knew Susan, but not really any of the rest of Katie's Space Force friends. She mouthed the word, "Sorry" at him.

He gave a little shrug. Lars understood she didn't have much time to touch bases with everyone, however little he liked it.

Just then, a new party arrived. It was mostly off of th *Resolute*, which was currently undergoing "special trials" in a distant off-limits section of Earth space. Katie no longer had the need to know what those trials involved. She doubted it was the simple evaluation of lessons learned that was the official story, but didn't actually know anything. Interestingly, the little group was led by Amy Sarkis, now a lieutenant, but only junior grade, not the senior one she might have expected. Amy had surprisingly jumped career tracks and was now the Deputy Engineering officer on one of the *Susquehanna*'s sister ships, the newest of the class, the Yukon.

Katie found it amusing that Amy was proving to be a natural leader. Amy had just needed goals she believed in. Katie gave her friend a small wave rather than trying to shout across the room.

Amy smiled and waved back. As usual, Amy understood the situation. She wanted to be here for Katie along with the rest of them, but she knew Katie was busy and couldn't spare any of them the attention she would have liked to. Amy turned to her little delegation and after a few words, they all began to sit themselves, gracing Katie with smiles and gestures of greeting as they did so.

Katie's Academy friends watched the little play with bemusement. Stephen grinned widely, and glancing at Susan, spoke to Katie. "Wow, you made some good friends on the *Resolute*. That's Amy, right? She's cute. Maybe you could find a little time to introduce us all?"

Susan, looking at Stephen, feigned being coldly unamused. "You're skating on thin ice."

Colleen, covering her face, suppressed what might have been a giggle. But , of course, Space Force officers don't giggle. Still, they all knew Stephen practically worshiped at Susan's feet. More surprisingly, Susan seemed to have developed a persistent attachment to Stephen. Their joking around belied the genuine strength of the bond they'd formed. The needs of the service complicated thebuilding of such bonds, and Katie felt a small twinge of jealousy.

When you were working with people, you built up intense attachments, but then the Space Force would split you up and make it hard to keep those attachments intact. With that, Katie decided she'd make a point of exchanging a few words with her former crew mates off of the *Resolute*. Haralson, in particular, had wide-ranging contacts and made a point of keeping up on everything that was happening. Fortunately or unfortunately, Katie didn't know which, she had need of whatever he could tell her about the situation out at the Mars Station.

As she pushed her chair out to get up, Katie spoke to Stephen. "Right oh, master. Apologies, Susan. I'll get right on with telling Amy of your interest, Stephen."

Stephen blinked and blushed red.

Katie laughed as she stood up. "I've got to talk to them, especially Lieutenant Haralson. Thor's pretty plugged in. He can probably tell me what's really going on out around Mars."

Stephen let out a breath and chuckled at himself.

Susan absentmindedly punched him in the shoulder. Her attention was on Katie. "Good idea. Pay close attention to what he says. Everybody knows something is not quite right out there, but they're reluctant to come out and say it, or guess at what. One thing for sure, they've been left out there for years longer than they should have been, because the ships that should have relieved them were diverted to either the Belt or the Jovian system."

"Don't imagine they're going to appreciate my part in that," Katie mused gloomily.

"Maybe not," Susan concurred. "Not your fault, but sometimes people aren't rational. Anyhow, get a move on, ask your questions, say your hellos, get back here, eat some of this good food, say bye, and get on your way. You've barely an hour."

"Yes, ma'am," Katie answered, throwing a mock salute. She walked over to her friends at the far end of the table who'd been watching the by-play with interest. She raised her arms and hands in a beatific greeting. "I come with brief greetings for all, and questions of urgent import for the great Thor," she declaimed.

"A single medal doesn't make you divine," Iris Gregorian faux grumped at her. Easy sentimentality wasn't in her repertoire.

"I don't know," Bobby Maddox said, grinning. "I thought she was pretty divine beforehand."

"Yes, and we all took your opinion with all the seriousness it deserved," Ravi Shankar chipped in.

Amy, who was sitting next to Thor, they were an on again, off again, item now, grinned broadly at Katie. She stood up. "You can borrow my seat. I want to go over and renew my acquaintance with Susan anyways, and you really do need to talk to Thor."

Katie looked around apologetically at her friends as she sat herself down. "Sorry guys, got to eat and then run to grab the shuttle up to Goddard in less than an hour. It's good to see you all. Thanks for coming out on such short notice." She turned to Thor Haralson and pointed at him. "You, I've got some questions for."

Thor raised his hands in a mock defensive gesture. The levity didn't quite reach his eyes. "Mars?"

"Yep."

"I can't tell you anything definite you don't already know," he said levelly. His words sounded considered. Katie figured he must have been thinking of what to say to her on the way here. "I can tell you it's at least as serious as you probably think it is."

Katie glanced around at her friends and colleagues. They were all looking on with barely concealed expressions of concern. They might be happy about her promotion, but they were worried about what she was in for. "Everybody knows something is not right, nobody is sure what or how bad it is."

"Yeah, exactly," Thor said. "We don't have much out there. A small presence on Mars Station. It's not much more than a recruiting office and a rather limited listening post, with even more limited support elements. A couple of squads of marines, not even a full platoon, and a couple of supply clerks. SFHQ, in its infinite wisdom, figured it would be more economical to rely on the civilian economy for most of their needs."

Katie waggled a hand in comment. "You can see the reasoning for a small detachment on a big station."

"Even if you don't agree with it," Thor said. He was easy-going but when it was work, he liked to have everything on the table and well defined.

Katie nodded. "Right. In any case, it's not enough to provide proper support for a warship. Not even a single small one like the Humber."

It was Thor's turn to nod. "No, it's not. Spaceships aren't as bad as, say, atmospheric aircraft or land based mechanical fighting vehicles when it comes to requiring on-going maintenance. However, as we all know all too well they do need a steady stream of parts and maintenance and properly trained and equipped technicians to remain fully operational. I think even we tend to overlook how much we depend on Goddard Sttaion for those."

Katie glanced over at Amy, who was deep into an animated

conversation with Susan and who was sending Stephen the occasional bright grin to the poor man's embarrassment and the amusement of both women. Her friends could be troublesome when they wished. Amy was also, outside of some old staffer who'd been working the job for decades, the single most qualified individual around to comment on the issue of the logistics of warship support.

Thor followed Katie's gaze. "Yes, it's too bad you don't have hours to sit down alone with Amy and work the issues through."

Katie smiled at him without humor. "So what can you tell me in a couple of minutes?"

Thor grimaced. "It's an issue, but not one that matters that much for you. Not directly."

"Not directly?"

"They've managed somehow now for years. What matters to you is how they did that, and how they feel about it."

Katie found that rather general. What was it that Thor wasn't saying? "Okay."

"You can be damned sure that, however they did it, that it wasn't by the book."

"Right. Nothing in the book to go by, even. Doesn't mean they did anything wrong or illegal. Anything they need to feel bad or defensive about."

Thor snorted in exasperation. Shook his head and gave Katie a hard look. "Katie, you know better. You're not that naïve. The Space Force bureaucracy frowns on anything not by the book, and there are enough rules that they can always find one you somehow broke."

Katie took a deep breath. It felt a bit like disarming a bomb that was timed to go off in a few minutes. You didn't have much time and couldn't waste it. You also wanted to be damned careful. "Okay. So pretty sure that even if nobody ever did anything outright criminal, whatever shifts they resorted to were kind of shady, in a very dark gray region. Also, they're likely not happy about that, are worried about being caught out, and resentful that they're not being appreciated for having managed to keep their ship going. That sound right?"

"Best-case scenario."

"Ouch. Really?"

"Really. Not even going to go into the relatively small issue that they've got used to running their ship without an XO and don't likely need some young hotshot coming in and messing things up. Look, Katie, if this was anyone else I'd be telling them to run, not walk away from this posting. Just the fact that they're asking for volunteers and not just ordering someone out there ought to tell you something."

"That nobody wants to be responsible for ordering someone to take a swim in the mess?"

"Precisely. It's radioactive. Explosive. Everybody knows it's going to need cleaning up. There isn't going to be any glory in it. Going to be ugly."

"So are you advising me to decline the posting?" Katie asked.

"No. You should consider it, but no," Thor answered. "Like it or not, you're the Space Force's hotshot wunderkind. There are those who think you can walk on water. There are those who think you're well connected and have been very lucky both and can't wait for you to get your comeuppance. A lot of the officer corps is just waiting to see what happens next."

Katie frowned. She wished she could just do her job and be appreciated for it. "Surely most officers have better things to do than think about me?"

Thor smiled ruefully. "Maybe, but you've built yourself quite the reputation. Ambitious as you are, that's natural. In fact, if you really want to make a difference in the Force, it's inevitable."

Katie looked at her one time superior and friend. He was right. She'd been working hard to be the best officer she could the last few years, but she'd been drifting a bit too. She'd thought she'd have a year or two more before having to grapple with the politics of climbing up the slippery pole of Space Force promotion. Surprise. Time's up. Make your choice. "So I decline this posting and the glow comes off. I take it and it's a swim in a pool full of crap at best. Could be worse. Could be looking at some real push back from people worried about going to jail."

Thor nodded. "Yep, and you're all on your own. You're not going to have any friends or even backup out there."

"Wow."

"Yeah, but I'm not sure you have much choice."

"No. I can't afford the hit to my reputation. I can't have people thinking that when the going starts to look tough I wimp out."

Thor looked at the table and the beer in front of him, some sort of Pale Ale he hadn't been enjoying. "A bad hand and it looks like you have to go all in. Again."

Katie flinched. She'd joined the odd poker game, and she rarely did well. She wasn't bad at calculating odds and keeping track of cards, but the other players always seemed able to figure out what she had. Her poker face must stink. She couldn't bluff, and they always folded to her winning hands. She didn't lose fast or badly, but she did lose consistently. There must be a lesson in there. "Ad Astra," she said.

"Going to reach for the skies?" Thor frowned. "So far it's worked."

"But sooner or later my luck is going to run out?"

"Yes, it is. And, Katie, would you ask so much of any other young woman in your place? You deserve to be happy too."

Katie looked around at all her friends, colleagues, and yes, her boyfriend, who she'd be leaving behind. "Maybe. But I want to make a serious difference, and you know that's not going to be easy. That it's bound to be risky at times."

Thor finally took a sip of his beer. "Yes, I understand. Just give it some real thought on the shuttle up, will you?"

"I will," Katie promised. "How have things been with you?"

Thor didn't have much of significance to share she hadn't already heard through the grapevine, but it was nice to talk to him about things less problematic than her once again rather rocky career prospects. It hurt when she had to make excuses and rejoin the rest of her friends. Even them she didn't get to talk to much. She made a point of eating a good breakfast. It wasn't what she'd have preferred to spend her limited time on, but she'd learned the hard way how she needed to take care of herself.

Shortly she was again making her excuses and on her way to the spaceport in the car she'd ordered earlier.

She would have liked to have napped the trip away. Only she had too much to think about.

2: LTSG Kincaid Takes a Trip

Leading Spacer (supposedly) Rob Hood (currently his name) was going home. He wasn't happy.

He'd had some happy years on Mars as a kid. It didn't make up for the dangerous, miserable years he'd spent as a tunnel rat, after his parents had died when the main dome of their homestead failed, and before a judge had given him the option of enlisting.

Enlisting in the Space Force was the best thing that had ever happened to him. He'd left Mars behind and would have been happy to have never gone back.

Theoretically, he was a reservist now and could have refused the assignment. Rob had a small, but global in scope, electrical contracting business now and had just taken on some major contracts. It really wasn't a great time to be swanning off across the Solar System playing silly bugger.

Practically, he hadn't had much choice. In addition to being a civilian electrical contractor and an enlisted ship's electrician, retired now reservist, he was an agent of SFHQ's Special Investigations Section. The section placed a high value on loyalty and they'd helped him start his business. Most of the section's investigations took place on Earth and so Rob would not infrequently mix business and duty. There was always some excuse for electrical work almost everywhere and nobody took much notice of the technical help.

There really wasn't any such thing as being retired from the section's service. And so Rob had found himself this fine morning in the third-class passenger's lounge for the Martian Queen, waiting to be allowed early boarding. He'd spend tonight on board. It was cheaper than paying for an on-station hotel. It'd also give him a chance to get to know some of his follow passengers. Maybe get a hand of cards started. Ideally, he'd find some fish to play poker with. It'd be good to get back in practice.

There wasn't going to be much else to do in third class except sleep or read in his pod. First class was luxurious and second class was less so, but still had a lot for tourists to enjoy. Third class was just about getting bodies to Mars as cheaply as possible. Ideally, perhaps he'd have gone first or second class to keep an eye out for people of interest. It was unlikely the Space Force was the only group interested in the developing situation on Mars, but his cover precluded that. The Space Force didn't waste money transporting enlisted hands.

Which brought Rob's thoughts back to the sprinkles on top of this whole crap cake. Looked like he was going to get to play babysitter in addition to everything else.

Normally, all the many action vids to the contrary, Rob's job didn't actually involve anything beyond keeping his eyes open and noticing what was going on around him. The Special Investigations Section existed to supplement SFHQ's sources of information. More often than not, to simply verify that the information being received through more regular channels was accurate and complete. It kept an eye on crooks. It didn't arrest them. It kept an eye on problems and bad actors in general. It might, if alternative sources could be attributed, pass on information to those that could act on it. The section avoided "direct action" almost religiously. Most of the time, Rob was a spy, not an action hero, certainly not an assassin. Most of the time.

Only now, in addition to being tasked with getting to the

bottom of whatever was going on with Mars and the Humber in particular, Rob was being tasked with protecting a certain Space Force officer. A young woman, newly made a senior lieutenant, by the name of Katherine Kincaid.

The granddaughter of an admiral with, from what Rob had seen of Kincaid's record, a real talent for finding trouble.

Rob was apparently supposed to keep Kincaid safe despite being barely able to talk to her without breaking cover.

So yeah, Rob was having to act as a glorified babysitter.

Great.

***

Noon hour had come and gone. Katie had made her decision and conveyed it to the *Susquehanna*'s XO. She'd take the posting to Mars. She was going to be the Humber's new XO. The electrons of the required "paperwork" were already winging their way to SFHQ.

The XO had expressed his regret that they didn't have time for a more formal parting, but she needed to have her affairs wrapped up, be packed, and be on the Martian Queen the next morning. It wasn't much time. He'd wished Katie well, said goodbye, and dismissed her to get on with it.

Katie was now having lunch with her grandmother. Her grandmother, the famous Admiral, who was supposed to be retired. At least for public consumption. There was some doubt regarding the reality of that.

Right now, the questions of what sort of spook stuff her grandmother might be involved in, and what relationship it had to the FTL programs everyone knew every organization capable of it was furiously pursuing in supposed secrecy, were all on back burners.

At this moment, Katie was dealing with her grandmother's skepticism regarding Katie's career choices.

"Katie, the heavens know I never wanted to discourage a talented young woman from having big dreams," her grandmother was saying.

Katie looked around at what must be one of the fancier dining rooms on Tsiolkovsky Station. Big, with lots of thick dark red cloth covering furniture that seemed to have mostly heavy dark wood or gleaming brass for its bones. Not the sort of place Katie ever expected to be in, let alone to have become comfortable with. She'd met her grandmother in a whole series of such places. Rarely the same place twice in a row. In a woman other than Admiral (ret'd) Katrina Schlossberg, Katie would have suspected flightiness. Given what Katie knew of her grandmother, she rather thought deliberate intent was more likely. It was particularly telling that this meeting was taking place on civilian Tsiolkovsky and not military Goddard Station. "I respect that you've tried to give me room," Katie said.

Her grandmother sighed in exasperation. "And I rather regret it at this point. The XO's slot on the Humber is a poison pill. That's harsh, but there's no other way to say it. You might think it's important to have a reputation as a junior super woman who fears to tackle nothing, but reputation derives from effectiveness, not the other way around."

"Grandma, you exaggerate. And that's rather rich coming from the woman with the most fearsome reputation in the entire Space Force. You know, I've seen grown men nervously hesitate at the very mention of your name. It'd be almost funny if it wasn't so exasperating. That couldn't have been all by accident. Anyhow, I don't think the link between effectiveness and reputation is one way in either direction. I'm convinced it's a chicken and egg thing. I think that they're mutually reinforcing."

Her grandmother responded by quietly and very precisely dissecting the steak in front of her. It was rare. Very rare. Katie could see the blood oozing from it.

"What?" Katie asked.

Her grandmother paused in her disassembling of her meal and looked up at Katie. "You're fond of classic literature and stories and heroes both, aren't you?"

Katie blushed. It was true. As true as the fact, her tastes did not confirm to those of the usual modern level headed, if young, officer in the Space Force. "True. True too that I believe in enduring principles. Doesn't mean I don't know things have changed since the Middle Ages or Classical times."

"Trying to head me off at the pass, young lady?"

"Trying to cut to the chase, ma'am."

Her grandmother smiled. "I wish we had longer to talk. I'm going to miss you, dear."

"I doubt it'll be much more than a year. The Humber has been out there around Mars too long as it is. She needs to come back here where she can get a proper refit. The crew will need a break and time to get to know their families again. I suspect much of what I'll need to be doing is preparing her for that return trip."

Her grandmother's next smile had no humor or amusement in it. It was grim. "I doubt it'll be that simple. I tried to get a sense of the Humber's readiness state from SFHQ. They don't seem to be entirely sure of it. That's a very bad sign. I repeat: This is a trap. You should have turned down this posting."

"I'm not sure of your experience, ma'am, but I don't think I've got the luxury of turning down the opportunities I'm offered."

Her grandmother looked over Katie's shoulder as if looking at something very distant she couldn't actually see. The ex-Admiral wasn't what anybody could call easy going, but Katie had rarely seen her this close to losing her patience.

Her grandmother sighed. She looked at Katie with a gleam in her eyes that ventured on sad. "Back to the classics and heroes. I had a point to make."

"Yes, ma'am."

"Shakespeare and Julius Caesar?"

"There is a tide in the affairs of men."

Katie's grandmother's smile was genuine this time. "Good girl," she teased.

"Makes my point, doesn't it?" Katie asked. "You have to seize the opportunities you get when they're presented and before they disappear, right?"

"Yes, I believe that's the conventional reading of the quote," her grandmother said. "Only think. It's Brutus, not Caesar speaking. Not the hero, not even a winner. Think too, that if you have to take the tide when it's running your way, you also have to wait for it to be doing so."

Katie downed her utensils in exasperation. It was a very fine meal in front of her and she hadn't been making much progress on it with all the talking. "In plain language, what's your point? I'm going. Can't change that now. Do you have useful advice? What is it?"

"Don't rock the boat. Don't wink at any obvious problems, and there will be problems, but don't go digging for them. It'll do no one any good. Any victories you achieve will be Pyhrric. Not worth what they cost you."

Katie frowned. Katie had asked her grandmother to be blunt. "I don't believe in ignoring problems and letting them fester. I don't believe in cutting corners."

Her grandmother nodded. "You set high standards for yourself, dear. That's good. Sometimes I think you expect too much of yourself. Only it's one thing to be harsh on yourself and another to be demanding of other people. You can rarely be sure of what it's like to be in someone else's shoes. It's easy to be inadvertently unreasonable. You ask too much of people and you'll get nothing."

"You think I should just be a placeholder?" Katie couldn't keep her distaste for the idea out of her voice.

"The XO's job is to implement the captain's policy."

That gave Katie pause. It was a simple statement of what the manual on a ship's organization said and something everyone knew. Only her grandmother's implicit point was correct. Katie had been thinking of what her policy would be and how she would enforce it. She'd been forgetting that it wasn't her job. That her job was going to be enforcing the captain's policy. Presumably the same one he'd been following the last few years. Presumably one of not rocking the boat, and winking at the odd thing that wasn't exactly by the book.

Katie looked at her grandmother hard. Her grandmother stared blandly back. Katie took a deep breath and exhaled. "Ouch. I guess my first job will be finding out what Captain Smith wants."

"That's right."

"And doing that regardless of what I think personally."

"Correct. And no playing games. You can't let any ligh appear between you and your captain."

Katie played with her food idly. A habit she detested in others. "I'm not sure I'm going to be comfortable with that, but I see what you're saying."

"Good."

"Honest. I'll keep your advice in mind."

"I hope so. Eat up. That's good food."

"Yes, ma'am."

***

So, it'd been over a month, but Katie had finally made it to Mars. Or, well, Mars Station at least. Who knew when, or even if, she'd get a chance to go down to the surface of the Red Planet.

Disembarkation of second-class passengers was about to begin. The Martian Queen was a large ship, but a small world. Katie had spent over a month confined with companions she'd not chosen. Companions who mostly thought of Katie as some sort of curiosity whose passage they, as taxpayers, were footing the bill for. Katie was eager to leave. She'd known the Space Force's reputation was less than sterling among the wider population of Earth, but not by how much. The last month had ground that home.

She was also bored. For all that she had mountains of study to do regarding her new position and Mars in general, she craved action and she'd not had much of that.

So yes, Katie was looking forward to getting off of the Martian Queen. Didn't mean her anticipation was unalloyed. In fact, her feelings were one part trepidation and fear to each part of eager anticipation. Her efforts at studying the history of Mars and the current situation there had left her feeling more concerned than informed.

Mars had been founded by people determined to escape the constraints and regulation of Earth. What they saw as the stifling hand of excessive government. And to this day there was little to nothing in the way of central government, less of any order, and peace was a sporadic luxury. There appeared to be more than a dozen large factions competing for a variety of goals. Reading between the lines, none of them were inclined to eschewing violence when it served their purposes.

Her study had raised as many questions as it had answered. And that was just with regard to the background situation on Mars. The actual situation on the Humber, which was her direct concern, was even more of a mystery. Whatever was going on with the officers and crew of the Space Force corvette, they didn't seem inclined to disturb their nominal superiors back in Earth space about it. Their reports were marvels of vague verbose non-information.

Katie snorted. She had to admit she was feeling rather strongly about it. People were hiding something. She wasn't sure what, but it was going to be her job to get to the bottom of it and do something about anything outright wrong or otherwise broken. That despite the admonishments of her grandmother and others not to unnecessarily rock the boat.

And that process was about to start sometime in the next few minutes. She would step off the Martian Queen, find the crew member that had been sent to meet her, and they'd all start to size each other up.

That they'd merely sent her a short text message about that was already an unfortunate straw in the wind. It'd stated that an enlisted hand would meet her and guide her to the Humber. Nothing major, but traditionally an outgoing XO would greet their replacement with a degree of formality. Then they'd introduce them to both the captain and the other officers at a minimum. In this case, there was no outgoing XO. Katie's predecessor had suffered a mysterious accident. But she would have expected to be met by the captain or at least another officer with a small greeting party. Apparently not.

Katie sighed. It wasn't just jittery feelings on her part, was it? She had real reasons to be concerned.

And, uncharacteristically, that concern was translating into hesitation.

The Martian Queen had both large reception areas and large passenger hatches. It allowed for rapidly embarking and disembarking passengers. There was one set each for each class of passengers. They were rather too large in Katie's mind. She felt the ship's designers had prioritized passenger convenience over safety to an excessive degree.

But be that as it may, the process of leaving was still not fast enough for most of Katie's fellow passengers. There was supposed to be a disembarkation order. They'd all been given numbers.

Katie, like many of the rest of the passengers, was ignoring hers. Only while most of the other passengers were trying to jump the exit queue, Katie was hanging back.

In addition to being in no hurry to leave, Katie didn't like being in a crowd. Raised out in the Belt on her family's ship, and on Ceres, she'd grown up used to there not being many other people around. She'd been used to having lots of privacy. True, there'd not been much privacy at the Academy. But the other people around her had been people who she'd gotten to know well. Disciplined and predictable people, too. Crowds of strangers in close proximity were not something she was used to. They certainly weren't something she liked. They made her uncomfortable.

And so Katie hung back. She didn't slip out onto the passenger docks of Mars Station until most of the rest of the other passengers had already exited.

To Katie's surprise, Mars Station was less organized for security than most passenger terminals Earthside. In addition to the crowd of former Martian Queen second-class passengers milling about in the middle of the space, there were crowds of apparent friends and family around greeting them. Luggage was being offloaded at various stations around the space's sides.

Katie was also surprised by how much of the space was consumed by big solid concrete planters and benches. The planters were large, a full meter and some high, coming up to Katie's middle. Some only had bushes and flowers, but some had actual small trees in them. Their presence exacerbated the congestion on the docks, and Katie wondered at the logic of the design.

Was it just an esthetic choice to keep the space from being too barren and imposing? Nothing Katie had read had suggested that the Martian authorities, such as there were, were very inclined to spending resources on making public spaces pleasant. She couldn't deny the evidence of her eyes, though.

Katie continued to hang back.

She had resolved to look longer before leaping than she had in the past. Katie had had her challenges in the past and not only survived them, but arguably triumphed. Only in reviewing how they'd gone, Katie couldn't help feeling she'd been very lucky. It wasn't possible to know everything ahead of time and be certain of success. Only Katie had gone headfirst and blind into the Academy and then repeated the process on her first posting on the *Resolute*. Katie wasn't inclined to being modest. She was a very capable young woman, and she'd worked hard, very hard, for her success, but she'd also had a lot more luck than she deserved. She couldn't count on that always being the case.

Also, in the past, her challenges had been more straightforward, and she'd had the aid of good friends. Neither was going to be true here in Mars space and on the Humber.

Katie was going to make a point of being more cautious than had been her wont previously. And so she hung back.

Having managed to clear the chokepoint of the exit ramp from the Martian Queen, she drifted to one side, away to the thinner edges of the crowd and the sides of the passenger disembarkation area. She knew there must be someone waiting for her, but she was in no hurry to meet them.

Rather, she took the opportunity to observe the rest of the crowd. Her fellow former passengers, to some degree to be sure, but mostly the individuals and small groups waiting to greet them. She wanted to get a better feel for the people in this new place.

There were a lot of expressions of relief as people finally located the people they were waiting for. A lot of awkward public intimacy, hugs, cheek pecks, and handshakes, as people greeted each other.

Some people were holding up pieces of cardboard with names scrawled on them. It struck Katie as an amazing anachronism in this age when everyone had a personal communications device, but she supposed you couldn't necessarily count on your phone to work with the local station network. It was a bit of an edge case. Having a technological solution didn't mean you could count on people to use it.

One of those posters had her name on it. The man holding it up was wearing a regular Space Force working uniform. Guess she wasn't worth dressing up for. He appeared to be a senior enlisted hand. A master chief petty officer, so one of the top three enlisted men on the Humber. He was a stoutly solid man with a florid complexion and sandy blond brown hair that partly manifested itself in a large bushy mustache. He also wore a big grin plastered on his face. That disturbed Katie. She was used to her senior NCOs being a sober lot and any sense of humor they had being rather subtle. She ignored him for the time being.

Katie continued examining the crowd. One gloomy young couple caught her eye. Not only weren't they interacting much with the rest of the crowd, they weren't having much interaction with each other. Additionally odd, because they had a big baby carriage in front of them. She supposed you could have a baby with someone you didn't much like, but how could you be completely indifferent to them? They were somewhat differently dressed, too. Dark sober clothing that didn't seem entirely practical. Katie was the despair of her friends when it came to fashion, but she suspected what the couple were wearing was edgily fashionable if somewhat deliberately toned down. Very odd.

They made quite the contrast with another nearby couple, Simon Adebayo and his wife, Marie, who'd been some of the few passengers genuinely friendly to Katie. It was just the way Simon, an extraordinarily tall, thin, and dark man, was. He was unrelentingly cheerful and helpful to all. He believed in making the world a better place. Truth be told, Katie had found him rather inspiring.

She'd just managed to take all that in when the heart wrenching, loud, and piercing wail of a baby crying began to emerge from the somber couple's baby carriage. The female half of that couple looked in Katie's direction before bending to attend to the crying.

The waiting man in the Space Force uniform also looked her way and then followed her gaze to the couple with the baby carriage.

Simon had also noticed them. Typically for Simon, he moved to help, obscuring her view of what was happening.

Katie glanced at the waiting man and saw his posture go stiff, his face hard and grim. He turned her way and sprinted towards her, knocking other people aside, his face angry and determined.

Katie bolted the other way. Only there wasn't far she could go. A few meters later, she was almost to the wall of the space, and slowing and turning to meet her pursuer, she was tackled. The man's heavy weight bore her to the deck, slamming her into it hard and painfully.

Before she could recover her senses, there was a bright white flash and a beyond loud "crack-thump" sound she felt in her very bones. A hot acrid wind rushed over those parts of her still exposed.

With what was left of her hearing, she heard a series of splattery thunks interspersed amongst a general pattering sound.

Looking out from under the man on top of her, she noticed bits of debris, some of it gooey hitting the wall a few meters away, and the surrounding planters, too. For a split second, she wondered what it could be. Then she noticed a larger bit sliding down the side of a nearby planter.

The skin on one side with the remaining traces of a tattoo's blue lines, and the reddish flesh on the other side, made it clear it was part of a person. A person who'd been alive minutes ago, but was now probably dead.

Katie barfed.

She gave up the contents of her stomach in one long, throat searing heave of vomit. She tried to lift herself up and roll over so she didn't have to lie in it.

"Get down," the man on top of her hissed angrily. "There might be a second follow up bomb, or a gun man waiting to finish the job," he said, following up himself in slightly calmer, more measured tones.

In the distant back of her mind, Katie realized the man had a point, and that he'd probably just saved her life. She couldn't manage to feel grateful for all that. Somehow, she didn't trust this guy. None of this agreed with her. Almost being killed in an explosion didn't agree with her. Being tackled didn't agree with her. And having to lie in her own vomit did not agree with her. Katie was pissed.

"Is this a normal greeting here?" she snapped.

"Welcome to Mars, ma'am."

***

Rob Hood wore his uniform for his disembarkation from the Martian Queen. Not only was it best that he report in to the Humber wearing it; it also signaled that he wasn't legitimate prey.

A majority of his fellow third-class passengers were indentured labor. A Martian labor organization had paid their fare to the Red Planet and it would now expect them to start paying that fare and more off.

The third-class disembarkation area of the Queen resembled a facility for processing livestock more than it did a tourist reception lounge. The passengers were herded down a set of narrow corridors, sorted out, and picked off by agents of the labor companies with facial recognition gear. They weren't beyond making mistakes and grabbing extra bodies that looked unclaimed and vulnerable.

And so Rob Hood wore his uniform.

It didn't make the close crowding better, or either the herding or the smell of his fellow passengers any more pleasant, but it did make him much safer.

Finally, the unclaimed remnants of the herd of third-class transportees from the Martian Queen came within sight of the exit from the spaceport docks. Slightly less pressed together, they slumped down a broad corridor that Rob knew led directly to the main concourse in the service levels of the station.

Rob didn't allow himself to relax. He remained alert.

A good thing because loitering next to the yellow and black edged emergency airlock doors at the entrance to the concourse, there was another gauntlet to run. A pair of typical, tall, skinny native Martian thugs. They had the look of men who never relaxed and who'd never had the luxury of a good meal. They didn't look like they'd ever had a proper bath, for that matter. They did look alert and eager.

Rob spared a split second to reflect how his time on Earth had changed his standards before returning to the moment. A lack of focus here could get him killed or worse. Somehow, although he'd not anticipated this, he had no doubt those men were waiting for him.

He shucked his heavy duffle bag off of his back, and, holding it in his hands, strode forward.

Rob's sudden appearance before them caught the thugs off guard. One to his left wasn't registering Rob's approach properly at all. Not yet. The other to his right reached for something. A knife appeared in his hand.

Rob threw his duffle bag with all his might directly into the young man's face. As he did so, he turned towards his left where the other thug had managed to get a knife out and was extending his arm.

Rob was faster. He didn't have the luxury of playing it safe. He stepped inside the man's guard and grabbing the man's wrist gave it a hard twist. The thug's knife dropped. Even as the sound of it hitting the deck penetrated Rob's consciousness, he was turning back to the righthand thug. That worthy had only been momentarily distracted by the duffle bag to his face.

Rob wasn't quite fast enough. Righthand thug failed to gut him, but he did get a good slash in across Rob's ribs. It burned. The thought of having to report on his new ship with his good uniform wrecked angered Rob.

Rob stepped back and down, and not even looking directly at the injured lefthand thug, smashed him in the face with one hand. With the other hand, he grabbed the knife that thug had dropped.

The knife forward, Rob pushed off low from the deck with all the strength his leg muscles had. Straight at the righthand thug who'd been moving forward, knife extended himself. It was not a safe move. Only Rob knew, from bitter personal experience and training both, that he wasn't getting out of this fight unhurt. All he could hope was that he'd deal out more hurt than he'd take and survive it.

Again, Rob got inside his surprised opponent's guard. The thug managed to recoil some and instead of gutting him, Rob only managed a stab to his hip.

Damn, there were still two of them, even if they were both injured.

At least rightmost thug was still off guard. He bent over in pain but didn't take his eyes off of Rob. Standing back up, he stepped back.

And tripped over the momentarily forgotten duffle bag. He flailed backwards and as he hit the deck, Rob was on him. Reacting instinctively on his training, he took full advantage, shoving his borrowed knife up under the thug's chin and into his brain, killing him. One down.

He sprang up and around, trying to locate the other thug. Said individual was fleeing, the watching crowd parting to make way for him.

Loud whistles pierced Rob's consciousness.

"Police! Police! You there, drop the knife," a voice yelled.

Rob did as ordered and was wrestled to the deck and his arm twisted behind his back for his troubles.

"They attacked me. I just defended myself," he said.

"We'll see," came a gruff, no nonsense reply.

"Leading Spacer Robert Hood. I just got off the Martian Queen."

"Well, Leading Spacer, welcome to Mars."

3: LTSG Kincaid is XO

They didn't make it to the Humber until some hours later. The enlisted man who'd come to greet Katie, who turned out to be Master Chief Petty Officer O'Conal, the bosun, had tried to hurry Katie on. Katie had insisted on remaining at the spaceport to help the other, more severely injured, victims of the blast.

And once she'd done what she could to that end, Katie had insisted on changing into a clean and undamaged dress uniform. Katie was no fashionista. In fact, Katie naturally tended to pay little attention to her appearance. But the Academy had taught her how to look sharp in her dress uniform. Her friends in the service had all made it clear to her that looking good in the proper way was important for an Executive Officer.

Executive Officers were supposed to rigorously impose the highest standards possible on their ships. Practically speaking they couldn't be too heavy-handed in doing so without raising a counterproductive resentment. Setting a good personal example was critical in squaring that circle.

And so, despite the expense and the picky effort it required,

Katie had a second dress uniform available and was able to dress spiffily in it. She also made a point of freshening up. All in a convenient restroom. Fairly quickly, but still at some cost in time.

The bosun's chagrin at this was clear, if unstated.

They'd arrived at the Humber well after normal working hours, well past 1600 hours, and into the evening routine. There'd been nobody there to greet them.

Katie wasn't clear if the single enlisted hand slumped against the bulkhead of the entry airlock was the regulation mandated guard or not. She glanced at the bosun in query. He returned her nothing but a bland smile. Katie settled for giving the able spacer in question a long searching look, at which point they struggled up into a position of attention and saluted. "Welcome aboard, ma'am," they said.

Katie returned the salute. Reading the man's name off of the name tag on his breast, she replied, "Thank you, Able Spacer Johnson. Glad to be aboard." A white lie, but she was determined to start off on the right foot.

"I'll escort the lieutenant to her cabin," the bosun told Johnson. "You let the captain know she's arrived."

"Aye, Chief," Johnson answered.

The bosun then started off without further consultation. Katie wasn't impressed but, again, didn't want to start making a fuss right off. She'd made a point of memorizing the Humber's layout on the way out. As it happened, it was, except for minor differences, the same as that of her sister ship, the *Susquehanna*. Katie had just spent several years on the *Susquehanna*, so she knew that layout well. She even had a pretty good idea of which cabin the bosun was taking her to. There weren't that many options.

So Katie didn't have to focus on memorizing her way around. She had plenty of mental cycles to spare for looking about her and assessing the state of her new ship. A state she was now going to be responsible for.

She didn't see any outright filth, or anything obviously broken, but the Humber had a distinctly shopworn feeling. The smell of its air was rounded, not musty, but not exactly sharply fresh either. Katie, from the Belt and a born spacer, was sensitive to the build up of trace contaminants in what were, after all, very small closed life support systems.

As a Space Force Academy graduate and officer, she also, very anachronistically, carried a pristine white handkerchief made of natural fibers. Trailing her fingers across a bulkhead as she followed the bosun she noted the surface was quite literally not squeaky clean. Her fingers slid across it rather too easily. A rub with the handkerchief produced a light smear.

It was hard, constant work keeping every surface on a ship clean, and not something most people, especially those who'd not grown up in space, were very eager to do. A ship's NCOs had to work hard to keep their ship's crew on top of the issue. Truth was, Katie had never been on a Space Force ship fully up to her own personal standards. Not even the *Susquehanna*, despite the professionalism of its officers and hard work of its crew. The Humber fell far short of the *Susquehanna*'s standard.

Looking at the bosun's back, Katie thought, pointing that out likely wouldn't be useful, let alone well received. "How are the CO_2 logs?" she idly asked the bosun.

"Engineering know that, ma'am," the bosun replied without looking back at her. "They're pretty busy keeping the vital machinery running though."

Katie choked back a strong urge to ask the man if he didn't think being able to breathe was vital. She took an indirect approach instead. "Where are you from, bosun?"

"Mars, ma'am. Lot of us are. A lot of the Earth born, even the Belters, bailed on us." The resentment was palpable, though Katie doubted the man had stopped smiling. Not that she could tell by looking at the back of his head. The senior NCO continued after a moment. "We know all about CO_2 poisoning down on Mars. It's not a problem on the Humber."

"Good to hear," Katie said. She decided to take a new tack. "Engineer's pretty busy? Earth born I guess? Where is everyone?"

"Whoa, ma'am," the bosun said, stopping and turning towards her. "That's a lot of questions."

"I'd like to get up to speed as quickly as possible."

"Yes, ma'am. We're below our minimum complement of

officers, even with you. Engineer's got no deputy. There's no supply officers at all. Pilot Officer got a medical back to Earth and hasn't been replaced. Ops got no deputy. Weapons got no deputy, and is busy acting as a co-pilot for the shuttle so we can get supplies from the surface. And, yeah, they're all Earth born." He looked back at Katie, a thinner smile than usual plastered on his face. For a second, his face seemed hard and thoughtful, and to honestly reflect the feelings behind it to a degree. "Space Force officers are nearly all Earth born, ma'am. Think you'd know that more than most being the exception."

Katie nodded.

The bosun gave an almost imperceptible nod back of his own. For once, they seemed to be on the same page. They both knew there were no good words on the topic Katie could voice. The bosun answered the rest of Katie's question. "We're due to do a patrol to the closer part of the Belt. Above my pay grade, but rumor has it SFHQ is less than pleased with the amount of patrolling we've managed. They want us to get at least one more in before they recall us."

Katie couldn't help thinking that the bosun was pretty well informed about something he claimed was above his pay grade. Also that his tone indicated he wasn't reluctant about having a strong opinion about it either. A rather disapproving opinion. The bosun appeared to think asking the Humber to go out on patrol was excessive. "The ship's not ready and that's keeping the engineer busy?" she asked.

"No proper source of spare parts out here. No qualified help. Been out here for years and no dockyard available. I'm no stoker, ma'am, but it does seem to be asking a lot. Engineer spends all day down in the Engine Room, day in and day out, and barely sleeps."

Katie chewed on her lower lip. A bad habit she'd worked hard to train herself out of. She'd thought she'd succeeded. Guess not. Her mind hung up on the trivial. She couldn't help Thinking it was weirdly anachronistic calling the ship's engineering crew "stokers". No one had shoveled coal on a ship for centuries. It'd been a long day, and she was tired. Maybe she could forgive herself for not wanting to grasp the nub of the matter. Some things don't change. Ships need maintenance. It always takes qualified personnel. Periodically, it's major enough that it needs to be done at a base equipped for such things.

Give the bosun one thing, as generally impatient as he seemed to be, he was giving her time to digest what he'd told her. Katie pushed on. "So the engineer's down in the engine room? What about the rest?"

The bosun nodded. He seemed to appreciate her not dwelling on the ship's state of readiness. "Weapons, Lieutenant Rompkey that is, and co-pilot Wentzell are down on the surface with the shuttle trying to get us stocked up on food and other consumables at a cost that isn't outright highway robbery."

"There's no ship's chandlers on Mars Station we can use?"

"None set up for a ship the size of the Humber, ma'am. And, if you'll pardon me for expressing my personal opinion, none that aren't crooks willing to fleece the Space Force for every dime they can."

"Ouch. And?"

"Well, ma'am, as you may have noticed, the Space Force likes to keep its officers busy doing paperwork, reports about how things are going, and they haven't asked for less just because we're out here at Mars short-handed. Fact is, from what I've heard, accidentally overheard you understand, they want more paperwork because we can't do things the regular way out here and they want that justified on the record."

Katie smiled at the bosun. She didn't have to work hard to force it. She understood all too well what he was describing. "Believe me, Bosun, I'm feeling the pain already."

"Yes, ma'am," the bosun answered. "Anyhow, paperwork is keeping the captain and my boss, Lieutenant Broomfield, who's Ops, busy. That answer your question, ma'am?" He raised his eyebrows in query. He wasn't going to actually ask Katie if they could get on with it, but the question was plain.

Katie smiled again. "Guess I'd better get to my cabin and get stuck in pronto."

"Yes, ma'am," the bosun said again, turning to continue there.

It wasn't far. Even a big ship isn't really large and corvettes are on the small side of big. The bosun fiddled with the entry pad to one side of Katie's new home, and opening the door for her, said, "Here you are, ma'am. You can change your entry key from your terminal in either the cabin, here, or your office."

Katie, despite a degree of untypical trepidation, marched through the door with a show of all the confidence she could manage. It was a small but comfortable looking space that all the same had a vaguely abandoned feeling. It was empty. None of the previous XO's personal effects remained, but it had the feel of having been quickly tidied up rather than rigorously prepared. Katie wondered if she wasn't just projecting the feeling the rest of the ship was giving her. The whole place had a feeling of just being adequate, but no more, to her.

The bosun had followed her in without asking. It made Katie uneasy, but she couldn't reasonably object. It was secondary anyhow. The terminal in the cabin was blinking urgently. There was a high priority message awaiting her attention.

The terminal wasn't passworded. She'd have to change that. The message was from the captain. The bosun peered over her shoulder as she read it. Unbeknownst to her, she'd had a crewmate as a fellow passenger down in third class on the Martian Queen. A badly needed replacement electrical tech. Somehow, he'd immediately become involved in a police incident upon disembarking from the passenger liner and was currently in police custody. Had been for a couple of hours. The captain wanted Katie to retrieve him. As soon as possible, which, ideally would have been a couple of hours ago.

"Sounds like something of a troublemaker," the bosun commented.

"Let's reserve judgment, Bosun," Katie said. "It's hard to see how he could have provoked any trouble in the short time he had after disembarking."

"Could be, ma'am," the bosun answered, "but, though I'm not engineering, I took the time to read his record. He's originally from Mars. Could have had trouble waiting for him."

"As did we, Bosun," Katie said coldly, turning to look the man in the eyes.

"Yes, ma'am," the bosun answered looking at the screen where the message he really shouldn't have been reading, lay. "Been a day full of trouble."

Katie turned back to the terminal and read the message there once again. The captain had recommended not only taking the two marines available but also asking the bosun for a couple of hands. Just in case the individual they were retrieving "proved problematic".

Katie was happy she wasn't facing the bosun. She could feel her jaw muscles. She had no doubt the expression on her face was not a happy one. She made a point of relaxing those muscles and trying to relax generally. She made a point of casually stretching her neck muscles as she turned towards the bosun again. It seemed the bosun was the go-to man on the Humber. "The captain has requested that I form a shore party with your help," she said. "And go retrieve our wayward new crew member. Two marines and two appropriate men of your choosing."

"Yes, ma'am. You want me to accompany you, ma'am?" the bosun asked.

"I don't think that should be necessary, Bosun," Katie said. "Doubtless I've been keeping you from other duties and the marines will know the way to the police station, right?"

"Yes, ma'am."

They found the two marines, a Corporal Bloggins and a Private Valdez, in the armory stripping down and cleaning weapons. The extra two hands required a foray into an enlisted hands mess where they found a group of men gathered around a central table full of beer containers, many now empty.

The chatter had died when they entered the space. Some of the men glanced at Katie before turning their wary attention to the bosun.

The bosun gave a hard look around before pointing to two of the larger men. "You, Anderson, and, you, Skorzeny, you're going ashore with Lieutenant Kincaid here. Seems the cops have gathered up a lost lamb of ours what came in with the liner. Got it?"

"Yes, Bosun," the men hastily replied, standing up. They took bare minutes to grab clothing and gear from nearby lockers before presenting themselves in front of Katie and the bosun.

With that, the little party made its way to the lifts down to the spindle where the Humber's docking port was situated.

The bosun left them there. "All yours, ma'am" was all he said.

A minute later and Katie had led them all into one now very crowded lift. "Know the way to Police HQ, Corporal?" she asked the senior marine.

"Yes, ma'am."

"Very well. Lead the way."

***

Pat wouldn't have minded a new XO who sat in their office and handled some of the ongoing torrent of paperwork SFHQ was always bombarding the Humber with.

It'd only been a few hours since he'd met Lieutenant Kincaid, the actual new XO, but Pat already figured that wasn't what he was getting. Too bad.

It was too early in the game to go all in on that proposition, and he couldn't afford to be openly hostile to the XO, anyway. Not until he had something on her or she was backed into a corner and beyond being able to complain to anyone, at least. Superficially, he had to appear to be friendly and helpful to the XO. He couldn't afford to indulge his irritation with her.

Fortunately, down here in the bowels of the Humber's main storage space, he had a useful target he could take his frustrations out on. Pat had risen to his position as bosun partly by being very competent at his job and good at pleasing people, especially senior NCOs and officers. With his peers and subordinates, he'd relied more on his fists.

Pat didn't get to do that very often anymore. He was finding he missed it. The simple pleasure of showing people who was boss in the simplest and most straightforward way possible. The smell of fear from someone that realized you could break them. The confidence that came from knowing that they knew their only hope was pleasing you. That you held their fate in your hands.

It was the most basic form of concrete problem solving.

The current problem being solved was the Humber's lead

supply tech. A man by the name of Wally Suresh. Pat vastly preferred dealing with men. He'd arranged an accident for Wally's female predecessor for that very reason. Main problem with women was that although they weren't that difficult to break, they tended to show it. Men would try to hide the fact they'd been emotionally crushed out of pride. Convenient for extortionists who had to keep a low profile. Also, women tended to be sneakier. You couldn't always depend on them to stay compliant. So Pat preferred men who he could beat the crap out of and who'd then know their place.

Wally was an excellent example of the type. At least, Pat had thought so before following him down to the storage space. Turned out Wally had been keeping an extra set of books. In real hardcopy physical ledger books and with a fountain pen of all things.

Pat pasted on a smile of faux sympathy and real disappointment. "Wally, Wally, I trusted you. I trusted you to keep a set of books that said what I told you they should."

"I did, honest, Bosun," Wally answered. He was gibbering. It was almost more disgusting than pleasing. "I kept those books. You can check on the terminal in the supply office using the password I gave you. The figures the officers and people back on Earth will see are exactly the ones you wanted."

"And these?" Pat asked, holding up a hardcopy ledger book. Its covers were fake leather around heavy plastic, or maybe even real cardboard. Pat wondered which. He also wondered where in the hell Wally had managed to find actual physical ledger books in the current day and age. Wasn't relevant to the current discussion as far as he could tell, though. The size and heft of the book was. Pat whacked Wally alongside the head with it hard. Hard enough to hurt, but not so hard it should leave permanent visible damage. Pat wouldn't take bets on Wally's hearing ever being the same again. "What the hell are these, Wally?"

Man was dazed. Practically crying and holding the side of his head. Pathetic. "Second books," he whimpered out.

"Second books?" Pat said, opening and flipping through the one he was holding. A master ledger it looked like. Pat was no accountant, but he didn't like taking things on trust. He'd taken the trouble to learn about the basics of accounting, double-entry bookkeeping etc.. Oddly enough, the textbook introductions always seemed to start with how it'd been devised and worked in the fifteenth century in Italy. Pat had wondered if that made sense. Proven more useful than he'd have expected anyhow.

Pat stopped his flipping of pages and read one entry. About the purchase of some potatoes from greenhouses on the surface. Pat knew for a fact that the amount purchased was lower than the official records would show, just as he knew for a fact that the price per pound was also lower. The difference being made up by a brokerage fee attributed to a company called "Green Fields Foods Distribution". Pat also knew it wouldn't take any serious investigator very long to figure out that "Green Fields" was a shell company. Might take them longer to determine that Pat was the company's main beneficiary if not exactly its official owner. He didn't doubt any serious investigator would eventually manage to figure it out. These books were enough to land Pat in jail if they ever fell into the wrong hands.

"Not very smart, Wally," Pat said.

"I know. I know, Bosun, but I needed them to keep track of our real supply situation," Wally sobbed. "Otherwise we'd start having shortages and be missing things and people would notice. Even the snots. Didn't want that. You'd be unhappy about that, wouldn't you?"

Pat couldn't help thinking that was a long and surprisingly sensible and coherent speech from a man hurting like Wally was. Seemed to Pat that meant Wally must have mentally rehearsed it ahead of time. So Wally had known he was offside and had thought up an excuse for it. Not good. Better keep Wally talking while thinking about that. "Not happy right now, Wally."

Wally looked blank. He really hadn't thought it through, had he? Man was a weak reed, as well as a likely traitorous one. Pat dearly wished he had someone better to fill his spot, and he didn't need the man. For a few months more, before Pat finally retired at least. Wally finally found some words to speak. "Didn't think anyone would ever notice them. The snots

I mean. Not you, Bosun." Wally looked as confused as he sounded for a moment before rushing ahead. "I mean, everyone knows you can't trust networks. We all learn that in school, but everyone's lazy too. Nobody keeps records on real paper anymore."

"So you thought sneaking down here to write things out in longhand wouldn't be obvious?" Pat asked. "You thought if anyone noticed, they'd think you were writing the Great Martian Novel of the 24th century, did you?"

For a brief moment, Wally looked more bewildered than frightened. Damn, Pat thought, he'd gotten carried away again. Imagination and smarts could both be useful, but in practical matters, it was best to keep it simple. Wally rallied. "Ah, no, Bosun."

Pat shook his head in mock exasperation. "You shouldn't try to be smart, Wally. You're no good at it. Got that?"

"Yes, Bosun."

The little twerp had figured out he was off the hook. Pat hammered him in the face out of real exasperation. Oops, that was likely to show. Pat hammered the little bastard hard on both sides of his ribs like he should have in the first place. That wouldn't show so much. "Really didn't want to do that, Wally," Pat ground out. "I'm going to be watching you from here on in extra careful. You understand, don't you? You're skating on thin ice here."

"Yes, sir."

"Don't 'sir' me. I work for a living." The line popped out of Pat's mouth automatically. "What are you going to do with these lovely old-fashioned books?"

"Burn them in the organic waste disposal. See to it myself. Alone."

"What did I tell you about thinking for yourself, Wally?"

"Don't?"

"Right, give me the books. I'll do it."

"Yes, Bosun. That all?"

"You don't have any other little secrets you want to confess? A third set of books? Little meetings that might look funny? A secret addiction or a mistress on the side? Anything that might cause us both embarrassment?"

Once again, Wally's bewilderment revealed his basic lack of imagination. Pat figured he'd been dealing with officers for too long. They seemed to relish long detours into imaginary worlds. Sometimes he wondered if, despite appearances, the hands and the snots were really members of the same species. Again, after a significant pause, Wally managed to say the obvious thing. "Ah, no, Bosun. I don't want to embarrass us. Certainly not. No way."

Pat figured he'd done what he could here. He wasn't happy with Wally, but he could likely string him along and keep him intimidated for another few months before folding the operation up and retiring to a new life on Mars before the *Humber* returned to Earth. It'd look reasonable, and even if someone back on Earth got suspicious, Earth based organizations would have a hard time getting to him down there.

"You're going to have an ugly black eye there, Wally," Pat said. "Best stay out of sight until it looks better. If anyone asks, you tripped and fell on your face, understand?"

"Yes, Bosun." Wally was back to being eagerly submissive now that he could see the light at the end of the tunnel.

"New XO comes asking questions. You act stupid. Shouldn't be hard. Right?"

"Right, Bosun," Wally answered, nodding vigorously.

"Good," with that, Pat turned and stomped out of the large but crowded space.

He reflected on the matter as he made his way back to the more inhabited parts of the ship. It was unfortunate the situation with Wally had come up, but he thought he'd solved it for the time being. The new XO, if she went looking around, wasn't going to find anyone willing to talk to her about anything untoward.

Pat would have hoped she'd not bother. A sensible older officer might have quietly warmed the XO's seat for the next year without stirring up trouble. Punched their ticket and gone on to their next promotion and eventually retired to some fancy, extremely well-paid position on Earth.

Not young Miss Kincaid, he was guessing. Belter girl extraordinaire and an Admiral's granddaughter, she probably felt she had something to prove. Too bad and very inconvenient.

All the same, she was only one young woman and alone and without help, there wasn't likely much she could do.

Pat would put a contingency plan in place to take care of her, just in case.

***

Katie was perfectly able to walk and chew gum at the same time. Chewing gum was unsanitary. Katie didn't usually chew gum, but she'd tried doing it and walking around once just to see what it was like. She'd mentioned the experiment to her friend Susan, who'd advised her not to spread that story around.

Be that as it may, Katie was capable of a certain level of multi-tasking. A fact she was currently proving by reading up on the Humber's errant new electrician as her little party made its way from the ship to Mars Station's police station.

And that despite several changes of gravity on the way. Both in strength and direction relative to the orientation of their surroundings. The Humber's main gravity ring was managing to maintain the illusion of regular one gee gravity despite the ship being docked. The benefits of a specialized ship design that allowed some gimballing of the gravity ring's sections between its spokes, and a special docking cradle. A sure sign that SFHQ hadn't planned its relative neglect of the Mars station. Those cradles only existed in three places; Mars Station, Callisto Station, and Goddard Station itself back in Earth space.

In any event, it was giving Katie a chance to demonstrate to the crew members of her new ship that she was no green Earth born klutz. The change in apparent gravity as they descended in the lift that took them from the ring to the *Humber*'s spindle was quite significant. It decreased from being a slightly skewed full gee to only a quarter gee but all the way to being from the ship's rear. That is from what was normally one side of the lift car.

Katie could tell out of the corner of her eyes that the enlisted men were surreptitiously observing how she handled the transition. Interesting that the bosun hadn't bothered on the way on to the ship. Amusing how now they were all quietly sizing each other up.

Even the most competent spacer can't climb down a ladder and read their tablet as they do so. For this section of the trip, at least, Katie had to lay off her reading. She stored her tablet in its holster to free her hands. She needed them to handle the gravity transition.

When she handled that transition with aplomb and ended by swinging herself smoothly down the hand holds acting as a ladder down to the *Humber*'s aft airlocks, she noticed her men suppressing looks of surprised appreciation. She fought to keep a smile off her face. This scrap of respect was the highlight of her day so far.

Once they were back in the quarter gee of Mars Station's docking area, and the increasing, but non-skewed, gravity of its lift to the full gee admin section, Katie was able to resume her reading.

Unfortunately, what she was reading about her new electrician, one Robert Hood, supposedly a Leading Spacer, didn't make her so happy. Didn't look like it'd be so simple to handle either.

There were no obvious inconsistencies in Hood's records that Katie could see. Only they seemed fishy. Strangely sparse, but what was there seemed a little too consistent. Two other overall data points presented themselves to Katie's mind. No, three really. The fact that Hood had been assigned to the *Humber* wasn't a single anomaly, it was two different ones.

The very fact that SFHQ had sent him from Earth to beef up the *Humber*'s crew was an anomaly in its own right. He was needed, it was true, but the *Humber* was short of qualified crew across the board and SFHQ hadn't done much to rectify the matter otherwise. The only new crew members they'd posted to the *Humber* in the last year were Hood and herself. She wondered what she and Hood had in common. That was suspicious in its own right.

Even more suspicious was that Hood was a reservist. Theoretically, he could have declined the posting. It was hard to see why he wouldn't have.

Which had triggered another major alarm in Katie's mind. A memory about something her grandmother had said in reaction to some weird rumors some of her Academy colleagues had shared. They'd claimed SFHQ had spies watching everything that happened in the Space Force. That you had to watch your p's and q's at all times because SFHQ was always watching even if they didn't always immediately act on what they saw.

It'd seemed far-fetched to Katie. Seemed like a crazy conspiracy theory that some less scrupulous cadets liked to peddle to the more gullible ones for shits and giggles, not to put a fine point on it.

She'd asked her grandmother, the crusty old ex-Admiral, about it just to be sure. To her surprise, her grandmother had confirmed an "internal intelligence section", the SIS, did exist. She'd gone on to note that if you were alert to the possibility it wasn't that hard to spot their operatives. The old Admiral had said they liked to use reservists, especially enlisted ones. Apparently because it was easier to gloss over anomalies in the agent's records and because many officers didn't pay much attention to their enlisted hands, let alone much to their backgrounds.

This Robert Hood guy didn't have a previous record of getting in trouble. To her surprise, Katie found herself suspecting it was more likely he was an SFHQ agent than that he was a troublemaker and a thug. Or, well, at least, an officially, if secretly, sanctioned troublemaker rather than a freelance one.

Like her life wasn't already complicated enough.

So by the time they had all arrived at the Main Police Station, Katie was feeling edgily unhappy again.

The senior police sergeant, apparently in charge of the reception area there, looked up, spotted them, and spoke without greeting or any other preamble. "Straight through those doors," he said, pointing. "Conference room three doors down on the right."

Katie nodded. "Thank you, Sergeant." And led her little group in the direction indicated.

Entering the conference room, she found several people waiting for her. None of them looked like the man she'd come to get.

"Lieutenant Kincaid. I'm the *Humber*'s new Executive Officer. I've come to fetch one of our crew members I understand you have in custody," she announced.

A slight man, a little taller than average, wearing a police uniform with a lot of gold on the shoulders and sleeves, extended his hand to Katie. "Police Chief Ken Kabukicho Lieutenant," he said.

"Pleased to meet you, Chief," Katie said, shaking his hand. "Wish it'd been under other circumstances. Where's my man? What's his story?"

"Your man," the police chief smiled thinly, "is in custody and under guard. He's dangerous. He killed a man. Claims it was self-defense."

"Which it fairly clearly was," said the man in the marine uniform. A uniform with a captain's insignia and a name tag reading "Von Luck".

"Which it is up to the courts to determine," an attractive woman in very sharp business attire put in.

Katie had the feeling she was older than she looked. "And you are?"

"Apologies, Lieutenant. Brigit Kharkov," she said, extending her hand. "Your Mars Station counterpart. I'm the Executive Officer for Mars Station and I handle most of the internal and day-to-day workings of the station. President Malik sets policy and works with other jurisdictions."

As soon as Katie had finished shaking the station executive's hand, the marine put his out. "Captain Heinrich von Luck, head of the Space Force marine detachment on-station," he said, confirming what Katie had already guessed.

A lot of cooks stirring this particular broth, Katie had to think. Also, she'd already had a long day despite having been on station less than twenty-four hours. She looked the Chief straight in the eye. "Is Hood under arrest? Have you charged him? Did he resist being taken into custody?"

The chief blinked.

Katie glanced at Kharkov and von Luck. They both had carefully blank faces, though Katie would swear von Luck was wearing a slight smile.

The chief threw Kharkov, nominally his superior, a questioning look. He wasn't getting any help there.

"Currently Leading Spacer Hood is not under arrest and we

haven't charged him with anything yet." He made a sound in his throat and looked around for help. Again, he wasn't getting any. Brigit Kharkov could have been watching a particularly boring speech and von Luck seemed outright amused at the chief's discomfort. Katie almost felt sorry for him. Almost. It had been a long day.

The chief continued. "As for being co-operative," he said, answering a different question than the one Katie had asked, "he did not resist arrest and hasn't been violent. He hasn't been willing to tell us anything other than to confirm who he was and to insist it was self-defense. He's insisting he won't talk except to you. We've been waiting for you to find out what his story is."

"To be clear," von Luck said, "he's been insisting on talking to you alone and in an unmonitored room. Apparently the man hasn't got a high opinion of the Martian justice system."

The chief didn't look happy about this interjection. Kharkov looked blander than ever.

Katie had questions, but wasn't feeling patient. She tried to look thoughtful before speaking. "Allow me to be clear," she said. "A Space Force member steps off of his ship and the first thing that happens is that he's attacked in broad daylight on your station, Chief, and your response is to take him into custody without legal reason and to attempt to interrogate him. Is that correct?"

The chief took a breath. "I wouldn't have put it that way."

Katie wasn't having that. "But that's basically accurate. Right? Was he off the direct path between the Martian Queen's disembarkation area and the *Humber*? Did he have a weapon? How many assailants were there? Do you have any witnesses? What did they say? Are you going to allow me to see him in private?"

Again the chief looked to Brigit Kharkov, the Station Executive, and, Katie was surer than ever, his de facto boss. Thi time, Kharkov relented. "Just the facts, Chief," she said.

The chief took a deep breath and let it out in something bordering on a sigh. "The incident occurred right at the outlet from the passenger docks. He had a knife but claims it wasn't his. Given that third-class passengers aren't allowed weapons on liners and that witnesses agree one of his assailants dropped it, this appears to be true. There appear to have been two assailants. One killed outright and one that escaped. We only managed to get two or three witnesses."

"Only two or three witnesses? You don't know how many witnesses you have? The disembarkation area wasn't crowded?"

The police chief cleared his throat and gave Katie a small tired smile. Katie was surprised. She would have expected embarrassment or hostility or some combination, but not this. The chief spoke. "My men report there were dozens of people present, but they only managed to nab three before the crowd dispersed. Their more immediate concern was subduing the man who'd just killed another one. Of the three possible witnesses we've detained, one of them plausibly maintains he was just passing by and didn't see anything. I'm afraid, Lieutenant Kincaid, that there are special challenges in policing in Martian space."

"Okay, but what have the witnesses you have said? Most importantly, are you going to let me see my man privately?"

Brigit Kharkov spoke up. "We'd all like to hear what he has to say. It doesn't seem to make sense to waste time and make him tell his story multiple times. I'm sure he'd like to get this over with as quickly as possible."

Katie gave the other woman a hard look. She hadn't been impressed with her so far. Von Luck had made it clear that Hood wanted to talk to Katie, or at least whatever officer came to collect him, in private. Somehow Kharkov thought Katie might have forgotten that and was trying to brush past it. Katie was sorely tempted to call the woman out on it in no uncertain terms. Katie took a deep breath and showed her teeth in what the misguided might call a smile. "You will allow me to talk to Hood now, and in private, or I will personally ensure that not only this incident, but the whole station, is audited by SFHQ, down to the color of the socks you're currently wearing. Am I understood?" Katie was impressed by her own relative restraint.

Kharkov stiffened and turned an unflattering color of red before her thoughts apparently caught up with her gut feelings and she turned pale. She took a deep breath of her own. She managed something resembling a smile, however insincere. "Forgive me, Lieutenant. I'm too used to being the one in charge here on Mars Station. As it happens, we're on the same side. I think we should be careful to avoid getting started off onthe wrong foot. I don't believe Chief Kabukicho plans to charge Leading Spacer Hood." She looked at that worthy."Correct?"

"No, pending further information, it does look like self-defense. Normally I'd ask he'd not leave our jurisdiction until the official investigation is complete, but as a Space Force member he's out of it as soon as he boards the *Humber*." The chief must have had a sore throat as he cleared it once again."I do assume the Space Force will be responsible for his behavior from now on in."

"Great," Kharkov said in the tone you'd use with a well-behaved dog. "And I don't imagine it will be any problem arranging a private interview with the man. You can decide if you want him after that. I don't imagine the *Humber* has long-term facilities for keeping a problem child in custody. Good?"

Katie looked around before answering. The police chief looked resigned. Von Luck was having a hard time suppressing an outright grin. Kharkov looked like she'd eaten something bad but was determined to be complimentary regards the cooking. "Good," Katie said. She turned to the marine leading her shore party. "Corporal Bloggins, you and the others will remain here. I'm sure the chief can show me the way to where Leading Spacer Hood is being held."

"Ma,am? We're responsible for your safety."

"I'll be fine, Corporal. Lead on, Chief."

It wasn't far. A nondescript door on a long corridor full of them. "This is a long-term holding room for non-suicidal witnesses or suspects," the chief said. "As you're probably aware, we're prohibited by Solar System Federal law from monitoring healthy non-suicidal citizens for more than a brief period after initial detention. You'll have the requested privacy here. I'm sending you a signed official certification of that over the local net."

Katie's personal device, her tablet, pinged. It was as the chief had said. "Thank you, Chief."

"I assure you, I'm probably more competent and sympathetic than you think, Lieutenant Kincaid," the chief said with what was his first genuine, if somewhat wan, smile. "You can find your own way back to the conference room when you're done. You can bring Hood with you if you wish. Also, I'm legally required to ascertain that you know your safety with him is not our responsibility."

"No problem, Chief," Katie answered. "I'm good. I know the way back. I doubt very much that Hood is a danger and I'm quite capable of defending myself anyway. It's okay."

The chief nodded and left.

Katie let herself into the little holding room.

The man she found sitting in the corner there on the end of a basic bunk seemed very ordinary. Certainly not someone you'd expect to be the center of a major incidence of violence. His uniform was slashed open and the white of bandages peeked through. It didn't have the dramatic impact you might expect. He had a slightly more solid and broodingly dangerous air compared to the average person, perhaps. But it was nothing that you could pin down. Dark haired, dark side of a white complexion, brown eyes, not ugly, but not really handsome either. Maybe a couple of centimeters taller than average. If the man stood out for anything, it was for being nondescript.

Katie looked at him and snorted.

Leading Spacer Robert Hood looked blandly back.

This seemed to be the night for bland looks, Katie couldn't help thinking. She had to be tired. Her mind was beginning to squirrel off in odd directions. Better get this over with. "I'm Lieutenant Kincaid, your new XO," she said.

"Yes, ma'am," he answered. He pointed at Katie's tablet and made some writing gestures.

Well, von Luck was right. The man didn't trust the Martian justice system or that this conversation was truly private. Katie quickly tapped some questions into her tablet. "What r u? Story?" Aloud she said, "This is a private unmonitored conversation." She handed her tablet to Hood.

Hood gave her a cynical smile in return. "That's good, ma'am. I'm sure something is very wrong here. I was attacked unprovoked as soon as I left the passenger docks." While speaking, he tapped something into Katie's tablet and handed it back to her.

"A man's dead," Katie said while reading what he'd written. "SIS. Investigator. Look out u 2," he'd wrote. She tapped her tablet quickly again. "Y? How?" Passed it back.

"Yes, ma'am. Two of them with knifes, and I was unarmed. I was fighting for my life. I wasn't in any place to pull my punches. Lucky they only scratched me, ma'am, really." All the while he was talking, he tapped away on Katie's tablet. Impressive display of multi-tasking.

"Well, there's going to have to be an investigation, but that story appears to match what the police have been able to learn. If I take you back to the *Humber*, will you come quietly and behave yourself once on board?"

"Yes, ma'am," Hood answered. "Not one to cause problems if I can help it, ma'am." He finished his tapping and passed the tablet back to Katie.

"Hmm," Katie tried to sound like she was in deep thought, considering his assertion while actually reading the tablet. "XO death, Audit. Ship net bkdr. Msg addr 2 'Merry Men of Sherwood' reach me any place time u need me on pdev." Katie nodded. "Okay, once back on the ship, I don't want to be seeing you again. Understand?"

"Yes, ma'am," Hood said nodding.

Katie faked a smile. She wasn't happy to learn that SFHQ had inserted back doors into its ships' networks. "Very good, come with me."

The rest of the evening was comparatively uneventful.

Nothing happened on their way back to the *Humber*. There were no attacks by knife-bearing thugs, gunfights, or people throwing baby bombs. Katie had Hood checked in the Med Bay and the medic gave him a couple of weeks light duty. Hood assured Katie he'd have no problem finding his berth on his own. She'd already dismissed her shore party.

Arriving back in her cabin, Katie messaged both the captain and the CERA, the chief in charge of engineering personnel, about having successfully retrieved Hood. She quickly showered and went to bed to get some well-deserved rest. It had been a long day.

Katie slept deeply and without dreaming.

**

It was the next morning. Katie had slept well. She didn't feel better for it.

So much had happened after she'd stepped off of the Martian Queen that she'd not had time to absorb it.

Now the gravity of what had happened, and the implications of it, were beginning to come home. It didn't make her happy.

Unfortunately, fate wasn't allowing her time to digest events.

It'd been a hurried breakfast and now she was standing in front of the door to her new captain's cabin. She was about to meet the man she was supposed to be running the *Humber* for. She had to figure out what he wanted her to do. She could only hope it both agreed with her and that she was capable of it. She could only hope the captain would help in seeing how to do it.

It was obvious to Katie that the *Humber* wasn't being run well right now and that she needed to change that. She could only hope the captain agreed. If not, it was his wishes that would prevail. Either way, as per what her grandmother had said, she could not allow any daylight to be seen between what the captain wanted and what she did. Katie took a deep breath.

Katie pressed the button to alert the captain of her presence. "Come in," came the response.

Katie had wondered if she should wear her dress uniform to this, her first meeting with the captain. Katie had chosen to wear her uniform ship suit instead. She was hoping it'd come off as unpretentious and down to business and not insulting.

The captain sitting in his darkened cabin was wearing a silk Chinese robe and slippers. He was sitting at a large table, working on what looked like a ship model in a large bottle. His work was brightly lit by the cabin's sole light. The ship he was building with a set of miniature waldoes wasn't a modern spaceship or a conventional nineteenth century clipper or schooner, but what Katie rather thought was an early modern man of war. Looked very fancy whatever it was.

"What ship?" Katie asked to break the ice.

"Sovereign of the Seas," the captain answered. "Charles the First's pride and joy. Arguably the Royal Navy's first major battleship."

Katie could have debated that. Katie rather thought Elizabeth the First and Hawkins, or maybe even, Henry the Eighth, Elizabeth's father, could have claimed to have begun the long building of the Royal Navy that had led to its dominating the world's oceans for a century or more. Herself, she believed the decisive date was 1649 under an effectively Republican Parliamentary regime when they'd reformed English finances and started using their new revenues to build a navy capable of wresting control of the world's trade from the Dutch.

None of which was relevant to the current situation. Also, Katie wasn't going to start off by arguing with her new captain, Lieutenant-Commander Ernst Anthony Smith, to give him his full name and rank, even over a shared interest. Might work out, might not. "Very ornate, very impressive looking," Katie said.

The captain smiled briefly without looking at her. "Yes, indeed it is," he said, "unlike your arrival yesterday, I'm afraid. Guess I can't blame you for getting caught in a terrorist explosion on arrival, but you do know the bosun probably saved your life?"

"Yes, sir."

"By tackling you while you ran away from him in fear? Not the best look, Lieutenant."

"I'd dispute the fear, sir. And, sir, I don't know your source for what happened, but may I suggest it may not have been the most unbiased."

"You may suggest, Lieutenant. In any event, I missed you yesterday as it was sometime before you arrived on board. I am pleased with how you handled the retrieval of our wayward electrician once you got here."

"Thank you, sir."

"Yes, you're a young firebrand known for being able to get things done, aren't you, Lieutenant Kincaid?"

"I can't speak to other people's opinions, sir."

The captain looked up at her, his eyes sharp, the fine wrinkles around them looking more like life experience than fatigue and age. "Indeed. Well, it seems to be a common opinion. Also, I'm well aware that SFHQ is not happy with the *Humber*'s failure to meet its goals. Both those of patrolling Martian space and the nearby parts of the Belt."

"I answer to you, sir. My role is to be your righthand man. How is up to you, but we both know traditionally the XO runs the ship for their captain. I don't answer to SFHQ any more than any other officer."

The captain nodded. "Good. That is how it should be." He fiddled with his ship model, affixing a minuscule yard to a tiny mast. "You know, Lieutenant, this is the apex of my career. It's not everybody that gets to be a ship's captain."

"Yes, sir. A very small number. It represents a lot of trust on the part of SFHQ and the system authorities." It was very true. There were some doubts about how the Space Force's ships would fare in a real naval battle. There was no doubt at all that in the hands of a rogue captain they could inflict devastating damage on civilian infrastructure and populations, both in space and on planetary surfaces.

"The *Humber* is probably my last ship," the captain said. "Finish up here in a year or two, a bit of time in some bureaucratic shore posting, and I'm retired. I'm about ready for it to be honest."

"Sir?" Katie wondered where this was going.

"So, I wish we were getting all the missions SFHQ has given us done, but given the circumstances, I feel we've done well to keep the *Humber* and her crew as functional as they are. Given our bad luck with XOs, we owe much of that to the bosun. He's stepped up and filled a vacuum beyond what he's formally responsible for."

"Yes, sir. What about the Cox'n and CERA?" The coxswain was formally the bosun's and senior enlisted engineer's boss. The senior enlisted engineer, the chief engine room artificer or CERA, was formally the bosun's peer.

"They're waiting out their time to retirement hoping nothing goes too wrong before then," the captain said. His mouth quirked. "I feel comfortable saying so, as they're friends. We often share the odd discreet wet together."

Great. The captain and two of the *Humber*'s most senior NCOs were just killing time until retirement, leaving the actual running of the ship to the third senior NCO. Apparently, the rest of the officers were too busy with specialist activities to fill the void. Katie didn't sense she was going to get much support in reforming the *Humber* from any of them.

Worse, although the captain was right, and the bosun had probably saved her life, which probably meant he at least wasn't responsible for trying to kill her, she did not like or trust the man.

"That's very frank, sir," Katie said.

The captain smiled thinly without looking at her. "Yes, I think there's too much room for misunderstanding as it is without beating around the bush. Also, Kincaid, you've got a reputation for being honest, if self-righteous and opinionated. I'm trusting you to be discreet." He looked her directly in the eyes for a few seconds before turning back to his work, apparently satisfied with what he saw. "Unlike myself, you're still young and ambitious. I don't think you're going to settle for leaving things as they are and just coasting. Waiting out the posting, punching your ticket, and progressing further on the fast track. You're very young for an XO. Went to the Academy young, been promoted very quickly."

"Yes, sir." It was all true. Katie couldn't deny it. She didn't understand why the captain was pointing it out. She feared she was being set up for some sort of dismissal or putdown.

"So, I fully expect you to try to shake things up, and try to ensure the *Humber* is available to do all her assigned missions, however ambitious and unreasonable they may be. I will support you in your efforts, Lieutenant."

"Thank you, sir," Katie said, surprised.

The captain indulged himself in another thin smile. "Yes, I'll be happy to take credit for whatever success you have. Let's be clear, I don't think it's the wisest course of action for you personally from a career point of view. If I thought there was the faintest chance you'd take my advice, I'd tell you to not upset the apple cart and just punch your ticket. Mars and the

Humber are a tinder heap. Misstep and you'll have a situation that's no improvement at all. You make things worse and I'll hang you out to dry. Understood?"

Katie still wasn't happy. If anything, she was unhappier than ever, but the captain had clarified the situation. "Yes, sir. Understood. If it's all right with you, sir. I'll schedule a general inspection of the ship for three days from now. Let everyone know there's a new sheriff in town and get a baseline fix on the *Humber*'s state."

The captain nodded slowly. "A solidly conventional approach. Still, be careful, downright delicate if you can, I know it's not your strong point. Try to praise what's right more than you condemn what's wrong. It's been a while since we've had a formal inspection and that alone will get a lot of the hands in a dither."

"Sir?"

"Remember, you get more flies with honey than vinegar, Lieutenant."

Katie had heard the expression before but still didn't quite know why you'd want to get flies at all. All the same, the captain was granting her what she wanted, although grudgingly and with significant reservations it seemed. "Yes, sir."

"Is that all, Lieutenant?"

"Yes, sir," Katie answered. Katie knew when she was being dismissed. She left.

4: A Rocky Start, Kincaid

So the time had come. Mid-morning three days after Katie's first meeting with the captain. Cleaning stations were done, and Katie's first formal inspection of the *Humber* was due to begin. Katie hoped the hands weren't feeling as keyed up and apprehensive as she was.

The bridge, wardroom, and officer's quarters were all exempt. The inspection would begin in the admin office part of the gravity ring.

Katie's goal was to assert her authority without stepping on anyone's corns.

If she managed to get a better fix on the state of the *Humber*, and perhaps inspire the crew to improve it some, that'd be gravy.

Katie had talked to the coxswain about who'd accompany her on her rounds. She'd wanted him to. To her frustration, he'd demurred. "I mostly do paperwork, ma'am," he'd said. "Bosun and CERA are the hands-on ones. They'll be able to answer any questions you have better."

And so, Katie was starting the inspection with the bosun at her side. The same blandly smiling man that made her teeth ache as always. Superficially, he'd been completely co-operative. Whenever she summoned him or managed to find him on her own, he'd say "Yes, ma'am" to everything she said and then leave as quickly as possible.

She got no feedback or information she didn't pull out of him almost physically.

That said, as they moved through the admin offices, she began to find herself pleasantly surprised. When she'd first come on board, she'd noticed a faint film on most surfaces that suggested they weren't scrubbed as thoroughly or as often as they should be.

Katie was checking to see if that was still true. She'd have not been surprised or even particularly displeased if it was. It was hard work keeping a ship squeaky clean. It was a standard she hoped to reach, but not one she'd had much hope of on her first inspection.

Katie was checking the surfaces with a disposable wipe. She had noticed that the use of a natural fiber handkerchief, as was standard at the Academy, had rubbed some of the hands on the *Susquehanna* the wrong way. Smacked of elitist snobbery, it seemed. Katie despaired of ever understanding the class politics of the Solar System outside of the Belt, but she tried to avoid its pitfalls as best she could.

In any case, the film she'd fully expected was missing. A good thing. "The crew seems to have done a very thorough cleaning job, Bosun," she said. Maybe there was hope for effective co-operation between them after all.

"Yes, ma'am," the bosun answered. "I made it perfectly clear to the lot of them that every surface was to be clean enough to eat off of."

Katie nodded as they moved from one cramped office to the next, past the clerks that worked in them, all standing rigidly at attention. She tried to look a couple in the eye, but none of them were having any of it. "I'm impressed, Bosun."

As they moved from the admin offices to the galley and the messes, and then the workspaces of the deck department, basically Ops, Weapons, and Supply, she continued to be impressed by how neat, tidy, and painfully clean the ship was.

She also became increasingly concerned by an unspoken,

but palpable, resentment on the part of the crew members. Stiffly correct, they continued to refuse to meet her eyes, and answered any questions she asked as briefly and coldly as they could.

"You must have worked the crew hard to achieve these results," Katie observed to the bosun.

Damned if the man's grin didn't broaden and his eyes didn't take on a mocking glint. It'd never stand up as fact in a court of law, but Katie was convinced that's what she was seeing.

"Yes, ma'am," the bosun answered. "Didn't give them any time off and rode them hard the whole last few days."

Katie gave him a smile she didn't feel.

When they finally reached the engineering workshops, she turned to him. "I'm impressed. Your people deserve a break. Give everyone that's not absolutely essential a day's stand down," she said.

There, that ought to take some of the edge off the image of her as an unreasonable hard arse that Katie had no doubt the bosun had promulgated.

"Yes, ma'am," the bosun replied. Of course.

Engineering proved to be an entirely different experience.

The CERA took over from the bosun.

The captain had identified the CERA as a friend but a time-server as well. Maybe, but that wasn't the impression Katie got of Master Chief John Carswell. At first the chief seemed like a less tubby, but shorter, version of the classical Santa Claus figure. A perfect little seventeenth century Dutch elf. A little rumpled and not skinny, if not fat either, he had round pale features with rosy cheeks. A pair of milky blue eyes looked out of the face those features formed. His hair was stereotypical wisps of pure white.

Appearances aside, his manner was all business and to the point.

He shook hands, and saying, "Follow me," led her off.

The chief described each space he took her to in a casual, matter-of-fact way. "This is the electrical workshop. Most maintenance and repair happens in place, but occasionally it's necessary to pull a component out and give it a careful going over here," was one remark he made.

His introductions to his crew were as matter of fact. "This here is Chief Petty Officer Tony Caligari. He's the head electrician," for instance.

In each case, Katie either shook hands with the engineering crew member or exchanged a friendly nod. Having done so, they stood aside to let her look around, but remained available for questions.

Katie was finding the engineering spaces less consistently and thoroughly clean than the ones the bosun had shown her.

They were all neat and well organized, though. It mightn't be fair, but regards engineering Katie was less worried about surfaces being squeaky clean. She was more concerned about gear being in good repair and well maintained.

For the most part, that seemed to be the case. Particularly up in the gravity ring in the workshops, everything looked fine. Down in the spindle that began to change. Everything still seemed to work, but it began to be apparent that it had required using non-Space Force standard components and parts here and there.

The odd lighting fixture would be what you'd usually see on a civilian survey ship, Katie was very familiar with them, not what the Space Force used. Much the same function but not certified to be as robust.

One first aid kit in an emergency station had obviously been recently replaced. Only instead of standard Space Force issue, an equivalent civilian kit had been used. Katie was familiar with both. Functionally, the contents were identical, only one was officially approved and one wasn't.

Moving down the spindle's central access way to the Engine Room, Katie found the most egregious example of ad hoc repair yet.

A piece of multi-function conduit was obviously non-standard.

One of the facets of her stay on Earth Katie had really enjoyed was the opportunity to visit ocean-going museum ships. Ships from both the Age of Sail and the Early Industrial Era that bracketed the twentieth century.

The cables and cabling racks of twentieth century warships

had fascinated her. An admittedly minority interest. Her friends had shaken their heads and commented, "Only you, Katie."

Be that as it may, the fact that early industrial ships had moved power and signals around through long strings of essentially hand-crafted pieces of metallic wire individually wrapped in insulation, and that they were placed in overhead cable racks, were things that had amazed and fascinated Katie.

Although bundled together, each of the wires was essentially a single point-to-point connection subject to interruption at any point. If such an interruption should occur, a good repair required replacing the whole length of cable. A time consuming and resource hungry process. In an emergency, splicing in a replacement stretch of wire was possible, but that required a skilled specialist, and still took some time.

Modern practice was a huge improvement. Modern multi-purpose conduits came in tough, pre-fabricated sections that ran between interconnection boxes, also tough and standard. A section could be pulled out and a new piece snapped in in mere seconds. The interconnection boxes would automatically re-rout power and signals around the damaged section. If the automatics failed, it was again only a matter of mere seconds to force the re-direction manually.

The intent was that ships should be able to continue working even in the event of massive damage, whether from being hit by a rogue piece of debris or as the result of enemy action.

Also, conduits were prone to being occasionally damaged in the course of normal operations. Although this was a fact no spacer had ever succeeded in getting through the skull of anydesk jockey, it was still a fact. Not so much on family owned and operated ships, where the ship belonged to its crew and they were careful to not damage it. Only many ships needed to hire outsiders. Those outsiders were often planet or station born. Those outsiders weren't always as careful and delicate in moving heavy cargo or gear around as they could be.

Even tough conduit could take only so much abuse. It had

to be accessible to be repairable. It could only have so much armor and crush padding before it became too expensive, and in aggregate, too heavy, to be practical.

And so, even without catastrophic accident, conduit had to be replaced routinely.

Therefore, Katie wasn't surprised to see a piece of conduit had needed replacing. She was surprised that a piece of largely civilian conduit had been used. Military conduit was deliberately designed not to be compatible with civilian designs. Ostensibly so that crews wouldn't succumb to the temptation of using less robust civilian product on Space Force ships.

Some careful and very skilled work had gone into grafting military connectors onto the piece of civilian conduit Katie was currently looking at. She was immensely impressed. And completely appalled.

"This is interesting, Chief," Katie said.

"Yes, tricky work that," the chief answered. "Our supply clerks couldn't convince their counterparts back on Goddard Station that we needed new military grade conduit. Said that was a yard supply, not a ship one first time around. Then they said shipping costs were excessive. Now they're saying they need a sign off from a commissioned supply officer. Not their fault we don't have one apparently."

Katie frowned. "I'll look into it, Chief."

The chief beamed. "Appreciate that, ma'am."

The rest of the inspection went quickly and comfortably until it was almost done.

Finally reaching the Engine Room, Katie decided to inspect the interior of a damage control station. Idly looking inside for anything out of place, she asked the chief a question that had been worrying her, but she hadn't been sure she could raise. Feeling a bit more comfortable with the chief she decided to give it a shot. "Looks like your crew put some effort into making your spaces all clean and proper, Chief," she said. "I know the engineer's been working overtime down here in propulsion. I hope this wasn't too much of a distraction from more pressing tasks."

"No, ma'am," the chief began before grabbing her arm in a

tight grip.

Katie had been reaching for a dedicated damage control communications box. She'd wanted to verify it functioned as it should. It was a standard sort of thing to check during an inspection.

Katie looked at the chief's hand on her arm and then up into his eyes. They were hard.

They directed her attention to the piece of conduit leading into the comms box. There were faint scratches around its fasteners.

"This work doesn't look up to the normal standard of your people," Katie said. Unable to keep a faint puzzlement out of her voice, she feared.

"None of mine would do this," the chief said, anger underlying his words. "They've got the skills and tools to do it right. This was some yob with a knife." He paused. "Rollins, get over here with a meter," he yelled to someone behind them.

Katie backed off to give the new arrival, room to squeeze in.

"Check the charge on the comms box case, Rollins," the chief said.

Rollins did as he was told. His face turned surprised, then grim. "Full charge of high power on the case, Chief," he said.

"Someone pulling a prank by giving someone a shock, Chief?" Katie asked.

"Someone trying to kill you more likely, ma'am," the chief answered grimly.

***

Katie was shocked. Not literally. Thank the Deity her father believed in and she didn't, not really, and the CERA too, for that. But emotionally, she was surprised and she was angry. Angry in a way she had no clear way to express.

At least here in her cabin, with the morning's inspection done, and lunch not quite arrived, she didn't have to school her face and body language to hide how she felt.

Which was a relief. It freed up energy and focus she could

use to think about what had happened.

For one thing, for all that she didn't much like him, and was convinced the man was working to keep her from establishing her authority over the *Humber*, the bosun had saved her life almost as soon as she'd stepped off of the Martian Queen.

It seemed to her he'd acted quickly on an unpremeditated appreciation of the situation. So she didn't think he'd known the explosion was coming. On seeing what was happening, his first instinct had been to protect her. Better, he'd succeeded in doing so.

Hard not to appreciate that on one level.

On the other hand, it was as clear as day he was used to running the non-engineering part of the *Humber*, at least, without any interference from pesky officers.

Theoretically, that didn't need to be nefarious. It didn't, theoretically, even need to be a problem if she didn't want to make it one.

Theoretically, she could do as the captain had suggested. She could warm her seat for what was likely to be a short posting before the *Humber* was recalled to Earth and likely sent into a prolonged re-fit. Have her stint as an XO ticket punched, probably get promoted again, and sent on to her next stop on the fast track. Easy-Peasy.

Only, not only was that not in character, but trying to be as objectively rational as she could be, she couldn't convince herself it was the right thing to do.

Something wasn't right on the *Humber*.

Heck, there looked like there were a pile of somethings on the *Humber*, on Mars Station, in Mars space, on Mars itself, and in the nearby part of the Belt that weren't right.

But her concern, her responsibility, was the *Humber*.

That a senior NCO seemed to be mostly running the ship while the officers either pursued hobbies or, at least, stuck to specialties like propulsion and piloting was one disturbing oddity.

That the ship had missed its assigned patrol missions was certainly another.

That someone, or heavens forbid maybe a couple of someones, had almost killed her twice in her first week on board was hard to ignore.

Katie didn't think sticking her head in the sand and trying to wait the thing out would work. The captain's suggestion wasn't really on her menu of choices.

She needed to figure out what was going on.

She had to act to fix it.

And there was no way she could wait to do that.

Whatever was happening in and around Mars, Katie had to get in control of the *Humber*.

And then she needed to put an end to whatever shenanigans had been going on.

If the bosun turned out to be one of the good guys, and helped, great.

If not, too bad.

***

Pat didn't generally waste time on regrets. Angst wasn't his thing. He'd long ago made the resolution to accept things as they were and get on with doing what he could. Cheerfully. Without pointless second thoughts. As a tangible sign of that commitment, he'd made a point of always having a smile plastered on his face. Whenever he spoke to someone, he was careful to always frame what he said in a positive, upbeat, and optimistic way. He was never explicitly negative.

Kincaid was trying his resolution.

Truth was, he was rather inclined to like the young woman, both from what he knew of her record, and from what he'd seen of her so far. She was a can-do sort. If she'd started blubbering, or even just locked herself in her cabin in a funk after almost being blown up on her arrival on station he'd not have been surprised. But she hadn't.

Kincaid had taken the reality of sudden death in stride. Good for her.

With that, Pat decided to propose another toast. "To our new XO. Guts, glory, and everything squeaky clean, no matter what!"

Someone snickered. "Gotta have priorities."

They all raised their beer filled beverage dispensers, personal, and drank. Most of the *Humber*'s non-engineering NCOs were present in the mess, enjoying the day their new XO had given them off. Most of them were active supporters of Pat's and in on, at least some of his little schemes. Those that weren't had long ago learned to mind their own business.

Out around Mars, men had to fend for themselves. Women too, but it was even tougher for them. The few that managed it were considered honorary real men, much more so than any floppy wristed pencil neck of indeterminate gender from somewhere around Earth.

Or so the prevalent mythology went. Pat thought it was all bull. The application of incongruous lipstick to a very ugly pig. Pat hadn't been happy when he'd learned the *Humber* and himself were being assigned to Mars space. He'd thought he'd escaped the damned place.

Probably what that poor, damned electrician they'd just been given had thought. Somebody higher up in the hierarchy of existence had it out for Martians. Pat wasn't sure about that man. Might be just another hard-luck story or might be an HQ plant. Pat didn't know, but he'd keep close tabs on him and figure it out, eventually.

That wasn't his main problem. Kincaid was.

"New XO going to be a problem, Bosun?" his lead weapons tech, SPO Sally Forsyth, asked. Apparently, he wasn't doing a good job of keeping his thoughts to himself.

"Could be, PO," Pat answered. "She doesn't seem to be one to leave well enough alone. Seems like she's a meddler."

"Seems like someone's got it in for her," the senior medic commented.

"Hell," Sally said, "everyone knows those Star Rat smugglers have given her the black mark."

"Everybody knows you read too many pirate romances, Sally," the Medic answered. "Like those bodice rippers, do you?"

"Fact is," Sally said, "anybody who hasn't had their head up their butts the last few years knows there's people with money and armed ships out there that have threatened to kill her."

"With the lady's talent for making enemies, I'm guessing it's a bit of a competition as to who gets to her first," an operations type muttered half to themselves.

Pat figured this was getting out of hand. "Girl's trying," he said.

"Certainly is," someone commented.

Pat ignored them. "As long as she's XO I'm going to give her all the support she deserves."

Sally smiled. She knew what Pat was really thinking. "I'll drink to that," she said aloud.

They all raised their beverage containers in a toast. They all knew the bosun had told them to change the topic.

Pat gave his table, and the mess in general, a broad grin.

Kincaid might be a problem that solved itself. Not in any manner that looked suspicious, let alone could be traced to Pat if he had his way, though.

Kincaid was a problem he'd make sure was solved. But quietly.

No way he was letting either Kincaid, or her likely early demise, interfere with his retirement plans.

He was too close to allow that.

***

Leading Spacer Rob Hood, both the *Humber*'s newest crew member and its newest electrician, was beginning to suspect his stint on board the ship wasn't going to be any picnic.

The knife attack, detention, and shore patrol that had greeted him upon his arrival had only been the first hints.

Supposedly, he was on light duties. That was according to the medic.

Rob wasn't sure his new boss, Chief Electrician Caligari, had gotten the memo.

Upon Rob's reporting for duty in the electrical workshop first thing in the morning several days ago, the chief had greeted him laconically.

"Welcome to the *Humber*, Leading Spacer Hood," he'd said in a monotone. "I'm dumping a list of tasks to your device. Get on with it. Goodbye."

It'd been a very long list that was taking Rob alone to odd unfrequented corners of the *Humber*.

Whether the *Humber*'s other electricians simply didn't like working anywhere other than the full gravity areas of the ship or it was something else Rob didn't know. At least he didn't have to work in the galley. He hated the grease, moisture, and heat of the place. Rob wasn't sure how the cooks managed to hack it.

On the other hand, Rob was working alone in odd parts of the ship for long periods of time. Bad things could happen to a man under those circumstances. Might be a long time before anyone noticed, too.

Rob had heard much of the rest of the crew had been given a stand down by the XO. Apparently Kincaid wasn't completely oblivious to issues of morale. Rob had not heard from the chief that this applied to him. So it pretty clearly did not.

It might be just the standard testing and trial period for a new guy. Rob suspected not.

The sudden appearance of a couple of burly weapons techs who should have been enjoying their day off confirmed that suspicion for him.

They had no good reason to be down in a non-weapons part of the spindle during their day off.

They were down here for Rob.

"Oh, look what we have here," the paler of the two said. "Our new tough guy electrician. All by his lonesome self. Wonder how tough he really is, Mike?"

They spread out to Rob's side and rear, malicious grins on their faces.

Rob figured he could take them.

Rob was tough. He was very well trained. More importantly, he was ruthless and decisive. He'd been in the odd fight before. It'd be wrong to say they held no fear for him. Rob was respectful of the risk any fight held, just as he was careful to avoid getting electrocuted while working on high power.

So he could take these two jerks, but that wasn't the problem. Taking these two out would only make things worse.

These two, whatever they thought, were mere messengers.

One of them reached in and gave Rob a hard shove. Rob resisted his instinctive reaction. His determination earned him a painful bruise as he collided with the open edge of a controller box and then the bulkhead next to it.

"What, the tough guy's going to let himself get pushed around?" the other thug asked.

"Not looking for trouble," Rob answered, playing his role.

In the end, they didn't break any bones. They certainly didn't cut Rob and cause any bleeding. They were apparently at least semi-professional thugs doing as ordered. Interesting factoid in its own right.

Rob got off with a variety of bruises and abrasions to his body. The bruises to his ego were deeper.

The lead thug had added insult to injury as they left, smirking at him. "Don't bother the medic with your whining. You're already on light duties, right? Don't want to end up in a hospital bed or on a slab, do you?"

They swaggered off, having delivered their message. Behave or else.

Rob had delivered his, too. Sure, I'll buckle under and not cause problems.

He meant it. He promised himself he'd keep his head down and try hard to avoid trouble.

Rob was going to be lucky to survive this assignment as it was.

5: Settle In, Kincaid

"Bosun, you're right here, right now and, believe you me, I know you can muck up my whole day," Leading Spacer Oliver Leblanc was saying.

"Got that right, Olly, and why shouldn't I?" Pat answered. "That's what you should be telling me."

"Because I had no choice, Bosun," Olly said. He looked sad and resigned, not frightened the way he should. "These guys, they've got connections with important people. They're bigger and scarier than you. Whatever you do to me, you're not going after my family, are you?"

Pat had found it necessary to cross a few lines in his day. And he still found himself wishing he was less principled and less cautious at times. "Probably not," Pat admitted. "Not into that whole sins of the fathers thing much. But, Olly, you will regret upsetting my apple cart. Got my retirement all planned and I don't need you giving the XO or SFHQ reasons to start stirring the muck up."

"Didn't want to cross you and got nothing against the new XO, but they said do her in or else."

Pat was curious about what could have induced the

normally phlegmatic and easygoing cook to attempt electrocuting Kincaid. "Or else?"

"Or else they'd not just do for me, but all my family and friends. And not in nice quick ways either." Now Olly looked scared. Haunted more, really, like there were things he wanted to unsee. "They were clear. Really clear about that, Bosun. I've got a younger sister. You don't want to know what they can do to young women if the wrong sort of people get a hold of them. You know people like us aren't safe if the big shots take notice of us."

Pat sighed. "I know, Olly. Sorry, but you understand I can't let this go by. You're going to have to pay. Turns out you've tripped and taken quite the fall."

Even with the warning, Pat's right hook caught Olly by surprise. Flipped his head back. His head hit the bulkhead behind him hard, stunning the man. Pat realized he'd overdone it out of anger and frustration.

He was more careful with the rest of the beating.

Stuck mostly to painful bruising blows to the ribs where it wouldn't show when Olly was dressed, but still hurt like hell.

Pat knew he had to send a message to the crew.

He also knew it wasn't enough. Apparently Kincaid had attracted the attention of powerful actors. Ones he couldn hope to handle. His best chance was probably to remove the target of their attention.

He had to hope that it was Kincaid, not the *Humber*'s possible patrol schedule, that was attracting their attention.

Pat really didn't like the situation one bit.

His planned retirement couldn't come a second too soon.

***

Katie had been surprised by the invitation from Brigit Kharkov, the station executive. It'd come out of the blue less than a week after Katie's arrival on the *Humber*.

It sounded like the woman wanted to mend fences after their initial somewhat awkward meeting with regard to Leading Spacer Hood's disposal.

"Captain von Luck and I like to spar regularly, usually twice a week, Tuesdays, and Fridays, in the Marine fitness complex. It's fun and a good opportunity to informally catch up on the news. Would you like to join us this Friday at 1600? We'd be happy to see you there. Yours sincerely, Brigit Kharkov," it'd read.

As it happened, the *Humber*'s exercise facilities were cramped, shared, and overused, and didn't permit of sparring sessions anyhow. After the biathlon, for which there were no venues any closer than Earth itself, sparring was Katie's favorite sport. So, just on a personal level, the invitation was an attractive one. On a practical level, Katie was acutely aware she had almost no idea what was going on on the *Humber*, let alone in the rest of Mars space. Since at least one someone was trying to kill her, it seemed, this was disturbing. Any sharing of news sounded very good to Katie, indeed. She needed to find out what the hell was going on.

So Katie had immediately accepted the invitation.

Following the directions downloaded to her tablet, Katie arrived at the reception area to the Marine fitness area to find Heinrich von Luck waiting for her.

"Spit your data over and I'll activate your associate membership," von Luck said.

Since both of their devices were Space Force issue that was no problem. Katie tapped in the necessary commands and they matched their wireless I/O ports and it was done.

"Great. Just a moment," von Luck said. "You know all your officers automatically have associate memberships here. Just need to be activated."

No, Katie hadn't known. Unfortunate, as it was one of her duties as the *Humber*'s Executive Officer to know such things. Maybe not the top of her priority list, but still part of her duties. "No, I hadn't," she said. "Thanks for mentioning it." She looked at a layout diagram of the facility covering most of one wall of the reception room. The place was quite large. Like on Ceres, it looked like the marine facilities here were much larger than was needed for the currently deployed marine detachment. "The facilities aren't overused?" she asked.

"Hardly," von Luck said, glancing at the layout diagram himself. "Mars Station is set up to have a much larger marine presence. Place got built and then that mess in the Belt and out around Jupiter happened. We've granted associate memberships to most of the station's executives and the place still seems empty. Your ship's officers seem to be mostly too busy or not interested."

"Mostly the first," Katie said. "I'll talk to them."

"Great. Then we're done. Change rooms through there. Sparring gym just beyond, but there are layout diagrams all over. See you in a bit."

One thing all Space Force officers learned at the Academy was how to be quick change artists. It was less than five minutes before Katie joined Brigit and von Luck in her gym gear. They had the sparring gym all to themselves.

Brigit was wearing bright red gear stretched tight over her very impressive super-heroine like figure. Katie noted that her business wear, as sharp as it was, had been designed more to emphasize her professionalism than how attractive she was. Interesting. Von Luck, on the other hand, was just as fit and as solidly built as you'd expect of a marine captain. He was in marine green, of course, just as Katie was in Space Force blue.

Brigit and von Luck had been talking. They nodded to Katie in greeting. "Glad you could make it," Brigit said. "We didn't start off on the right foot. I was afraid it might have led to hard feelings."

"It was an awkward situation," Katie allowed.

"One I intensely regret," Brigit said. "Somehow working relationships between Mars Station and the *Humber*'s people just haven't been as close or effective as we would have liked."

"That's even true of the *Humber*'s crew and those of us in the Space Force posted to the station," von Luck put in. He seemed more worried than accusatory.

"It'd been our fond hope," Brigit said, "that your arrival here might mark a new era of better co-operation."

Katie nodded. "Glad to hear that."

Brigit smiled slightly, but as best Katie could tell, genuinely. "Your almost getting killed in a major bombing attack, and then an attempted knifing of one of your crew members were not what we had in mind."

"I hadn't planned on them myself," Katie answered.

Brigit and von Luck both grinned at that. They seemed relieved Katie was taking it all in stride. That she was even willing to joke about it. "In any event," Brigit said, "Captain von Luck – Heinrich – and I want to offer all the help we can. We want you to know we're on your side."

Off to one side, von Luck nodded in agreement.

"Great," Katie said. She couldn't argue with the sentiment.

"We thought maybe we could start off by giving you a briefing on the local situation while we spar. Okay?" Brigit asked.

"If you're guessing SFHQ didn't give me an in-depth briefing on it," Katie answered while walking over to one side of the mat and squaring off against Brigit, "you're not wrong. I'd really like to know what the heck is going on."

"We don't know exactly what's going on ourselves," Brigit answered as she adopted a fighting stance, "but we can at least tell you who most of the serious actors are."

"That'd be a great start," Katie said as she eyed Brigit, waiting for her to make the first move. If the woman followed the usual informal rules for this sort of thing, it'd be a slow-motion move without any force behind it. The lack of any protective equipment and her declared intention to carry on a friendly conversation during the bout hinted as much. Of course, there were always degrees to these things.

Brigit started with a slow, clearly telegraphed high kick. "First off, there's no higher authority with any real power in Martian space with the ability to make and enforce law."

"That's not just distressing, it's very odd," Katie answered as she ducked back from Brigit's kick. She wondered if the woman's aggressiveness was cousin to a fondness for hyperbole.

"I know my history too," Brigit answered, just as if she'd heard the unspoken part of Katie's reaction. She shuffled to one side as if looking to flank Katie. "Usually the various parties let one dominate because even if they don't agree completely with either their principles or how they divide the common pie, any degree of order and predictability is preferable to violent chaos."

"Well put," Katie answered, hoping to assuage the woman's pride while she shuffled to one side herself to avoid being flanked.

Brigit smiled. Obviously, she liked to be buttered up even if she could see what was being done. She stopped her motion and waited alert. "Not the Martians as it happens," she said. "About the only thing they all agree on is that they don't want anyone else to be in a position to tell them what to do."

Katie remembered hearing as much, but hadn't realized how seriously they still took it. She stepped towards Brigit and threw a slow but very extended strike. "I'd heard about the Founders. That's the right term, yes?"

"Yes," Brigit answered, motioning a block and possible retaliation for getting overextended. "That's right. The Founders were the initial settlers. They put a ton of capital into reaching and developing the place all with the goal of being allowed to do what they damned well wanted to."

"And it's been that way ever since?" Katie said while backing off warily.

"Exactly," Brigit answered while watching Katie.

Katie wondered if the woman was surrendering the initiative for the time being. "Okay, but there have been follow-on groups, right? Some of them crooks. I understand the migrant workers have it hard and are a breeding ground for criminal activity."

"True, as far as it goes," von Luck contributed from the sidelines. Katie had almost forgotten he was there.

"Not to get too far ahead of ourselves," Brigit said while starting to circle in the other direction. Apparently she had a plan of presentation here she didn't want upset. "Yes, the migrants are a large and important if not very internally cohesive group."

Von Luck snorted by way of comment.

"Not that any of these groups are that cohesive internally," Brigit said, dropping her guard and giving von Luck an exasperated glance.

"Except these new Star Rat smugglers that have put out a bounty on Lieutenant Kincaid," von Luck answered without much in the way of contrition.

Katie moved in on Brigit, who brought her guard up again. She was annoyed. She'd been directly threatened by Guy Boucher, who was probably one of these "Star Rat smugglers", but she hadn't realized she had an actual bounty on her head. "I hope it's a big one," she said.

"Really?" Brigit asked.

"Oh yes," von Luck answered, "anyone who manages to off you is going to be rich. Set for life. Flattered?"

Katie supposed so, but it was a complication in her life she didn't need. "Sure, but I didn't know that it was a Martian group."

"Isn't really," Brigit answered. "We don't know who they are for sure or what they want, but it appears to be a system-wide criminal conspiracy with its roots on Earth. They've taken advantage of the situation here to establish a considerable presence though."

"Getting some pushback on account of being outsiders throwing their weight and a lot of money around," von Luck said.

Brigit launched a slow-motion flurry of punches Katie backed away from. "Not that that helps you any, Lieutenant. The more established players seem willing to overlook their newcomer status as far as it concerns you. None of the factions want the Space Force meddling in affairs here. They're happy to let the Star Rat smuggler faction remove you from the board."

"So I'm already contributing to co-operation between Martians? Great," Katie said, stopping and standing her ground.

Brigit moved back warily. "To get back on track, the next group to arrive after the Founders were the Homesteaders."

"The people the Founders promised farms of their own to for making the trip and doing the necessary work to get set up," Katie said to show she wasn't entirely ignorant of Martian history. To save them all some time, maybe. As she did so, she slowly circled Brigit, looking for an opening.

"Taking a degree of risk too," Brigit answered, "Not all of Mars' underclass came here as migrant workers. You might ask your boy Hood about that. In any case, if the Founders are the Martian version of aristocracy, then the Homesteaders would be the gentry."

"And the migrant workers they've both since imported are

the poor damned peasants. Three classes, that's rather traditional. Doesn't seem that complicated," Katie said. She moved towards Brigit, more to see what she'd do than because she saw any opening.

"Oh, don't worry, that's just a start. It gets more interesting," von Luck said from the sidelines.

Brigit easily countered Katie's attempts to knock her off balance. "In addition to your Star Rat smugglers, Mars has a variety of homegrown criminal groups," she said. "Good old fashioned regular legacy smugglers. Mobs running vice and extortion down on the surface. Our own organized crime group of long standing here on station. Gambling, prostitution, and extortion, all the usual stuff, not that most of it's formally illegal under Martian law, just shady and undesirable. We can't legally step in unless someone actually steals from or assaults someone."

Katie could hear the woman's exasperation with that in her voice. Brigit launching a set of slightly too fast attacks was another hint at her unhappiness with the situation. "Can see how that's rather annoying," Katie said.

Brigit cooled perceptibly. Interesting that she wasn't simply an emotionless business drone. "And with all due respect, the Space Force has added some variety and spice to the mix."

Well, that was interesting. Katie made some slow-motion efforts at attacks which Brigit met effortlessly. "How so?" she asked.

"It appears that the *Humber*'s crew was not picked for its gentle adherence to law and order," Brigit said. "Some of your crew are reoccurring and frequent guests in our holding facilities. The least annoying are the ones that just get drunk and start fights every Friday night."

"What our friend the Station XO is trying to say," von Luck said, "is that Earth seems to have recruited the worse of Mars' scum and sent back just the ones that couldn't reform themselves and fit in back in Earth space."

Ouch. That was bad, and a definite failure of personnel policy. Katie would have to ask her grandmother about it if she ever made it back to the home planet. "I'll see what I can do about that," Katie said. She'd at least have to try.

"Good luck with that," Brigit answered. She sighed. She dropped her guard a little. Katie took advantage. Brigit gave ground, but managed to get her guard back up. She smiled. "And thanks." She paused and looked grimly pensive before going on. "It'd be nice if you could manage to put the worst of your animals on a shorter leash. Only that's not your major problem."

"It isn't?"

Brigit put her guard up solid and gave Katie an ugly grin. "No. We don't know who they are exactly or their precise methods, but we're certain there's a tightly organized group on the *Humber* that's skimming from the supply and procurement budgets."

Katie sighed. Senior hands who were trusted, but disgruntled, abusing that trust to take a little extra for themselves from government stores were a perennial problem in the Space Force, as were kickbacks and doing favors for old friends who might have retired into the private sector. "Worse than the normal nonsense?" she asked. She let her guard down a bit as she did so, and Brigit took a lackadaisical advantage of it.

"Yes," Brigit answered. "In a way it's no surprise and not even the fault of the crooks, given that your SFHQ stuck your people on the *Humber* out here with no regular way to properly supply themselves with either consumables or the spare parts they needed."

Katie remembered the ad hoc repairs she'd seen in engineering. "Okay, but there are channels and they don't have to be stealing for their own benefit. Even if they are, how's that a threat bigger than smugglers trying to kill me?"

"Probably started with someone just thinking that if they were going to take the risk of being prosecuted for irregularities, they might as well profit some from it," Brigit said. She wasn't even pretending to be sparring now.

Katie dropped her guard, too. "But?"

"Now there's a gang of them in on it and they seemed to have taken enough that they can buy the ringleaders, at least, posh, well-established homesteads down on Mars where the Space Force can't in practice reach them. Comfortable retirements for the rest if nobody blows the whole scheme wide open."

"Which I'll have to do if I'm doing my job," Katie finished for Brigit. "Ouch." All she wanted to do was make the *Humber* into an efficient ship that did its patrols and prevented smuggling. That was supposed to be her job. She didn't want to get into a fight with her own crew. Only that seemed to be what Brigit was telling her was bound to happen. Might already be happening, though she suspected neither the explosion on her arrival nor the attempt to electrocute her originated within the *Humber*. She figured the crooks on the *Humber* were likely waiting to see if she'd be a problem for them before acting so drastically. Sadly, they were just as likely now reaching the conclusion that she would be. So Katie was going to have even more people gunning for her shortly.

Brigit had just stood there and watched as Katie absorbed the situation. "That's right," she said.

Katie took a deep breath and looked at Brigit's and von Luck's grim, if rather sympathetic, faces. "Is that all?" she asked.

"No, that's the worst of it," Brigit said, "but you've got crew that are trying to do their jobs honestly but are afraid of the bad actors. And," and with this she nodded at von Luck, "given the lack of established order and direction, other actors like the marines here and your SIS are likely to improvise in ways they might not otherwise be inclined to."

"The SIS?" Katie asked. She was pretty sure they avoided direct action, but she didn't know much about them. Nobody did.

"You've heard of the SIS, the Special Investigations Section of SFHQ, right?" Brigit asked. Von Luck looked curious too, but didn't say anything.

"Mostly vague rumors," Katie admitted, "but I thought they were solely an information collection body and kind of small too."

"Maybe, but we've heard rumors they're sometimes a little more proactive and Mars is just the sort of extraordinary situation that might call for extraordinary measures."

Katie grunted. She was tempted to mention Hood and his revelation of a backdoor in the *Humber*'s systems and promise of support if needed. Only she didn't think SFHQ would approve. "Great. Don't suppose you thought of writing any of this down anywhere?" She wouldn't blame them if they hadn't. Their appreciation of the situation could be explosive if committed to a form that had to be officially recognized.

Brigit grinned. "Yep, Heinrich will dump the whole presentation to your device. It has all sorts of extra gory details you'll wish you never heard of as well as what I've already given you."

"Then why did you bother with this?"

"Sometimes it's easier to get someone's attention with a personal talk than by dumping a doorstop of a document into their in-box," Brigit answered. She didn't seem in the least apologetic.

Katie could see that. She could also feel a headache coming on.

"Right," she said. "Have you or the marines any practical help beyond information to offer?"

Von Luck shook his head.

"No," Brigit answered.

***

Katie was scrambling. Too much to do, too little time to do it. Too few clues about what was going on, and even fewer about what to do about it as well. She did now realize she should have sat down and had a good talk with her fellow officers on the *Humber* some time before this. About that, at least she felt more guilty than confused.

But hey, better late than never. Right?

So, here she was in the wardroom for Saturday breakfast. It was the day after her ever so informative little sparring session with the Station Executive and Marine commander. Basically, almost a week after arriving on Mars and joining the *Humber*.

"I'd like to apologize for not talking to you guys earlier," she was saying over a plate of rather good scrambled eggs. Light, and fluffy, and with just the right amount of butter. Likely it was real butter at that. It tasted like it. Nice that some things on the *Humber* were better than average. The food in her wardroom might not have been the most important thing, but Katie certainly wasn't complaining.

"We've all been busy," LTSG Kegan Rous, the engineer, said. The other officer present, LTSG Brian Broomfield, the ops officer, nodded in agreement.

"Yes, I know, and I told myself that you in particular were so busy making sure propulsion would be up and running for our planned patrol to the Belt that it'd be best not to disturb you," Katie answered. She turned and looked at the ops officer sitting beside the engineer. "And you, Brian, I know what sort of planning SFHQ expects for the simplest evolution. I know you've probably been going crazy trying to get all the paperwork done for them."

"Yeah, remote control micromanagement by document," the ops officer replied. "Never realized how insane it was back in Earth space. There you have lots of extra officers to spread the effort around to. And you can tick off standard boxes and paste in a bunch of boilerplate most places. Out here around Mars everything seems like an exception you have to submit explanations in triplicate for." He grinned wanly at Katie. "I mightn't have minded too much if you'd seen fit to interrupt me. I think I went down the rabbit hole a bit."

Katie nodded in turn. She wasn't totally unfamiliar with how nervous uncertainty could lead to obsessive overwork and getting lost in the details of a task. If you don't know what to do, try doing a bit of everything. Doesn't really work all that well usually, but we're all human. "All the same, I dropped the ball by not having a few words with you guys several days ago. Guess I should have really consulted you before calling that inspection for the whole ship. Hope that didn't mess up your efforts,Kegan."

"No, for better or worse, we're bottlenecked on our anti-matter containment overhaul and calibration," the engineer said. "Sort of thing you want a few very well-trained and competent people for rather than a lot of hands. Too many cooks spoil the stew. And spoiling that particular stew could wreck everybody's day."

Katie threw the engineer a quick, humorless grin. Anti-matter was no joke. "Imagine you've been keeping a close eye on that."

The engineer gave a little nod and a wry grin of his own. "Yeah, maybe to the exclusion of taking care of some of my other responsibilities, XO. Maybe making sure the workshops are clean and tidy and personnel records up to date, and taking a few moments to greet a new XO, aren't as important as making sure the *Humber* can launch on its planned patrol, but I should have made a little time for it all. Sorry, XO."

"Apologies accepted, Kegan," Katie answered. "I think we're all doing our good faith best in difficult circumstances."

"I've got even less excuse, XO," Brian the ops officer said. "Just got used to being heads down in my immediate tasks. I wasn't paying attention. No excuse, but we've got pretty used to doing our own thing out here without much in the way of guidance."

Katie nodded. She certainly wasn't going to go into the captain's apparently very hands-off command approach. "Not great, but understandable," she said. "All the commissioned clerks back at SFHQ seem to imagine themselves as stand-ins for admirals. It's hard not to get carried away with managing up with all the demands they make. Managing sidewards and down naturally tends to get neglected."

"Yeah," Brian answered, "but it makes it all the more important to make a point of it. Although I have to tell you, Bosun O'Conal is a good man and doing a great job of keeping the department ticking over efficiently despite the fact we're so far away from the normal support available at Goddard Station."

"He does seem like a very take-charge, competent kind of man," Katie agreed. She couldn't very well criticize the man to his boss for working too hard and grinning too much, could she?

"One of the men said he saved your life," Brian said. "Is that true? What was that all about? Do they know who was behind the bombing yet? And who they were targeting? And why?"

Katie smiled. Seemed the ops officer had been saving questions up. "Basically that's true. I owe him. Going to make it hard being a hard arse if I need to be. As for the explosion, from what the station authorities told me, they're not sure. Not clear they'll ever be sure. Bombers were professionals up from the surface. Could have been they were targeting a new homesteader to get his newly acquired property back, or it could have been paid for by the Star Rat smugglers who want me dead. They just don't know."

"That's awkward," the engineer said.

"Sure is," the ops officer agreed. "Makes our problems seem small."

"Maybe, gentleman, but we all share one goal. We all want to get the *Humber* out on patrol and throw a wrench into the plans of all smugglers. Agreed?"

"Yep."

"Amen."

***

Against all the odds Rob had a winning hand. Which was not what he wanted. Not in this particular game. He wasn't in it to win. Very much the contrary today. Today he was trying to ingratiate himself with the rest of the crew.

It was the first weekend after Rob's arrival on the *Humber*. His bruises from the welcoming message he'd received hadn't faded and still hurt. Rob was desperately trying to keep his head down as directed.

He was also trying to fit in.

An old mate had once philosophized to him about ship's crews. "A ship's crew is either an organic whole, Rob, me boy, or it's a festering mess. Our job is to see it's an organic whole, more or less functional. If a festering mess develops, we have to lance the infection as quickly and ruthlessly as possible. No fussing about or anything. Just fix the problem. Kapeech?"

Yeah, kapeech, old buds. It wasn't about what was fair or reasonable, it was about what worked for the whole. Rob really didn't want to be the infection that needed cutting out. He wanted to fit in.

And so, when a Petty Officer stoker in his mess had invited Rob to join a friendly poker game, Rob had agreed. Unlike on the *Martian Queen*, he wasn't playing to win. Not a lot anyway, maybe a little. Be better to lose a little, though. Rob's goal was to show his new ship mates he was a standup, somewhat clueful guy, a reasonable, friendly sort of guy. Give them a chance to know him better and like what they saw, or at least, not find it objectionable.

There were a half dozen other players besides Rob sitting around the mess's central table and they'd been playing for over an hour before trouble began to develop.

It'd all been routine play. Rob's luck had been rather good, but he hadn't pushed it or placed large bets to take advantage of it. They'd all been feeling each other out. It'd seemed increasingly relaxed. All very copacetic. Rob had even begun to enjoy himself in a mild sort of way.

Only there's always one hothead in a group. One guy who doesn't feel life's been entirely fair to them, doesn't understand what's wrong, and is simmering with resentment.

In this case, Able Spacer Paul Zimmerman, a stoker, an engineering type, on his first tour. A very long, an admittedly unfairly long, one that it seemed had resulted in Zimmerman's girlfriend back on Earth leaving him. Seemed it'd thrown "Paulie", a nickname he seemed to resent, into a funk his mates would occasionally tease him about. Something he also seemed to resent.

Spacers don't like emotional weakness. They'll pick at it until it resolves itself one way or the other.

Zimmerman wasn't dumb. He was probably smarter than almost half his ship mates. He obviously understood he couldn't take his frustrations out on them. It wasn't so obvious regards the new guy.

Zimmerman seemed annoyed Rob was constantly winning, even if it wasn't much.

When Rob made a bigger than usual bet on an inside straight draw, he expected to lose. He'd hoped that'd alleviate some of Zimmerman's unhappiness.

Only he hadn't lost. Against the odds he'd won the bet and Zimmerman was furious.

Rob looked at him.

"You're cheating," Zimmerman said.

The whole table, and the collection of spectators around it, went quiet.

At first, Rob didn't know what to say. He just looked calmly back at Zimmerman. The man was being immature and silly. It wouldn't do to say so. "No, I'm not," Rob said. "It's just luck."

Zimmerman stood up and Rob followed suit.

They moved around the table to face each other and the spectators hastily made them space.

Zimmerman threw a haymaker.

Rob ducked it and hit Zimmerman hard under the chin and up, knocking him back. No way anyone was adding to the bruises Rob already had on his ribs. Rob pounded the stunned Zimmerman in his ribs instead. Then he followed up with another blow to Zimmerman's head, and since this was no boxing match, knocked his feet out from under him.

While Zimmerman lay on the deck, stunned, Rob placed his foot on his throat. From the quiet murmurs of shock and concern from the men around him, Rob realized he'd gone too far.

"I don't cheat," Rob said before removing his foot and turning to the others. The poker players had mostly remained seated. "Guess the game's over," he said.

"Guess so," the PO that had invited him to play said.

Rob made his way through the crowd back to his sleeping pod.

He left his money on the table.

Guess he'd made an impression.

Not exactly the one he'd intended.

6: Do Your Job, Kincaid

It was the proverbial Monday morning, the beginning of yet another week tackling problems that might not be solvable.

Not that that was going to stop Katie from trying. She was down in the Boat Bay doing her best.

She'd met the boat on its return from the Martian surface several hours before. It'd been loaded to the gunwales wit badly needed supplies the weapons Officer and co-pilot had managed to scrounge.

The place had been like a combination of Christmas morning and a circus as ratings from multiple departments crowded in to see if eagerly awaited supplies had been obtained. Katie had been less than impressed by the hectic disorder. It'd been basically impossible to be sure who was present, let alone to properly account for what supplies they'd received. She'd decided to give it a pass this time. Her main priority had been meeting the two officers who'd conducted the supply run.

The weapons Officer, LTSG Thomas Rompkey, and co-pilot, LTJG Tammy Wentzell, had both looked tired. Haggard and like death warmed over in truth.

"Business on Mars isn't like business in Earth space," Tom Rompkey had said. "They've got trust issues. They like to get to know you personally. They like to see you drunk and tired, not to put a fine point on it."

"They like to see how you react to raunchy floor shows, too," Tammy had added.

Tom had given Tammy a faint smile at that. "Glad I've got you, Tammy, or I'd have to be dodging honey traps left, right, and center."

So standard Martian business practices weren't entirely innocent. Big surprise. It did please Katie to see that, although Tom and Tammy obviously liked each other and worked well together, that there didn't seem to be any romantic spark. Thank the heavens for that. She had enough complications to deal with, some semi-domestic relationship issues would have been an extra dollop of them she didn't need.

Katie was also extremely relieved, sadly and pathetically relieved almost, to see that the two of them seemed competent and doing their level best at their jobs. Also friendly and not unhappy to see Katie. Yep, extremely relieved.

Katie had been afraid that some of the *Humber*'s officers might be in on whatever was wrong with the ship. She'd been worried she'd meet outright hostility from them. She'd been concerned she might find deliberate dereliction of duty or outright incompetence.

None of that seemed to be the case.

The *Humber*'s officers mostly seemed to be working hard at their jobs as they understood them.

Narrowly defined, they even seemed to be doing well at the tasks they'd given themselves. Problem was, they weren't working together as a group. As a group, they weren't inspiring the ship's company to do the job it was here to do. That job being to assert Space Force control of local Martian space at a minimum and ideally of the nearby Belt too.

The most obvious and immediate result of asserting such control would be to prevent wholesale smuggling by the ship load in local space. Stopping local smuggling wasn't Katie's real goal, though. Indeed, low-level retail smuggling, although criminal and undesirable, wasn't her concern at all. Not in her jurisdiction, quite literally.

Katie's concern was that the Space Force's lack of control of a part of its inner stellar system amounted to a lack of sovereignty by the political authorities that claimed to represent humanity. When humanity met the wider galactic community, Katie was sure it was going to be sized up by that community and, if it couldn't even assert control of its own home system, be found lacking.

Not if Katie could help it.

And, to that end, she needed to get the *Humber*'s officers working together. On the ship's common goals, not just their own narrow self-assigned tasks.

And her current contribution to those grand goals was to have just finished supervising the unloading of the ship's boat. The boring stuff left after the most critical and interesting items had already been carried off.

Mostly she'd stood around and watched as a Leading Spacer deckhand supervised other enlisted hands in lifting and moving stuff. The term "deckhand" was yet another anachronistic import from the days of oceanic surface ships. In practice in the current Space Force, a deckhand was a specialist in the general housekeeping tasks - cleaning, moving things around, and minor maintenance - that all the technical specialists only did part time.

If she'd been a civilian with a crew of Belters, Katie would have been expected to pitch in to help and would have done so. It was different in the Space Force. Katie wasn't convinced it should be, but she didn't want to rock the boat more than she had to. She'd had enough problems fitting in when she'd first joined the Space Force and gone to the Academy that she never wanted to repeat the experience. She chose her battles carefully these days.

And so, despite being generally overworked and busy, Katie had basically killed time watching other people work.

At least by doing so, she'd taken the place of either Tom or Tammy, or more likely both. Katie had the impression that not being sure who was senior and basically making things up as they went in an irregular situation, they did everything as a pair. Not the most efficient way of working, but likely not only did it provide them both moral support, but helped keep them on the same page about how they were doing things.

The relief they'd shown when Katie had offered to not only supervise the boat's unloading but also prep and secure it for its next mission had been palpable. They'd both been happy to be able to immediately retire to their sleeping pods.

Their gratitude alone was rewarding. Katie had hopes too that it might also free them up some. Free them up, especially Tom, to attend to the administrative and supervisory tasks they'd been giving short shrift to.

If there were irregularities in how the ship was currently being run, and Katie was sure there were, just not sure how serious, then maybe they could be the ones to find them and have to figure out how to fix them.

It was in Katie's job description as the XO that she had to be the bad guy, the one who held everyone's nose to the grindstone. But she'd rather not bear the whole burden herself.

In addition, Katie was herself a qualified pilot. With a third pilot available, it might be possible to start getting more work out of the *Humber*'s single boat. Katie was hoping she might be able to schedule some local space patrols. Show the Space Force flag some. Put the local smugglers on notice.

Things were looking good in that regard. Both the *Humber*'s Boat Bay and the boat in it showed signs of hard use. They were also well maintained and in good repair, as far as Katie could tell, and she figured she was pretty good at telling such things.

The flight engineer had finished up while the unloading was still in progress. They appeared to have topped up all the consumables before leaving.

Katie inspected the boat and its bay, carefully taking much longer than she usually would have. She also checked the maintenance logs. It looked good. It looked, in fact, like the only constraint on using the boat more had been the availability of pilots. And here Katie was, eager to keep her piloting hours up. Life was looking a bit brighter.

Katie was feeling pretty good as she finished up.

Then she punched the button to open the hatch out of the Boat Bay, and nothing happened. Bad sign. If something is not right, assume the worst. Katie immediately retreated to the hatch to the boat itself. She didn't want to be trapped in the bay if the fire system went off or the outer airlock was to cycle. The boat hatch was locked. This couldn't be coincidence.

Katie didn't panic. She'd been doing emergency drills for these sorts of situations since she was a toddler. She knew where the emergency locker was. It was a matter of seconds to get to it and only seconds more to don an emergency vacuum suit.

That done, she paused to think, holding herself firmly in place while doing so in case of decompression.

The Boat Bay hatch could be locked down remotely, but only in the case of an emergency. An emergency of the sort that ought to be accompanied by blaring horns and seriously annoying flashing lights. The boat hatch wasn't remotely overridable. It must have been finagled locally.

Unlike every other Space Force officer Katie knew of, Katie was space born. She'd also had a much greater concentration on engineering topics in her training than most officers. Certainly more than any but the small minority on the engineering career track. Most other officers in this situation would have to try to communicate to the ship's bridge and call someone to come and get them out. That would be very embarrassing. Not the sort of thing that gave the impression of a competent leader.

Worse, Katie hadn't checked yet, but the communications might be sabotaged too. In that case, she might have been here until someone found her either accidentally or noticed she was missing. Hours, likely, maybe days.

Fortunately, Katie knew exactly how the hatch mechanisms worked, where the access covers to them were located, and where the tools she needed could be found.

She did the boat first. It was interesting, for some value of interesting. The fasteners of the outside access cover for the boat hatch mechanism showed none of the scratches that had been left by the earlier sabotage. Either their earlier saboteur was a fast learner or they had a second, more competent one. Katie suspected the latter. The saboteur had had only a very short window to work in right after the boat's return. The sabotage had been performed quickly and unobtrusively. The idea of a second, very competent saboteur did nothing to make her happier.

In any event, the sabotage had been clean and neat. A connector with one end lifted and insulating tape wrapped around it. The boat had been designed for easy maintenance and repair, and that, ironically, had made the sabotage neat and easy too. Even more ironically, it also made fixing that sabotage quick and easy.

So, no problem getting access to the boat. Katie did a nominal comms check, and they were working. Emergency essentially over, but Katie still had clean-up to do.

Katie did another thorough check of the boat, including systems not normally on the checklist. She didn't find anything more wrong.

Next, still in the emergency vacuum suit, Katie checked out the Boat Bay hatch, which had been sabotaged in an almost identical way.

After that she checked the Boat Bay's internal intercom to the rest of the ship. And then the repeater station for relaying signals from personal devices. Once again, key connections had been neatly broken.

All done and finished with her repairs, Katie reported the issues and what she'd done to the CERA. Asked him to keep it under his hat, and sat herself down to think.

What did this mean?

Whoever had done this hadn't been trying to kill her.

Which was sort of nice, but different from whoever had been behind the terminal explosion and the damage control comms sabotage. That party or parties had been trying to kill, though it was unclear if she'd been the target in both cases.

It suggested at least two hostile factions. More likely, given the differences in approaches, three of them.

Katie wondered if hiding in her cabin and pretending to be a potted plant would convince them to leave her alone.

Probably not all of them.

Didn't matter anyway. It wasn't in Katie's nature to give up.

She was going to find out what was going on.

She was going to get control of the *Humber* and its crew.

She was going to institute patrols of local space by the boat.

She was going to root out any smugglers.

And, by all that was sacred, she was going to make sure the *Humber* left on its next patrol on time.

And if someone wanted to kill her for that?

Well, bring it on.

***

Pat was beginning to realize he might find his planned retirement rather boring. It was possible that keeping an established Martian homestead running profitably might be an adequate challenge for him, but he was beginning to doubt it.

Pat had come a long way, and it'd been a tough slog at times. He'd smiled through it all, but there'd been plenty of risk too to worry about.

So, Pat had thought a comfortable place with an established position in society and free of much in the way of risk was something to look forward to.

Thanks to the Kincaid girl, he was beginning to realize he may have miscalculated.

Right now, thanks to her, he was involved in a knife fight. He'd attempted to take her down a peg and send her a warning, just like that one he'd sent that Hood thug, and thanks to some unexpected resourcefulness on her part, that attempt had backfired.

The engineering PO he'd pressured into doing the deed was scared now. Silly bastard that he was, Petty Officer Johanson, was running more scared of Kincaid and the possibility of a Space Force court martial than he was of the bosun.

Stuck between a rock and a hard place, apparently he'd decided Pat was the easier problem to take care of.

And so, Pat found himself spending this fine Tuesday morning down in the spindle alone with Johanson. Johanson had pulled a knife in what was supposed to be a friendly debrief and tried to use it on Pat. Bad move. Pat hadn't managed to disarm the man, but he had evaded the blow.

Pat intended to finish what Johanson had started. Johanson, to give him a little credit, apparently realized this was a fight to the finish. The two men were circling each other in the confines of the main weapons access area. It wasn't a big space, and it wasn't likely they could avoid each other for long.

A sensible man would have been tense, at least worried, and not happy to find himself in such a situation.

Not Pat. To his own surprise, he found himself happy, almost gleeful at the prospect of taking direct decisive action and dealing with a problematic individual personally and in a final fashion. Pat had no doubts who'd win this standoff.

Pat's main concern was avoiding a hard to explain injury. A difficult thing to do in a knife fight no matter how good you were.

Pat looked to a point behind Johanson down the main passageway and put a startled frown on his face.

Stupid bastard fell for the old trick. He glanced behind himself and in that moment Pat lunged forward. Stuck his knife up and under Johanson's ribs with one hand. And grabbed his startled victim's knife hand with his other one. Kept the man from doing the same to him.

Pat pushed the stunned Johanson hard up against the bulkhead and held him there while he bled out. Took a while and Pat wasn't exactly proud of the pleasure he felt in watching the life fade from Johanson's eyes.

He was happy that the engineer's ship suit absorbed most of his blood, and that none of the rest ended up on Pat. It was going to be tricky enough to clean the area without anyone noticing. Fortunately, he had a delivery to the station pending he could fit the body in with.

He had friends who could arrange for it to look like Johanson had been mugged on station.

The same friends who would help him take care of the problem the Kincaid girl was posing for all of them. Take care of her in the same final way he'd just dealt with Johanson.

To his considerable surprise Pat found himself feeling a fair degree of respect for the Kincaid girl. Lots of guts and not afraid of a little trouble. Not unlike Pat himself, he now realized.

It occurred to Pat as he lowered Johanson's body to the deck that if he'd been a little more risk averse, he could have avoided all this trouble. By the time he'd made bosun on the *Humber*, his days of having to resort to desperate measures to get ahead had been behind him. The chance of skimming some of the money being misspent on the *Humber*'s deployment to Mars had seemed too easy and lucrative to pass up. All the same, he could have done so. Done so and have looked forward to a very good retirement on some beach on Earth. A little time topping up his savings in a useless, but well paid, civil service job. Then a little time after leaving government employment working his contacts on the behalf of a private contractor and he'd have been set up pretty well.

The risk he'd taken, as minimal as it had seemed at the time, had been unnecessary.

He'd failed to note his own taste for trouble and flouting the rules. Well, live and learn.

It's a funny old world and full of surprises.

He chuckled to himself as he worked Johanson's dead weight into a disposal bag.

Wasn't it ironic that his newfound respect for Kincaid was exactly why he felt he had to deal with her?

Deal with her finally.

***

If you'd asked him a year ago, Rob would have told you he'd done pretty well in life.

That he'd had some rough breaks early on, but, through mostly good choices and hard work, ended up in a pretty good place. Right now, he wasn't so sure.

He wasn't being reflective out of self-pity or self-indulgence generally. It came as a job requirement. He had just finished composing his first major report back to his bosses in SFHQ and was now on his way to deliver it to a dead drop on station. It wasn't the sort of thing you sent through normal channels.

In one sense, it'd been an eventful first week and a half. On the other hand, he didn't have much solid to report. Nothing that wasn't already available through regular channels.

Sure, somebody on Mars wasn't happy at his presence, and the crew of the *Humber* was tense and acting extremely defensive about something. It was verification of something wrong here, but they'd already been fairly sure that was the case.

Not a lot of new information there.

Rob had also reported he was feeling increasingly worried

about his own safety and that of Kincaid. The degree of danger was something of a surprise to Rob. He wasn't sure it was going to be that much of one to his bosses. He allowed himself a moment of annoyance at them for that.

In yet another of life's little ironies, he almost missed the immediate danger he was in while worrying about it generally.

Fortunately, one of the thugs waiting to ambush him got antsy and careless. Moved a bit. Just a small shift of weight, probably. It was enough for Rob's old instincts newly reawakened to catch, though. Instantly, Rob knew an ambush was waiting for him in the corridor ahead.

Too close to make running for it a viable choice. Not that that was Rob's inclination, anyway.

So, should he call them out? Learn how many of them there were and maybe get a sense of what sort of threat they posed. Only at the cost of alerting them to the fact he knew they were there. Or should he let them think they were surprising him and try to turn the tables?

Rob paused and pretended to check directions on his device.

Gave his would-be assailants just enough time to relax again, and strode off briskly towards where he knew one of them was waiting.

That man was ready for Rob. He wasn't ready for the ultra-bright light Rob flashed directly into his face.

As he stood there blinded, Rob took the opportunity to first stab him, then slash his throat, and then knock the man off his feet. For good measure, Rob kicked him in the head as he fell.

Almost took too long about it. Almost.

Still, Rob got around fast enough to face his second attacker on even terms. He was almost insulted. You'd have thought they'd have sent more than two attackers. At least after how he'd handled himself the last time. As insults went, it was one he could live with.

Even odds against a man like Rob were anything but. It took a little time and a few more tricks, but the second man went down in good time. Rob got off with no more than a surface scratch.

Rob knew there were adrenaline junkies who got off on this

sort of thing. He wasn't one of them. It just bugged him. Also, as confident as he was in his own abilities, he knew every time he went to the well there was a chance luck would fail him. He'd rather not keep playing a lottery where the prize was premature death in a back alley.

Also annoying was that an inspection of his would be killers didn't provide much in the way of new information. They looked like station dwellers this time. They hadn't been total amateurs, but not particularly professional either. Unfortunately, professional enough not to have any identifying information on them.

Just the same, Rob took time to make an addendum to his report. That done, he proceeded to a place just short of the neglected park where the bench that was his dead drop was installed. Prying the tiny internal chip out of the outer case of the storage device the report resided on, he stuck it on the pre-arranged part of the bench's underside with a bit of gum.

That done, he went in search of an all-night diner.

Some strong coffee, along with warm food rich in fat and sugar, seemed like a good idea.

Best to enjoy life as much as possible while he could.

**

So it was the wee hours of Wednesday. A great time to visit her compatriots on Mars Station and look at bodies with them, Katie felt. Well, not really.

Katie really hoped her newly acquired knowledge of where the station's morgue was located wasn't going to prove too useful in the future. A few bodies went a long way as far as she was concerned.

Even more than that, she hoped to avoid being one of those bodies.

At least this was giving her an excuse for being on the station this morning.

"So, do you recognize any of them?" Police Chief Kabukicho asked.

"No, Ken, I do not," Katie answered. "Even Petty Officer Johanson, I only recognize because of his uniform. No idea who the other two are."

It was worse than that. Until Brigit, the station's XO, had

called and woken her from a sound sleep a little over an hour ago, Katie hadn't even realized Johanson was missing.

She'd had a few words with the CERA about that. Apparently, engineering didn't keep close track of its people working regular daytime hours on routine maintenance. Not when they were senior techs, like most of them were. The last time a superior had laid eyes on Johanson had been Monday morning. Two days ago now. Katie was not happy.

"We found Johanson in a corridor not far from the cheap apartment he was renting," Brigit supplied. In the background, von Luck the marine commander smirked. Katie wondered exactly what his excuse for being here was. Surely he didn't get up in the early hours and visit morgues just to watch her squirm.

"Do you know if he routinely spent his nights ashore?" Brigit asked.

Katie grimaced. She hadn't even realized many of the crew had shore accommodations. Made sense for the few with family. Back at Goddard Station, most of the enlisted crew on the *Susquehanna* had had families and lived ashore when not required on duty. It was a fact Katie realized she'd never absorbed. She'd been born and lived on board ship most of her life before joining the Space Force. And then she'd gone on a long deployment and after that simply found her cabin on ship more convenient.

She'd never given any thought to the fact that wouldn't be true for most of the ship's enlisted crew. Yet another blank spot in her knowledge she needed to fill in yesterday.

Brigit cleared her throat to get Katie's attention.

"Sorry. No, I'm afraid I don't," Katie said.

"I had to ask," Brigit said. "Don't feel too bad. You're new and you've had a busy first week and a half. I heard there was another accident."

Katie sighed. There was no one here she had to impress. "A mispacked and labeled container of acidic reaction fuel. Blew up in my face when I was checking our inventories against the manifests."

"And would have disfigured and blinded you, maybe for life, if you hadn't just happened to be wearing an environmental suit with the face plate down. Paranoid much?" von Luck said.

"Prudent and the environmental suit needed to be tested. I was killing two birds with one stone," Katie answered.

"About that," von Luck pressed on, "an accident like that mightn't have outright killed you, but it would have likely gotten you medically invalided back to Earth, and out of the way."

"It wasn't very subtle, was it?" Katie said. "I think I must be getting close to something sensitive. In fact, I'm planning t meet a possible smuggler informant for breakfast this morning."

It was Brigit's turn to sigh.

Von Luck just looked worried. "I'd advise against this. It's likely a trap, but I will provide a squad. Keep them as close to you as I can."

"The chief will provide you and the marines the fullest support," Brigit said.

"Thank you," Katie said.

She just hoped it was enough to keep her alive in case it was, in fact, a trap.

7: A Warm Reception for Katie

Hey, diddle, diddle, right up the middle.

Sometimes there was just no way to be clever. Sometimes you just had to take direct, simple action without anything resembling finesse.

Katie was glad those times were mostly things she'd read about in old books on heroics in ancient Earth wars. Simply charging straight up the hill was apparently something that occasionally worked. There'd been a famous unplanned and unordered instance of it by pissed-off troops at Chattanooga in the American Civil War.

It was also something that seemed to be anecdotally common in Boys Own stories before a succession of mechanically murderous total wars killed off the traditional concept of heroism for a while.

Truth was, the old generals had always known the direct approach often failed and almost always at great cost.

It'd been young men barely out of boyhood who'd mostly been heroes then. As far as Katie could tell, the girls mostly got to be merely plucky. The odd heroine would be a nurse braving the battlefield to clean up the messes the men's heroism had resulted in.

Katie was feeling nervous and exposed, and without good choices, hence the ruminations on heroism.

Katie believed in heroism, and in heroes, less so in glory. But she did believe heroes were sometimes necessary. That sometimes there was no easy way forward and courage was needed.

Currently, Katie was sitting on a "patio", a portion of broad corridor with chairs and tables, eating a rather decent breakfast. Not quite the same as slogging uphill through mud and a hail of bullets.

She was waiting for an informant to arrive. Or rather, someone she hoped would be an informant, but was more like a contact that Tom and Tammy had given her. Someone they'd arranged supplies from who'd hinted at the possibility of more lucrative but shady arrangements. The two pilots had foregone that opportunity, but when Katie had asked for suggestions about people who might be able to give her inside information about illicit trade on the station, that was all they'd been able to give her.

It wasn't much.

Katie had actually expected the man to blow her off when she'd contacted him. She'd been surprised when he'd nervously agreed to meet her. Apparently, he had information he wasn't willing to trust to any communications system. That's what he'd implied. He'd also given the feeling that he wanted to size her up in person. "This is a business that relies on personal relationships," he'd actually said.

Katie agreed with Brigit and von Luck. It seemed more like a trap than anything else. Nevertheless, it'd been the one thin lead she had, and here she was.

There were marines and police waiting only minutes away, ready to support her. Minutes are too long when seconds count, but that was the best they'd been able to arrange.

So, Katie did have something in common with those old-fashioned heroes. She was putting herself in harm's way. She was deliberately going into an uncertain situation because of a lack of alternatives. It was dangerous and it could get her hurt or even killed.

She wished the man would show up so they could get the whole thing over with. She really hoped being brave was something you got better at with time, because otherwise maybe she wasn't cut out for this hero business after all.

Katie almost didn't spot him before he spoke. "Most of the people in the business aren't morning people. It's a good time to meet," said the skinny, dark complected stranger she'd been expecting.

Katie nodded. "Makes sense."

Her contact sat down to the meal of smoked fish and fried potato she'd ordered for him. "Assuming they're not already on to you."

Katie didn't know what to say. It was obvious she'd been an object of interest even before arriving at Mars. She didn't know how closely she was being observed. "I'm just doing my job looking into the *Humber*'s supply arrangements. Also, I had to visit the station's morgue this morning for a perfectly legitimate but unpredictable reason. I don't think anyone could have anticipated that. I think anyone who did get on my trail as I left the ship would have been scraped off there. Very official, lots of police, and multiple exits."

Her contact, who was calling himself "Saul Ansall", nodded slightly and managed a thin smile. "Could be worse," he said.

Katie grunted. "It can always be worse. Being a superstitious Belter girl, I try not to tempt or tease the great Murphy myself."

Saul's brief smile seemed a little more genuine this time. Still thin though. "No need of Murphy stirring the current Devil's brew," he said acerbically. "It's coming along fine as it is."

"For certain counterintuitive values of fine, I assume," Katie said.

"There were a variety of Martian factions already working at cross purposes in too tight of a space even before the *Humber* arrived."

"Had a number of official briefings to that effect," Katie said, trying to be agreeable.

Saul snorted. "If the pooh-bahs back on Earth had the faintest clue, they'd have never stuck themselves into this mess half-assed like they have."

Katie shrugged. "Not always entirely a fan of Earth-centric bureaucracy myself. Only I don't think they could have predicted the messes out on Vesta and in Jovian space. Those diverted limited resources."

Saul shook his head. "Seriously? They should have known before you uncovered the mess on Ceres. After that, they had no excuse at all. It was all as clear as day."

Katie sighed. "To those of us living out here and who are paying attention to what's happening, sure."

"It is their job. They've failed to do it."

Katie was astonished. The man sounded for all the world like an offended tax payer annoyed that his government wasn't performing the tasks he was paying it to do. Okay, she had a lot of questions she wanted to ask, but if she understood how this was supposed to work, she was supposed to establish some rapport first. "Earth's people provide most of the Space Force's budget and I think they mostly think its main job is to keep nasty people from dropping space rocks on their heads."

Saul snickered. Looked like Katie had scored some points. "To do that, they need to control space and the people in it. Again they've failed to do their jobs even from an Earth centric point of view."

Katie was almost finished with her own breakfast. She was also tired of new things appearing out of left field when she already had enough problems. "So what's that all got to do with our current situation here?"

Saul looked up at her with what looked like genuine exasperation. Not all aimed at her, Katie hoped. "They should have had the sense to figure out what they were doing. Either that or done nothing. Blundering around in ignorance has brought a bad situation to a head."

"You think it was a mistake their sending me here?"

Saul inspected her and frowned. "You're a Belter, but awfully young. Don't imagine you want to buck your bosses if you want to get ahead."

"But excuses aside, not a good idea?"

"No," Saul began and just then Katie realized their time had run out. A pair of stout but hungry looking men had appeared at the entrance to the breakfast place. Katie recognized the type. They were one of the sorts of people Saul had said you didn't usually see at this time of day. Katie was willing to bet on it. She was, in fact, betting life and limb on it.

Seeing one of the men reaching for a pocket, she half stood and pushed the smallish metal table between them into Saul. Trying to knock him over as quickly as she could.

The sharp slap-whine of a very low caliber high velocity kinetic pistol, one of the ones often called a "needler", indicated she hadn't acted too soon.

A spray of blood from one of Saul's shoulders indicated she'd been a bit late, but at least quick enough that his head was still intact. The whizzing sound close by one of her ears invoked a quick exhilarating relief that she still had her own head.

Only the fight was just beginning, and Katie and Saul were sprawled in a tangle on the deck.

Adrenaline is a wonderful thing.

Otherwise, Katie wouldn't have had the strength to spring to her feet, grabbing the little metal table in one hand as she did so and flinging it at her attackers. The metallic rat-tat-tat that ensued verified the fact that although needlers were great shredding flesh, they wouldn't penetrate even thin metal.

Following her protecting chair in its flight, Katie ran at the attackers. She jumped over an intervening chair and, pushing off another, leapt over a low railing directly at the man who'd shot at her, screaming the whole way.

Katie was mad. She had her hands out and she was going to claw that man's eyes out if it was the last thing she did. Which it very well might be. Not that Katie cared anymore. She'd had enough.

The startled looks of surprise on the thugs' faces made her blood sing with happy, homicidal glee. Apparently, they'd thought she'd run the other way.

Luck was on Katie's side. She had enough momentum to not only tear deep scratches across her victim's eyes, but to carry both of them to the ground. Despite being caught off balance initially, and having to be at least half blind and in pain, her victim managed to grapple with her and roll them over so he was on top. Later, Katie, analyzing what had happened, was to figure this was fortunate, as it likely kept the second man from shooting her.

At the time, she was just concerned with keeping the first man from pinning her down.

Katie had read that Colt's revolver was the great equalizer. She'd always figured that in the gender wars that it was the fact that God had given sensitive dangly bits to men that hung between their legs where they could be easily kicked or kneed.

She took advantage of this. The half blinded thug forgot about pinning Katie down for a moment. Katie took advantage of that to break his nose with the heel of her hand.

And at that point, the marines finally arrived.

Not too soon.

They'd been busy though dealing with a second pair of thugs who'd been approaching from the other direction. Katie saw the bodies as one of the marines helped her to her feet. Others were securing her pair of thugs.

Katie also saw Saul's body. Its upper part was thoroughly shredded. In this case, it seemed she hadn't been the priority target.

Katie stared at Brigit and von Luck as they approached.

In a while, she knew she'd be feeling very emotional about what had happened.

Right now, she was just numb.

***

The captain seemed to be in a dry mood as he sipped some amber colored liquid in a fancy thick glass. Scotch, Katie imagined.

Katie herself was alternating between hot anger and black depression. Whichever mood it was, she was still hopped up from the events of little more than an hour ago. She was trying not to show it.

Katie had been called to the captain's cabin immediately upon arriving back on the *Humber*. She was still in the civvies she'd met Saul in. They were rather the worse for wear. Dirty and torn from her little wrestling match with one of the men who'd tried to kill her.

Who had succeeded in killing Saul.

No, Katie wasn't happy, but that wasn't something she

could share with the captain.

"So, XO, first an explosion, now a shooting," he was saying. "Don't imagine I can blame you for either."

Katie blinked. "No, sir," she answered.

The captain smiled. Glad someone was amused. "Well, at least this time you did your screaming and running in the right direction."

Seemed the captain had had at least a preliminary report about the incident.

"Depends on context, sir," Katie answered. It hadn't been his butt on the line either time, after all, had it?

Another little smile. "Wouldn't know, XO," the captain said, "I generally avoid such activities. I don't remember many firefights, explosions, or much running being involved in my stint as an Executive Officer either." He paused as if to recollect something. "Don't remember much screaming, either. I rather think we tried to avoid that too."

"Yes, sir."

A thoughtful look. "As regards the more normal parts of your duties, it's only been a week and a half, true, but you seem to have made a good start."

"Thank you, sir."

"Having to bail a technician out of jail, and having another go missing and turn up dead, was rather unfortunate."

"Yes, sir."

"But again, I really can't blame you for that, can I, XO?"

"I don't think so, sir. I did my best to handle both situations properly."

"Yes, and don't think I'm unhappy with your performance."

"Yes, sir. Thank you, sir."

"You know, Lieutenant Kincaid, I'd heard you were a trouble magnet, but that it wasn't your fault. I found those stories hard to believe. They didn't make sense to me."

Katie swallowed. She was starting to cool off. "Yes, sir."

Seemed the captain hadn't expected anything more. "And, you know, Kincaid, they still don't make sense to me. Only you can't argue with facts, can you? Trouble follows you like a stray dog, but as far as I can tell, you're never to blame. Even if something you've done precipitates a situation, you've always acted with the best of intentions."

"I try, sir."

The captain sighed and looked unhappy. "In any event, due to the ongoing investigation into the incident, our planned patrol next week has been delayed. SFHQ is not going to be happy, however good our excuse is this time."

"Yes, sir."

"Might I suggest, XO, that more of a focus on your shipboard activities regarding the running of the ship, and less on criminal activity outside the ship, is a good idea?"

"Yes, sir. I thought the two were connected, but there are no leads now anyhow. I'll concentrate on purely internal shipboard tasks. The station authorities have informally asked I remain on the *Humber* as much as possible."

The captain gave that a twitch of a smile. "Yes, I'd heard. They're doubtless afraid that after a couple of years of your presence they might have no station left. Please, try to leave me my ship intact if you could."

"Yes, sir."

"Good. So, XO, do you think we've covered all the outstanding issues?"

"Yes, sir. I do have one idea I think is worth pursuing."

The captain's expression was neutral, perhaps slightly bemused, as he regarded her. "Go on, XO. What is it?"

"My presence provides the *Humber* with a third fully qualified pilot," Katie said.

The captain nodded. "Yes."

"So, sir, I think we should take advantage of that to get more use out of the boat. I think occasional patrols of local space with the boat will give us a greater reach, and I think it'll signal to whomever may be concerned that we're paying attention."

The captain pursed his lips and looked into his Scotch. "I can't see any problem with that. You will consult with Lieutenants Rompkey and Wentzell to make sure that it doesn't interfere with their other duties."

Not much chance of that, Katie thought. "Of course, sir," she said.

"Very well, I imagine it'll look good on both of our

resumes," the captain said. "I can't see how it can go wrong. Please, don't take that as a challenge, Lieutenant."

"Of course not, sir," Katie answered, happy with the idea of some useful action she could take. And she enjoyed piloting too.

The captain smirked. "That it, XO?"

"Yes, sir."

"Good. Now get cleaned up. Change into a proper uniform. Have lunch, and maybe taking the afternoon off to get some downtime would be a good idea. A little rest and everything becomes a bit more copacetic I find."

"Yes, sir." Katie turned and left.

***

Rob wasn't used to failure.

It was late on Thursday, almost two weeks since Rob arrived on the *Humber*, and he wasn't breathlessly anticipating his weekend. Didn't look like he'd be going ashore for a good time with his mates. His shipmates weren't warming up to him. It'd also been made clear he should avoid going ashore with friends or otherwise.

Besides, he was probably going to be working overtime just like he was now.

Alone, down in the weapons access bay of the spindle, fixing every little job that had piled up during the *Humber*'s long deployment, it seemed.

The chief electrician, for whatever reason, was running him ragged. He'd been given an extraordinarily long list of tasks to do. And not enough time. The chief had gone so far as to criticize him in front of the other electricians in this morning's muster for his slowness. Told him if he wasn't so slow he wouldn't have to be working overtime to get his daily quota done.

Which was bad form and nonsense both. You don't tear men, or the odd woman for that matter, down in front of their mates. Leadership supposedly required correcting one's subordinates from time to time, but it was never supposed to involve humiliating them. Also, Rob was competent and knew his job. Far more experienced than his cover allowed him to appear. He knew damned well that he wasn't working that slowly.

Admittedly, he was significantly slower than he would be if he wasn't working so carefully. Both Kincaid and he had already been attacked and there were obviously people on the ship notabove indulging in potentially fatal sabotage. He needed to be careful.

It wasn't at all clear he could be careful enough.

Rob wasn't one to wallow in self pity. He was no "Paulie" Zimmerman. Though truth be told, Zimmerman had been a bit of a pleasant surprise to the upside. It seemed a shock to the system was what Zimmerman had needed to snap him out of his self destructive rut. Zimmerman had sought Rob out in his rack after their aborted poker game. He'd collected Rob's winnings for him. Gave them to Rob and muttered an embarrassed, only half coherent apology. A sincere one, it appeared.

Zimmerman seemed to have gotten over his resentment of Rob and the world in general. Good.

That was nice and rather edifying.

Didn't do much to help Rob with his problems.

He'd had several mission goals. First, find out if there were genuinely serious problems on the *Humber* and around Mars generally. It was possible that the death of the ship's last XO was just an unfortunate coincidence.

Well, not likely. He'd succeeded in his first goal. Yes, indeed, there were serious problems both on the *Humber* and around Mars generally.

Unfortunately, his second explicit goal of figuring out what they were wasn't going well.

And then there was Kincaid. He was supposed to be watching her back. He'd been told to keep her safe.

Ha. Rob was barely keeping himself safe.

Also, he needed to focus on his work. He'd arrived at the site of his next job. Internal Signals Repeater Station no. 29, which, according to reports, was failing to repeat correctly.

In a fit of absent-minded habit, Rob checked the case for high power. Which was totally unnecessary. Repeater stations do not have high power routed through them and so there's no risk of it getting accidentally shorted to their cases.

Only in this instance, Rob's meter lighted up indicating a high voltage charge was present.

Rob was so surprised he double checked. Yep, high power to a signals station. That wasn't an accident. This was a trap, not an accident. A potentially fatal one.

One suspiciously similar to the one that had been laid for Kincaid during her first ship's inspection. Rob had thought that trap had probably been laid by that PO stoker that had turned up mysteriously dead on station. His reward for failure.

He wondered if this current trap had been laid days ago by that man or if there was a second saboteur on board the *Humber*. A very important question, and Rob had no idea how to answer it.

Annoying. Also annoying that they'd tried the same trick twice and on a trained technician. Rather insulting. Worse than that, it'd almost worked. Even Rob, at his most paranoid, wouldn't have normally checked the case of a low power signals station for being hot.

Ouch. So currently, Rob's main goal had to be keeping himself alive.

And maybe he needed to emulate Zimmerman and rethink his attitude some.

Sure, Rob might be tough and competent, but this might be something neither he nor Kincaid were going to be able to tough out. Maybe he ought to get a hold of SFHQ and Kincaid both.

Tell them they needed to consider bailing out.

Recalling Rob and Kincaid both.

Placing marines and a new crew on the *Humber* and having them bring the ship back to Earth sooner rather than later.

It'd be seen by SFHQ as an embarrassing failure.

It might be the best they could hope for.

***

Pat wasn't the sort of man to show fear.

That didn't mean he didn't have his worries.

For one, he'd have been happier if the local mob enforcers being paid by the local smugglers had succeeded in their job of taking Kincaid out. Even some severe injuries would have got her medical leave and sent back to Earth. And even if she'd managed to raise a fuss there about the state of affairs on the *Humber*, Pat would have been retired before SFHQ got around to doing anything effective.

Retired and comfortably settled down on the Martian surface, where nobody on Earth, including SFHQ, could do much to him.

Locally, it was all settled. Broomfield the ops officer, formally his boss, was convinced he'd talked Pat into staying for one more patrol and had in recompense put all the necessary paperwork in place.

Kincaid hadn't mentioned anything about Pat's pending retirement to him. He wondered if she was aware of it.

It would have been so much more convenient if those hit men had succeeded. The girl had the luck of the devil.

What were the odds that a team of four armed and professional hit men would manage to surprise her unarmed and alone on the station and then still do no more than scratch her up some?

Not great. Not something Pat would have bet on. And still Kincaid had managed to survive the attack without major injury. Amazing.

Pat must have let his smile slip. The Leading Spacer Pat was following about, supposedly checking his work, was panicking.

"Something wrong, Bosun?" Leading Spacer McDonald was saying. "I'll see it's fixed. I promise. Even if it takes all weekend."

Pat could do his formal job pretty much on autopilot. Didn't mean he liked to make a habit of it. "Not bad, Mac," Pat said judiciously, giving the nervous man a warm smile. "Good enough for me, I'd say. But, you know, the new XO is a stickler. Squeaky clean and sparkling, and no excuses accepted. Might be a good idea to have the boys go over it again this afternoon, and Monday afternoon too. No need to spoil anyone's weekend. I'll tell the XO as much if it comes to it."

McDonald wiped the back of a hand across a sweaty forehead. "Thanks, Bosun," he said. "Trying to make a mark, our new XO, is she?"

"She's young, and she's got a lot on her plate," Pat replied, trying as hard as possible to sound like he was making excuses for Kincaid, but wasn't totally convinced himself.

"Yep, guess we were all young once," McDonald muttered.

"Too true, Mac, too true. Seems a long time ago, doesn't it?" Pat said. "Anyhow, best get on with it. We're both busy and our boys and girls won't want to be any later for happy hour than they have to be."

And the rest of their little tour was completely routine.

Turned out Friday morning wasn't too early to start preparing for the regular Tuesday morning inspections Kincaid was instituting. Definitely a silver lining on the dark Kincaid cloud in Pat's mind. Gave him an excuse to keep everyone very busy and resentful of their new XO both.

That Kincaid herself seemed to be busy with setting up a set of boat patrols was another positive development. Anything that kept her from spending time on the internal running of the ship was good, but her planned patrols had the additional positive feature of bringing her into conflict with the local smugglers and the armed ships they weren't supposed to have.

Could be the local bad guys would solve Pat's main problem for him. Without his fingerprints having to appear on the solution. He'd certainly appreciate that.

And, in the meantime, it still amazed Pat how well feeding everyone some bullshit, and then keeping them too busy to question it, worked.

Yes, Pat had his worries.

But he'd manage to cope.

And too bad for anyone in his way.

8: A Pause for Katie to Think

Rob didn't have quitting in him.

He might not survive this mission, but damned if he wasn't going to keep trying as long as he was breathing.

And so, he was out on the town this wonderful Friday night, sneaking into a warehouse. A warehouse that his research had been unable to determine the ownership of.

A "hole in the water" to use a twentieth century nautical analogy. You had to love crooks who were too lazy or too cocky to cover their tracks proficiently. Just hiding information isn't enough. You have to provide plausible facts to fill the space where it should be.

Whoever owned this storage facility hadn't done that, and so, here Rob was. As it happened, his technical familiarity with control systems translated into an ability to bypass alarm systems quite well.

Not for the first time, Rob found himself envying those hackers who could access a security system remotely and not have to put their own personal fragile bodies at risk in doing so.

Wouldn't have worked here, though. There was neither any

surveillance system in this warehouse nor any human guards. Which was rather odd and spooky.

Suggested the place's owners weren't worried about physical intruders. Rob, as he lowered himself carefully into the dark cavernous space through an emergency rescue hatch, wondered why.

Even with night vision gear he'd picked up from a blind drop, he couldn't see a thing. He listened attentively for anything odd. He moved very slowly and carefully. If there was some security precaution here he hadn't foreseen, he wanted to know about it sooner rather than later.

At least if something happened to him here, he'd managed to get off a second report to SFHQ. He hadn't quite demanded that he and Kincaid both be evacuated immediately. Neither had he pulled any punches. He'd made it clear that the both of them were in imminent danger from multiple sources and that at some point a major intervention was going to be needed in Mars space.

In the meantime, he continued to do his job to the best of his ability.

He felt his way around the warehouse by touch alone. He found an odd packing container of a sort he'd been briefed on. One with atypically rounded corners. One of a style known to be used by the Kannawik, their alien fellow inhabitants of the Solar System more popularly known as "Star Rats". A species that seemed to have crooks just as humanity did. Ones willing to do a little illegal smuggling.

His heart was in his mouth all during his slow, careful opening of one of those containers. Again, something he did completely by touch.

He chanced a very low, covered light to see what was inside.

Star Rat terminals doubtless full of Star Rat data, and neither of them legal by what the Star Rats had told humanity of Galactic law.

Great. New information. Not precisely what Rob had been looking for. He doubted the Star Rat smugglers had a significant presence on the *Humber*. All the same, his superiors would be, well, not exactly pleased, but let's say, appreciative that Rob had found what he had.

Rob was very careful not to let his guard down as he withdrew from the smuggler facility, trying to leave no trace of his having been there as he went.

Again, his caution didn't seem to have been necessary.

Not something Rob ever intended to take for granted.

Life had enough problems and little surprises you couldn't do anything about.

No excuse for not guarding against what you could.

**

Nelson had gathered a group of like-minded friends around him. A group of genuine brothers-in-arms who were eager to help him. Brothers-in-arms who saw things the same way he did. Colleagues who could be counted on to do the right thing, even if orders were lacking. Even, in fact, if those orders were to do the contrary.

Katie knew she was no Nelson in this respect.

The very fact that she would never admit, even to her closest friends, all of them now back in Earth space, that she patterned herself on heroes like Nelson was an indicator of that.

Not for the first time, Katie found herself doubting not just the practicality of what she was attempting to do with her life, but her very sanity.

She was being very ambitious. Extraordinarily so.

It was Friday evening. Most of the *Humber*'s crew were ashore, blowing off the week's accumulated steam.

Katie was sitting on a bench in a food court. The food court, being in an administrative section of the station that was only busy during normal weekday work hours, was currently deserted.

Katie didn't intend to be seen to be working through a funk by her shipmates or anyone else, for that matter.

Strangely enough, people trying to kill her didn't depress Katie. If anything, it was a kind of back-handed compliment. Somebody thought she was important enough to take the trouble of trying to remove her from the board. They were saying through their actions that she mattered to the game.

Maybe.

Or maybe Katie was just in the position of an oblivious pedestrian who stepped out into the street in front of a speeding bus.

Katie had never actually seen that happen. She had read news stories about it happening. She'd seen some near misses. She'd had a stranger grab her and keep her from doing it at one point. The shock of adrenaline had given her a dizzy pins and needles feeling. A near death experience that would never sound as impressive as nearly getting blown to bits.

After her family ship the Dawn Threader and Ceres, the bustling, crowded, and yes, not entirely safe, downtowns of Earth had been quite a shock to Katie. Exciting too, but she'd definitely been a fish out of water and her experiences in them had left a definite impression upon her.

So it turned out travel was broading. It gave you more metaphors to express how lost at sea you were emotionally.

For all that she seemed to spend an inordinate amount of time lost in self-doubting angst, Katie was basically someone who believed in action. Sitting still immobilized by analysi paralysis never got anything done. Act, see what happens, adjust, and act again. That was what Katie liked to do.

Good thing she'd grown up in a space ship where that sort of going off blindly half-cocked could get you killed. Katie had learned from an early age to have a plan before acting. To read the safety manual and do all the recommended checks. A bit of dirt in a valve that you didn't check could lead to no air. No air meant death.

There were many other ways of dying in space, all of them omnipresent.

No spacer ever willingly gave Murphy an opening.

Spacers had plans and protocols, and they all involved assessing risk and trying to minimize it.

Katie was a spacer to the core.

Katie believed they had the right of this and not just when working in space on ships. She believed it was the right approach to take to life and problems in general.

It was what she was trying to do now.

Katie had taken her position as XO on the *Humber*

without much of a plan other than to do the best she could. She hadn't had, and really still didn't have, any sense of the risks involved. She didn't have much in the way of plans to deal with the risks she hadn't assessed.

Katie needed to up her game. She needed to change course.

Katie had felt the need of some quiet time to think it over. Some place away from a long list of tasks to do and people she had to keep up appearances for.

So she'd gone for her second weekly sparring session with Brigit and von Luck and then instead of returning right to the *Humber,* had sought out this part of the station she knew would be deserted. For all the inefficiencies it imposed, people still liked to separate work and their personal lives. Not easy for anyone in the Space Force or spacers in general, but any study of how people lived when they had a choice showed it.

People wanted their commutes to be as short as possible, but they also wanted a line between where they did things because they wanted to and where they did them because they had to.

And this great geographical and social insight had led Katie to this deserted food court.

Who knew that wool gathering while avoiding thinking about difficult things could be so over-the-top and wide ranging?

Okay, first assess. Collect and organize your facts. Don't eliminate any as irrelevant at first.

Brigit Kharkov and Heinrich von Luck weren't friends. Not yet. Hopefully that'd change. They were friendly, though. Also determined to help though so far Katie wasn't sure how useful their help had been.

No, scratch that. If they hadn't provided backup for her meeting with "Saul", she'd be dead. Dead, just like Saul. She had to work on appreciating what people had already done for her. She couldn't just be annoyed they weren't helping more.

Personal issues aside, and despite the fact that emotionally she appreciated their support, it was apparent that Mars Station's authorities felt that they had a problem with criminal elements and were determined to do something about it.

Good.

However alone Katie might feel, she did have allies.

Even SFHQ, who'd for some reason stuck her in this predicament, had sent that Robert Hood guy along as backup.

Katie for the life of her couldn't see how he'd be useful, and his very existence had all but slipped her mind the last week. She wasn't at all clear on how she could check up on him, let alone use him, without blowing his cover.

Katie needed to think on that more, but not right now.

So what was she doing?

She was thinking about other people who could be useful to her and how.

Katie contemplated that. As much as she liked things cut and dried and not to waste time, when you wanted to think things over and gain insight, you had to step back and let things come as they would. You couldn't force it.

It occurred to Katie that her approach was cold and utilitarian and profoundly self-centered. The thought hurt and she wanted to reject it as just more self indulgent angst.

It made her think of Lars. It didn't make her feel good. Whatever they might have agreed formally, Lars had loved her. He'd loved her and gone out of his way to treat her well and she'd dumped him cold on short notice.

Katie still thought it'd needed doing and yet she hated herself for doing it. Katie didn't feel like a good person. And in truth, she missed him, too. It left a cold, sick, empty feeling in her stomach.

So Katie needed people to do what she wanted to and yet more and more she was cutting herself off from them emotionally. It wasn't like she'd ever been a touchy-feely social butterfly.

Maybe she couldn't ever do as much for other people as they would have liked, as she'd like even, but maybe she needed to think about what she could do for them more. More than just what they could do for her.

There. It hurt, that idea, but it felt right.

It was a finger hold she could grasp and pull herself up with and use to progress on this long, difficult climb she was making of her life.

She needed to build on the insight and she couldn't forget to catalog the rest of her facts. Right now, however, maybe that emptiness in her stomach wasn't just emotional. Maybe she was also hungry because it was supper time.

Katie had had the duty steward in the wardroom pack her up a boxed meal before leaving the *Humber*. "I'll probably be eating on the fly and so far I haven't been overwhelmed by Martian cuisine," she'd told him.

Boxed meals don't tend to be overly inspiring, but still Katie was curious to see what she'd got when she opened hers.

There was a sandwich. It had decent looking bread but an egg salad filling. For some reason, Katie hated egg salad. Eggs in most other forms were fine, but not egg salad and not on bread. The drink pack, veggies and dip, crackers and cheese, and tiny fruit cup all looked fine.

It turned out Katie wasn't the only living thing in the food court. A pigeon had appeared from nowhere as soon as Katie had opened her food container. Katie wasn't sure rats with wings and beaks were a great idea on a space station, but she did have to admit it gave the place a more Earth-like flavor.

Knowing it was wrong but unable to resist the bird's entreaties, Katie fed it bits of egg salad sandwich as she chomped on carrot sticks dipped in ranch dressing herself.

It made her feel better. It was peaceful. Just a couple of life forms far from their home planet getting on with the simple basics of living.

And then the pigeon started acting weird.

Distressed and confused. It stumbled around in a couple of small circles and then fell over.

Dead.

***

Katie was cold with rage.

And it wasn't just that someone had tried to poison her.

Nothing new or surprising about someone deciding to off Katie. She was almost getting used to that.

No, someone had wrecked Katie's quiet Friday evening, during which she'd hoped to get some useful perspective on what she was doing. She'd been trying to get away from being overwhelmed by events.

Well, here she was in the captain's cabin and Friday evening, all but a couple of hours of Friday night, and now most of Saturday morning had been spent talking to various people at great length and with no results.

Katie was tired. She was pissed. And she'd had just about enough.

And she could not afford to indulge her temper while talking to the captain.

"You should be flattered, Lieutenant Kincaid," he was saying. "There aren't many lieutenants anybody would consider worth making multiple attempts to kill."

"It's an honor I could do without, sir," Katie answered.

"Careful now, XO," the captain said.

"Yes, sir."

"*Yes, sir*' is an amazingly useful phrase. Pleasantries aside, the station authorities weren't able to help?"

"They tried, sir. They did everything they could. Forensics teams went over every location I'd visited with a fine-tooth comb."

"Every location on the station and the docks, too?"

"Yes, sir, but not the ship. They don't have jurisdiction here."

"Yes, we don't want to set any unfortunate precedents," the captain said. "All the same, if you want, I'll invite them aboard to do their magic."

"Like you said, sir, it'd set a bad precedent. I don't think it'd do any good."

"That bad? They didn't come up with anything? There couldn't have been that many people who had access to your meal. Your own investigations here didn't turn up any leads?"

"What we've been able to determine at great length, sir, is that we have no idea when the rat poison was introduced. It could have been any time and place between just after lunch here on the *Humber* and supper time at the food court. It could have easily been while the meal was unattended at the Marine sports complex. They have a lot of associate members and support staff there."

"Someone can poison an officer's sandwich and no one has any idea who?"

"Disconcerting, isn't it, sir?"

The captain smiled. "Yes, but restrain yourself. I

understand how frustrating this is. In a way, it's a relief it wasn't necessarily done on the ship. The thought that the people feeding us mightn't be trustworthy is beyond disconcerting. It's outright alarming. If I really thought the problem was on board the *Humber*, I'd have to insist you did something about it."

"Yes, sir," Katie answered. "Only, sir, frankly if we can't trust our people there isn't much we can do about it."

The captain smiled again. It wasn't a happy expression. "I'm glad you can see that. It's an awkward insight."

"Yes, sir. Practically, we only have the two stewards and we can't have them double up and watch each other all the time. Even if we were sure there were only a few bad apples and that doubling up and having everybody always watched by someone else would work, we don't have the manpower for it. Also, not incidentally, it'd generate a paranoid sense of not being trusted or being able to trust anyone else that would destroy the ship's morale."

"Couldn't have said it better myself, XO. It's a pretty dilemma we're in, isn't it?"

"Yes, sir, but what do we do about it?"

"Do? We do what we can, XO, and we try not to make things any worse and we hope it works out."

Katie barely kept the words "Hope is not a plan" off of her lips. Maybe sometimes plans weren't possible. She really didn't like that thought. "That's not very satisfactory, sir."

Another little smirk of a smile. "Life's the pits and then you die. Nobody is guaranteed a satisfactory life, Kincaid. Take your wins where you can find them and don't sweat the rest."

"Sir?"

"Specifically, in your case, you're still alive. You seem to have quite the knack for staying that way."

Katie couldn't help thinking she'd been awfully lucky and wondering how long that could last. "Yes, sir. Thank you, sir."

"Also, you still have plans for doing some boat patrols in local space, don't you? I understand Wentzell and Rompkey are good with that."

"Yes, sir. They both seem rather pleased by the idea and believe they can spare time from their other tasks for it."

"Great. Remember, Kincaid, just by being here and a potential threat, even if we do nothing else, we're putting a crimp in any potential smuggler's plans. Sure, we'd like to shut them down completely, but we are keeping them from running completely free. As long as the *Humber* is here and cannot be ignored, the Space Force and the System authority can claim to be in control."

"Claim, sir?"

"Appearances count, Lieutenant. I suspect they count a much with that wider galactic community I believe you're concerned about as they do with Earthside politicians."

"That's a reassuring thought, sir."

"Yes. Remember Lieutenant, do what you can, accept what you can't. I think that's all."

"Yes, sir." She'd been dismissed. Katie left to get some badly needed rest.

***

Rob's job was interfering with his mission.

First thing Monday and he was going to have to go outside into the vacuum as part of his first task. The whole ship had been turned upside down as a result of an apparent attempt to poison the new XO.

Another attempt on Kincaid's life Rob hadn't been in place to do anything about. He was definitely failing in that part of his mission. He was having trouble keeping himself safe, let alone Kincaid.

Rob had no doubt whatsoever that someone had got to the chief electrician and asked them to keep Rob busy. Busy at jobs that allowed that someone to make repeated attempts to permanently compromise Rob's health. Somebody was trying to kill Rob as well as Kincaid, but he suspected they'd settle for scaring him away or so badly injuring him that he ended up in a hospital somewhere. Mars or Earth, it likely didn't matter to them.

Didn't make for much peace of mind. It was downright distracting, in fact.

And it didn't do to be distracted when you were preparing for an EVA.

Rob had learned on a trades course that this stood for Extra

Vehicular Activity and dated from the early years of spaceflight. He'd never heard anyone actually use the full term. Everybody used the acronym and knew it meant going out into the vacuum where there was no gravity and you were expected to do delicate work with the functional equivalent of oven mitts on.

Rob had heard people brag about how it didn't bother them. He'd never heard anyone claim they liked it. The sometimes spectacular views didn't make up for the risk and awkwardness of it.

Rob wasn't going to get to spend the morning in contact with his crew mates finding out what they knew or thought about the latest attempt on Kincaid. Despite the safety rules supposedly in place, he was going to be alone in space out on the hull, checking out the control box for communications antenna number three. It was interesting how so many of the problems he was being assigned involved communications gear.

A clue as to where to look, but nothing solid to go on yet.

And he needed to get his head into the game. EVAs are not the sort of task you ought to be doing while distracted.

A visual inspection of the entire suit and the life support pack, especially the air tanks, was standard procedure. Rob never skipped it.

In fact, he made a personal point of checking more carefully. The gauge for how much air he had showed good green numbers. Rob had been taught informally by a grizzled old chief not to trust that.

"Sure, ninety-nine percent and better of the time, it's accurate, but seeing as how that remaining fraction of a percent can get you killed, just maybe you want to check the gauge is working right. You follow, son?" the chief had said. He had a certain studiously casual way of speaking that made you hang on his words. Years of instructing cocky young know-it-alls, Rob supposed. Rob regretted never picking up the knack of it himself. It'd be handy as a bossman back on Earth.

So Rob punched the quick vent valve from the tanks very briefly and looked, expecting to see the air pressure numbers flicker just a fraction in response. That would show the gauge was working.

Only the reading didn't budge. It stayed rock solid.

Rob tried the exercise again. Again, the gauge reading went utterly unchanged.

For some reason, the gauge wasn't working.

After some finicky disassembly, Rob got eyes on the inlet to the gauge. It was an analog and mechanical design hundreds of years old. It worked and it was incredibly robust and it was, not at all incidentally, immune to remote hacking.

But not, it appeared immune to hands-on physical sabotage. There was a tiny bit of wood shoved into the gauge's inlet port. Rob repurposed a tiny jeweler's screwdriver from his kit and pried the obstruction out.

Reassembling the thing and checking the air tanks out revealed two things. One, the gauge was working properly now. Great.

Two, there was just enough air in the tanks to allow Rob to get out all the way to the control box and maybe to start working. Only not enough to let him get back to the external air lock from there. Not so great.

Somebody had just made another attempt on Rob's life. Somebody close by who knew his routines and was clever and subtle. The attempt could have easily have succeeded if Rob had been a fraction less professionally paranoid. Damn.

Rob needed to up his game. Otherwise he wasn't going to survive this mission, let alone achieve its remaining goal of keeping Kincaid alive too.

Standing there staring at the life support gear that had almost failed him, Rob realized he was facing a different sort of problem than he was used to.

Rob was used to working in secret. Usually, nobody knew he was a spy, and he did nothing but observe and report. That was sort of the essence of being a spy. On very rare occasions, he'd been required to take direct action.

On those prior occasions he'd acted quickly and decisively, hitting hard, and then immediately extracting himself from the context, leaving as few traces as possible.

His current predicament where his opponents had made him, but he wasn't sure who they were, and he was being required to hang around being a target for them, was new to Rob.

Rob needed to adapt.

Specifically, it was clear he couldn't do this entirely alone and without support. He had to find allies and friends among the crew. Going this alone was going to get him killed.

And if he got himself killed, he'd also fail the rest of his mission requirements. He wouldn't get to make more reports. He wouldn't be able to help Kincaid.

And it was pretty clear Kincaid needed help, too.

If she wanted to stay alive.

9: A Chance for Katie to Help Some

One thing that any large institution of any duration could be counted on to develop was bureaucracy.

And it's an iron law of history that bureaucracy runs on paperwork.

Not that the "paperwork" need involve much actual paper. That term was an artifact of the fact that it was coined during the great industrial revolution of the 19th and 20th centuries. During that period, paper, first from rags and then from wood pulp, had been the main media upon which reports and accounts were written.

But that technical quibble aside, bureaucracy and paperwork were an historical constant. Starting with the hen scratches on the clay tablets of Mesopotamia in the third millennium BC and running up to the artfully arranged electrons within a ship's computer on a ship in orbit around Mars in the 24th century, it was a constant.

And, in the specific case of the current Executive Officer assigned to the *Humber*, it had piled up beyond all belief.

Katie's inbox was overflowing. Many of the more recent messages were red-bordered warnings that she'd exceeded her storage quotas. Which was insane given how little space it took to store text. Katie suspected the quotas were more to keep an unmanageable backlog from building up than they were to conserve storage resources.

In which case, they'd completely failed to serve their purpose. And were contributing to the problem they were supposed to be solving.

It was amusing in a depressing sort of way.

Katie had always managed to be proficient at IT, but had also always found it rather boring. Very abstract and full of persnickety artificial constraints, it seemed to her. Maybe she ought to re-visit that attitude. Could be the bit twiddlers weren't totally out to lunch all the time.

She simply didn't have the time, not even if she stopped eating and sleeping, to handle the problem of her overflowing inbox the way she'd like. She'd have liked to have glanced at their contents and outright deleted as many as she could. And then roughly binned the remaining messages by importance. Wasn't going to happen. There were so many that even that wouldn't work.

Ignoring the issue wouldn't work either.

Katie was sorely tempted to ignore the backlog. To cherry pick some of the more important messages out when she had spare time at most. Answer current messages for her specifically and leave it at that.

Apparently, this wasn't an uncommon urge. Some programmer back on Earth decades, or as far as Katie knew perhaps centuries ago, had anticipated it. Or maybe been required to deal with the fact of it. Turned out there was an algorithm in place to prevent such behavior. After an initial grace period, the e-mail program was becoming increasingly insistent that she deal with the backlog. It was now threatening to lock her out of being able to use her account for anything else unless she did so. She'd taken the trouble to read one of the more recent warnings.

It'd been informative.

Not in a nice or edifying way.

Once her account was locked, she could appeal to the captain for a week's temporary reprieve. If she didn't clear her backlog, she'd have to get one each and every week. Katie didn't think the captain would be impressed by that.

Alternatively, she could appeal to a properly trained and certified IT professional. Such a personage could up her quotas. Or they could work in concert with her to develop a set of rules for the automated clearing of the backlog. That set of rules would need to be approved by a special office in SFHQ back on Earth.

The quota increase would just be another, albeit longer, deferment of the problem.

Katie had no intention of bothering SFHQ with her e-mail problems either. Somehow she sensed that was not the sort of thing an up-and-coming officer wanted on their record. And she knew SFHQ, it would go on her record.

Didn't matter, anyway.

On checking, Katie found that there was no "properly trained and certified IT professional" on the *Humber*. There didn't appear to be any such creature any closer than Earth.

Okay.

So, Katie was going to have to deal with this herself.

As it happened, the program provided a plethora of tools for doing that. A confusing surplus of them. With a matching surplus of constraints.

The ancient and distant programmers that had written them weren't going to let any poor Space Force officer get away with anything so simple and as straightforward as simply deleting all the e-mails before a certain date, for instance.

In fact, Katie had to look long and hard before she found anything more than the function that allowed you to delete a single e-mail marked as "read" at a time.

There were a lot of rules for sorting and binning messages and you could send them to almost any sort of folder you wanted. You could create an arbitrarily complex tree of such folders.

One of the few pieces of advice that the *Susquehanna*'s XC had found time to pass on to Katie before her hurried departure for her new posting on the *Humber* was that she should avoid doing so.

"You're going to get a lot more e-mail as XO than as a mere

departmental officer," he'd said. A significant understatement that. "Resist the temptation to over complicate it. Look at everything as it arrives. You can delete almost everything right away without doing anything more. Do that. Answer or act on what you have to. Whatever you do, don't store things in some complicated prioritized folder tree. That way lies madness and whoever takes it over will hate you for the rest of eternity." Well, that seemed like useful advice.

And not necessarily something she'd have figured out on her own. Most of the rest of the world used forms of communication that were inherently temporary. But not the Space Force. No, it was a bureaucracy still stuck back in the 20th century. It wanted to store everything until it could be "curated for archival purposes".

Katie pitied future historians. Maybe she could help them, she mused. One of her heroes, Churchill, had written history would be kind to him because he'd write it. Might be an idea to emulate that trick if she managed to survive early death by e-mail.

Anyhow, too little time already. She needed to find a way to act and do so. Not something quite as simple as reading each message one by one and then deleting it. She'd already figured out that wouldn't work.

There was no avoiding it. She was going to have to read the help file. RTFM.

It was a long and tedious effort, but eventually Katie found something useful.

There was provision for finding and deleting duplicate e-mails. Clunky, and not at all straightforward to use, but it existed. Yeah!

Even better, the parameters for "duplicate" could be tweaked. And tweaked meant they could be subverted in Katie's mind. This was a challenge she could handle.

It was also one that turned out to have more than a few quirks. For one, it turned out that for e-mail purposes, Katie was four different entities. She was Katie herself personally. She had broad permissions over those messages, although that was qualified by the origin of the messages. Apparently, the people who'd created the e-mail program wanted to make sure those permissions couldn't be abused. They didn't want official business being handled through personal channels.

And, second, of course, she was the official Katie. That was LTSG Katherine Kincaid, the Space Force officer, independent of her specific assignment.

And, third, she was also Lieutenant Kincaid, the Executive Officer of the *Humber*.

Fourth, strangely enough, she also counted as the Executive Officer a second time. A certain amount of current e-mail came to her, independent of who she was personally. It was e-mail for the *Humber*'s Executive Officer without regard to what individual might be filling those boots. All of the e-mail that had been addressed to the post when it was empty or to prior XOs who'd not disposed of it fell into that category, too.

It was this category that Katie had the least control over and which composed most of the messages clogging her in-box.

Fortunately, it was possible to bin messages by those categories. Thank the Lord for small favors. It was a small step, but it was also a start on the problem. Forward progress if only baby steps.

Katie was sure in her bones that she could correctly categorize all the messages. If so, she could manage to put the bulk of them into bins where most of them were close duplicates, varying in some cases only by the timestamps on them.

The anal bastards back in the SFHQ records section still wouldn't allow her to completely delete the entire contents of most such folders. The only exceptions were messages that were clearly personal to her. What they would allow was removal of all but one copy of close duplicates. So long as a record of the deleted messages was kept along with a log of the differences from the retained copy.

Figuring all this out took Katie hours, well into the wee hours, and well past the time she should have gone to sleep. It gave her something of a headache, too. But also a sense of accomplishment, a feeling that she could beat this thing if she just persisted and pushed hard enough.

She had to be careful. Especially in the early stages of initial categorization, she had to get it right. If she goofed and misfiled some significant number of messages, she might be forever cleaning up the mess she'd made.

Katie had this weird vision of herself as an old graying lieutenant. One still stuck in orbit around Mars because of not being allowed to retire until she managed to get her e-mail account cleaned up. She saw herself slumped over her terminal, having died of e-mail exhaustion. Her destiny unfulfilled. Her very existence forgotten. The fact of that existence having been lost in some personnel officer's overfilled in-box.

She snickered. She was tired and kind of spacey, wasn't she?

Katie hated to quit while she was actually making progress of some sort, but she had to get some sleep tonight.

She decided to further categorize the messages by date and do a quick random sample of each of their contents. Then she'd sleep on what step to take next.

There, that was a reasonable plan.

Katie thought about it and decided on a set of dates. The best ones would be those that matched the periods each of the *Humber*'s XOs had been present for, and each of the gaps between them. Those gaps annoyed her to no end. Katie thought they were a clear failure of someone at SFHQ to do their job. Didn't matter really, she had to deal with the fact they existed. The *Humber* had had three XOs since being deployed to Mars and before Katie had got the job. There'd been three long gaps after each of them, during which the *Humber* had had no XO present at all.

It took a while for the sorting of the messages into Katie's newly created bins to complete. She got herself a coffee and watched it happen. It was frustrating, but there was nothing she could do to hurry it up. She killed time thinking about how she might write about what she was doing. Something to help other XOs. Certainly to help whatever poor jerk got to be her successor. She wondered why such a document didn't already exist. Could it be that the few dozen XOs in the Space Force had already informally adopted the process of handling e-mail proactively? Deleting much of it out of hand with the barest glance as soon as it arrived, and, therefore, never faced the problem of an overflowing in-box? That Katie had been assigned to the one ship in the fleet where it was a problem?

An annoying thought, to be sure.

Finally, before Katie could get too worked up, the process completed. Apparently, sorting and binning by dates was comparatively quick. Good to know.

The longest of the six main periods was that for the first XO, LTSG Thomas Robertson. He'd been XO for seventeen months before taking an early, but full, retirement. There was very little in the bin for his period in office. Katie checked a couple of them and looked over the titles. Looked mostly like archived instances of standard ship's reports with some logs of how the reports varied from month to month. A couple of information requests from SFHQ and Robertson's replies to them. He'd made some requests for a waiver of normal procedures for getting supplies and doing maintenance. They were all related to not having a dockyard present. Katie checked SFHQ's reply to a couple of those. One had been refused outright, the other had been a request for further supporting documentation.

Okay, looked like Robertson, an older man who'd been around the block, had known enough to keep his e-mail in check or at least to clean up before he'd left.

There was a three-month period before Robertson was replaced by LTSG Mary Cortez. Where Robertson had been a little old for the post, Cortez was on the young side for it, although nowhere near as young for it as Katie was. It looked like Cortez had made a start on cleaning up the messages that had arrived in the gap after Robertson, but never finished the job.

Cortez apparently had never got the advice Katie had from Katie's old boss on the *Susquehanna*. The e-mails from Cortez's five months as XO were a mess. They were already organized in a complicated and confusing way. At first, it sort of made sense, but later it was just confusing.

Katie remembered being told Cortez had been relieved of duty because of medical problems. Some other officers had hinted that they weren't just physical problems. Katie's grandmother had been more blunt. "She started having psychotic episodes and spouting conspiracy theories. A very sad end to what had been a promising career up to that point."

At this point, Katie wondered if perhaps drugs instead of poison might have been introduced into Cortez's food. It was a frightening thought. One that very much seemed like a conspiracy theory she wasn't going to share with anyone.

At any rate, the folder with the messages that arrived during Cortez's watch was only moderate in size. However, it looked like it was going to be a bear to whittle down.

Katie moved on to look at the messages from the eleven months after Cortez's departure. An unconscionably long time, Katie thought. And, Katie suspected, it was only eleven months long because someone at SFHQ had thought leaving a ship without an XO for a year or more would look very bad. A real problem if the press ever got a hold of it.

Seemed like a lot of officers besides Katie had thought Cortez's fate looked odd and had wanted to shy clear of a similar one. Could be they'd been the smart ones.

Looking at the messages that had arrived after Cortez's departure, Katie found that was when the in-box overflow warnings had started arriving. It never rains, but it pours.

Hard to be entirely sure with only a quick perusal, but it didn't look like van Eych had made much of a dent in the eleven month back og during his tenure.

Forgivable maybe, given that van Eych's time as XO had only lasted seven months before he was killed in an on-station mugging. Moving on, Katie found that he'd managed to mostly keep up with the inflow of new messages that arrived while he was present. He'd made a number of starts on clearing up the backlog of prior messages. He'd had to ask the captain for a number of formal reprieves to keep his account up and working. The very fate Katie was trying to avoid.

Only things had only gotten worse in the two months after van Eych's death and Katie's arrival.

Katie decided that the period after van Eych and before she arrived was probably the first one she needed to get to work on. Maybe not tonight, but it wouldn't hurt to sample what was there to get an idea of what she was facing.

The first couple of messages she picked out at random were standard reports. More of the sort that had been prevalent throughout the earlier periods. The next one she looked at was addressed "Personal - Urgent - To the Executive Officer for Immediate Action". Rather shocking considering there'd been no XO at the time it was sent.

Turned out it was a desperate plea for help from a young female rating who'd somehow managed to become pregnant. It was the ship's medic's job to make sure female hands didn't suffer such accidents. They were issued long term contraceptives to that end. They were expected to make sure every female aboard took them unless granted maternity leave. The Space Force planned around the idea that every young woman would likely want to have at least two children. It wasn't averse to granting leave for a third child, in most cases. Fifteen months was the normal period. It didn't help a career true, but for a not too ambitious thirty to forty year life timer, it wasn't a huge handicap either.

Katie had a lot of problems with the young woman's situation. She lost track at about three. One, the woman should never have got pregnant in the first place. It was primarily her responsibility in theory not to, but Med Bay was supposed to make sure it didn't happen, too. In this case, the young lady claimed she'd gone in for her medicine as required and become pregnant anyway. The med bay had no records of it, surprisingly. That was a second major problem. Another problem was that this hadn't come to Katie's or some other officer's attention immediately. Katie noted the young woman was a fire control tech and, therefore, in the operations department. Katie wasn't going to be able to avoid talking to both Broomfield, the ops officer, and the bosun about this.

Wonderful.

Finally, having become pregnant, the woman wasn't being given the chance to decide what to do with the potential child that she was entitled to. Not only was the Space Force liberal in granting women maternity leave for the odd unplanned pregnancy, they actively encouraged them to take it. It'd been found that both miscarriages and abortions had unfortunate impacts on the mental health of many women. The Space

Force liked to avoid such complications. It also liked to seem like a sensitive employer.

Only in this case, the young woman in question, a LS Alice Younghusband, hadn't been granted that leave. Nor an allowance to make the accompanying trip back to Earth where most of her family was. The young lady claimed to not be sure of who the child's father was. Katie didn't attempt to enumerate the ways that annoyed her. Still, formally, it should make no difference. The choice of having the child and how to raise them was legally and morally the potential mother's.

Whatever was going on here was not kosher.

Just to round out the thing was the reason given for why Younghusband wasn't getting the leave she deserved. It was because the *Humber*'s XO needed to approve it and hadn't done so. There mightn't be an official rule, but in the absence of a XO, common sense said the captain should have been informed.

Oh, boy. Katie saw red. She could hear someone's teeth grating. Hers, apparently. She took a deep breath, and tried to be, if not calm, at least not overwhelmed by anger.

She checked Younghusband's dates. There was still time for her to get to Earth and have her child there. Katie wrote an e-mail instead of reading one for the first time that evening. Morning really now. Katie granted Younghusband immediate maternity leave. She tacked an extra three months on to it to allow for travel time and preparations. She checked the next departure date for a liner to Earth and bought the young woman a ticket. A second, not third, class one. She attached a copy of it to the e-mail. Katie also authorized a travel allowance. She forwarded copies of the message to SFHQ, the captain, ops officer, bosun, and Med Bay. She added comments for SFHQ and the captain to the effect that it was urgent that the matter be settled fully and completely. At least if the Space Force wished to avoid a nasty lawsuit complete with rather serious political fallout. She added her personal belief that this was a simple matter of basic moral responsibility. She wrote that they had badly failed one of their members and that she was looking into it. To the others, she simply wrote that the matter was urgent. Also, that if for some reason Younghusband didn't make it on to that liner, happy and healthy, Katie was going to look into it personally and heads would roll.

This, at least, was something Katie knew how to handle.

Just as a last thought, Katie checked to see that Med Bay was getting the contraceptives it should be. It turned out that it was. More than enough, in fact, for a normal ship's complement of female spacers. A normal complement that the *Humber* hadn't come anywhere meeting from the very start. No sensible young woman wanted to be stuck out around Mars. The *Humber* had had fewer women on board than was normal from the very start. The ratio of men to women had only become ever more lopsided during its long stay in Martian space.

Med Bay was ordering and apparently using a lot more contraceptive medicine than it needed. So what was happening to the extra? Katie could guess. It was yet another indicator of what was wrong here.

She'd hold off acting until she had firm evidence.

Her first priority right now was the boat patrols.

But sooner or later she was going to clean up the mess on the *Humber* itself, too.

Come hell or high water.

But that was going to be quite the battle, she had to think.

Not one she wanted to go into half dead from lack of sleep.

Right now, she needed to go to bed.

She needed to be at her best for all the battles ahead.

***

Pat didn't believe in getting angry.

Anger had killed his dad. Drinking had been the immediate cause, but it'd really been his deep persistent anger that had done him in. He'd been a bright man with a real talent for figuring out how things worked. Only he hadn't been a patient one. He couldn't easily explain how he fixed things, and he wasn't much for training courses or certifications. He'd done good work while others goofed off or worse, messed up, but it was the others that got the raises and good pay. And so, he was always disappointed and angry. It'd driven him to drink.

Late one night, when Pat was still a boy of seven, his father had either fallen or jumped in front of a transit train. Left Pat and his mom high and dry.

Pat had loved his dad, but he'd resolved there and then not to make his mistakes.

So, Pat made a point of not giving into anger.

Sometimes it was harder than others. Like this morning, when he'd gotten the message about Alice being given maternity leave and sent back to Earth. Worse, though the message made no mention of the med bay or its failure to keep Alice from getting pregnant, Pat had no doubt Kincaid, and every other officer who became aware of the incident, would be wondering what had happened. There was going to be an investigation of the med bay as sure as God had made little green apples.

And so, Pat was in the med bay talking to the medic with the aim of making sure that investigation found exactly nothing.

The medic was nervous, rubbing his hands together and blowing on them as if they were cold. Made no sense; it wasn't cold in the med bay. "Don't worry, Bosun," he was saying, "there's nothing out of order. Paperwork's all done signed off by me and you, and Broomfield, too. Our friend in medical disposal on-station will swear himself blind that he regularly disposed of our expired drugs by high temperature incineration. Exactly like regulations require, and it leaves absolutely no evidence for anyone to check. We're fine."

"You just be sure of that, Doc," Pat answered. "You be sure there's no loose ends I have to tidy up when they come looking. Even Broomfield is going to have to go through the motions now. You understand me?"

The medic rubbed his hands harder and nodded. "Don't worry about me. I've got it under control. We're a team, right?"

"That's right, Doc," Pat said to reassure the man. No point to pointing out that there were always loose ends, the documentation was too complicated and there were too many checks and balances to ever hide fiddling if someone wanted to dig long and hard enough. Worse, the longer it went on the greater the chances someone complicit would crack, or someone cowed would discover a backbone.

"Good to hear, Bosun. Good to hear."

"Anyhow, Kincaid's distracted with that boat patrol project

of hers." A project that was likely to get her killed. Possibly by one of the armed ships the local smugglers had while she was out on patrol. That'd be the ideal outcome. Kincaid would be off of Pat and his boys' backs without them having to get their hands dirty. Or the smugglers might take more direct action against her personally again. And do a better job of it this time. That would certainly result in an in-depth investigation by a team from SFHQ. Only it'd take so long Pat would be retired and safely down on the Martian surface before it unearthed anything incriminating. And who knew, maybe they'd be satisfied with just taking the smugglers down.

"She is the nosy one, isn't she?"

"Yep, and it's likely to get her killed."

"Sad."

Pat snickered. "So sad."

***

It was a disturbingly normal and peaceful scene.

Tuesday, just after work and school, and people on Mars Station going home from both were stopping here at this food court in a local shopping area to have a bite to eat. One that they wouldn't have to cook or clean up after themselves. A minor treat to themselves, maybe, or perhaps for children that had been obedient.

It was almost enough to make a man let his guard down. Rob wasn't going to make that mistake, though.

Not ever. Particularly not given the shady character that had set this as their rendezvous spot. And certainly not after what had happened to Kincaid and her informant doing something almost identical to what Rob was attempting.

Which was to find out what the local smugglers were up to.

Rob didn't really care much about moderate scale smuggling, intended to avoid local duties and taxes. Wasn't his job. What he cared about was any complicity on the part of Space Force personnel. Also, about keeping Kincaid safe. That was quite enough already.

Too bad there wasn't any chance of talking to the criminals, not of much interest in this case, and convincing them to adopt a live and let live attitude. His bosses probably wouldn't approve anyhow. So Rob kept an eye out.

So he took notice when a skinny, strung-out man appeared, someone who seemed to belong in the dingier, skid row, part of the station rather than this pleasant residential one.

And, when that man threw something at him, he yelled "Get down!" and followed his own direction. Hitting the deck, he rolled away from where he'd been as fast as he could.

The bomb, when it went off, still deafened him and then pelted him with debris.

It turned out it'd only been a small bomb compared to the one that had greeted Kincaid on her arrival.

Standing up, strangely wobbly, Rob looked around. The bomb thrower, to his disgust, had hightailed it and was nowhere in sight.

There was one woman bleeding from a deep cut on her arm. Some other people seemed to have bruises or abrasions from following his advice, but no one was severely injured. Rob thanked the heavens for that.

A good thing he'd been anti-social and sitting by himself away from all the other people. Also that the place hadn't been that crowded.

He resisted the urge to just return to the ship and get some shut-eye. Rob found he was very tired all of a sudden. Only he knew the station police would not approve, that they'd want to talk to him about what had happened. Wasn't likely to be a very friendly conversation. Rob waited all the same.

While he did so, he thought about what had just happened. Also, about the situation overall.

Wasn't good. Local smugglers seemed rather hostile. Murderously so. Figured Kincaid had to be a priority target for them too, given her now well-known plan to institute randomly timed boat patrols of local space. She was in danger of putting a serious crimp into the local unofficial import and export business.

Rob sighed. Leaving Mars had been the smartest thing he'd ever done, and coming back the dumbest.

Anyhow, his supposed informant was another dead end. He was also sure he couldn't protect Kincaid against all the possible threats she faced.

He might, however, be able to combine his day job and

looking out for her to a degree.

Some of the many shit jobs he'd been assigned were in or around the boat bay. Rob would be surprised if the bad guys, whoever they were, didn't attempt to capitalize on the fact the boat bay was an inherently dangerous place. Add some intentional danger and sooner or later Kincaid's luck was bound to run out. Rob could run interference and check the place for such shenanigans.

It was something.

Not much.

But, something.

***

Truth be told, Katie was happy to be doing something besides admin work.

Technically, it wasn't her job to be down here in the boat bay doing pre-flight preparations for the coming patrol. She'd presented it as a favor of sorts to Tom and Tammy. It was a sacrifice she was more than willing to make.

These boat patrols were how Katie was going to show the local bad guys that there was a new sheriff in town. They weren't going to be able to blithely ignore the *Humber*. She was going to put a crimp in their operations.

Katie had just checked the fuel levels and those of the various life support consumables too, water and air, but also the various chemicals for things like removing carbon dioxide. Right now, she was doing a visual inspection of the boat clamps. Next up was the mechanism for opening the external boat bay hatch, but she needed to concentrate on what she was doing right now. And that was inspecting the boat clamps.

A failure of the mechanisms for releasing the boat and ejecting it into space would be catastrophic.

The *Humber* itself might largely survive. The living quarters, weapons, and propulsion would probably be unaffected. Only the boat bay, and the boat itself, would probably be out of commission for a good long time. The rest of the ship's tour, most likely, given the lack of a local naval dockyard.

And wouldn't that put paid to Katie's patrol plans?

Fortunately, such failure was very rare. Also, normally, any gross physical damage to the involved mechanisms would be glaringly obvious to even the most cursory visual inspection.

Only things weren't normal right now. Katie had to consider the possibility of deliberate sabotage. Sabotage that might not be so obvious. So her visual inspection was very careful, and she was using a handheld meter to check both metal tensions and structural integrity.

In her concentration, she almost missed the hissing.

Katie didn't know how long it'd been going on when she noticed it. It was bad news and she couldn't have much time.

Holding her breath, and leaving her instruments behind, she pushed off towards where she knew one of the damage control lockers was located. That was one motion. It took a couple of seconds.

Less than a second to open the locker. Another motion.

She grabbed an emergency vac suit and pulled it on over her legs and torso in another motion. Another second.

Katie was still holding her breath. Not easy while being so active, but she'd been training herself to do it since she was a girl.

Getting her arms into the suit was another motion, and a further second.

The motion of zipping it up didn't take so long.

Flip the helmet up, seal it, and hit the emergency air input hard to push out whatever had been in the ambient air. Another three motions, maybe another couple of seconds.

And Katie could breathe again. She took a deep, blessed breath. And a moment to let the adrenaline subside a bit, and wonder what exactly was happening. She'd been going on urgent auto-pilot up to that point.

It didn't take long to figure out the fire suppression system was working, even if the alarms that were supposed to accompany its activation weren't. There weren't any loud klaxons, or urgent verbal messages sounding. There were no bright lights flashing.

What there was, was a boat bay full of a gas designed to rapidly neutralize all the oxygen in it.

A gas that, if she'd taken a deep breath of it, would have killed her. A whiff of the stuff would only have severely damaged her lungs. Landed her in the hospital for months, likely one back on Earth.

Only bright spot would have been the Space Force paying for the prolonged and painful operations to replace those damaged lungs.

Katie suspected either outcome would have satisfied whoever had laid the trap.

Somebody didn't want her to succeed in her patrol plan.

In a way, it was a good sign. She and her plan were threats to somebody and their plans. She only wished she knew exactly who and what they were trying to do. There were too many actors in this little drama.

All she knew was that she was going to play her part to the hilt.

Even if it killed her.

Which it well might.

10: Katie On Patrol

Katie loved to fly and had given herself the pilot's seat. Poor LTJG "Tammy" Wentzell had been relegated to the co-pilot's seat. Formally, it was her designated position anyway, and she didn't seem to mind too much.

Being woken up without warning at a random time that happened to be the wee hours of Thursday morning hadn't bothered her much more.

Katie was relieved at that.

As co-pilot, Tammy arguably had the more important role of the two of them. It was her job to track the local traffic and determine what was legit and what wasn't. Not only did she have to use the boat's not so great sensors to the best effect, she also had to co-ordinate with several different traffic control centers. Mars Station traffic control for starters, but then the overall center for near Martian space, and finally it seemed each region of the Red Planet had its own local traffic control center that controlled local take-offs and landings.

It was a chaotic, messy, and inefficient system. Also typically Martian. They hated centralization. They were willing to sacrifice a lot to retain local control wherever possible.

So Tammy had a tough job that was best done by a fully engaged and motivated individual. Not a tired, resentful, unmotivated one. Fortunately, Tammy seemed to be happy, alert, and performing well.

It was keeping Tammy quite busy, but Katie was rather impressed with how well Tammy was handling it. Lots of experience, it seemed.

In the meantime, it was Katie's job to get the *Humber*'s boat out where it could do some good keeping an eye out for possible bad guys.

They wanted to loiter over the far side of Mars from Mars Station, where the *Humber* was docked, for as long as possible. A highly eccentric orbit with its high point, "apoares" technically, over the far side, and its low point, or "periares", beneath Mars Station was the ticket.

Katie spent the first hour and a half of their twelve-hour patrol and their first trip around the planet getting them inserted into that orbit.

It was a standard sort of maneuver and one every pilot trained for constantly, but it was good to be out in the boat and exercising the orbital mechanics part of her brain for real.

It was good to be out on patrol and showing the flag.

Finally, they were making a difference.

The slight surprise most of the traffic controllers Tammy was contacting showed that.

This was something at least some of those people trying to remove Katie from the picture had been trying to prevent. And yet, here they were out on patrol. Space Force eyes out where they hadn't been before. An armed Space Force vessel, if only a boat, present where it hadn't been seen before.

The boat should be enough. As poorly armed as it was, it should be able to handle an unarmed merchant.

They were half way between periares and apoares and on the ascent when Tammy spotted it.

"Medium sized merchant," she said with no introduction. "Looks like a Liberty class transport. Just clearing the far horizon. No transponder. Nothing on it from traffic control. Rapid ascent. Looks like they're optimizing for speed of transit, not fuel economy."

Hot damn, looked like a smuggler. Katie would have never dared hope for this. They'd got lucky. Smuggler mustn't have even bothered checking for a patrol ship. They'd caught them by surprise. "Intercept course?" she asked.

"Punching the numbers in now," Tammy answered.

Katie checked the indicated course. Not perfect. It looked like they were going to have a long stern chase. "Prepare for maneuvers," she said. No way Katie wasn't going for this. Once aligned, the gees pressed them back into their seats. "Have they altered course?" she asked. "Any sign at all they've noticed us?"

"Not yet," Tammy answered. "Should we hail them?"

"No, not yet. The longer they wait before trying to evade us, the better our chances of catching them."

Whoever that ship was, and Katie was convinced they were somehow illegitimate, just not having a transponder was illegal, they were pretty complacent. Fat, happy, and dumb. It was almost fifteen minutes before they altered course and upped their acceleration in an apparent attempt to avoid interception by Katie and Tammy.

"Okay," Katie said, "I think they've noticed us. Hail them and order them to cease acceleration and maneuvering and prepare to be escorted back to Mars Station for inspection. Suppose you can ask them to identify themselves and explain what they're doing first."

"That would be according to the book," Tammy commented dryly. "Unknown ship on course," she broadcast before giving the probable smuggler's course. "This is the Space Force boat *Humber Alpha*. Identify yourselves and your business. Your transponder is not operating. Immediately cease all acceleration and maneuvering. Prepare to be escorted to Mars Station upon interception. *Humber Alpha*, out."

There was no response.

Tammy tried again after a few minutes.

Again they waited. "No response?" Katie asked rhetorically. "Course changes?"

"None. Rock solid on optimal evasion course and acceleration is unwavering."

Now that was interesting. Whoever was in charge on the

presumed smuggler was assuming they could outrun the *Humber*'s boat. A good assumption because although the maximum acceleration of the two spacecraft was probably comparable, their fuel loads weren't.

Katie's boat was going to run out of fuel a long time before that smuggler did. Long before she managed to bring it within normal effective weapon's range.

The boat's dinky little missiles didn't have anywhere near the delta vee to make up the gap.

As for the 12mm railgun, its rounds didn't need fuel, and they were fast, only fast still means a long time in transit over even short astronomical distances. Even small changes in course would result in clean misses over the distances involved.

Only it looked like they were all new to this sort of thing. The smuggler wasn't making even small changes to its course. Katie would be willing to bet they didn't have the sensors to detect the boat's railgun firing or its round in transit either.

"No changes in course at all? Not even small evasive ones?"

"No, nothing," Tammy confirmed.

"I want a firing solution for the railgun on the engines based on their current course then."

"Okay," Tammy answered in a drawn out tone of skepticism.

"You mean '*yes, ma'am*'," Katie said sarcastically. "Seriously, I know it's a long shot. Literally. But if they don't alter course even slightly, it's just math."

"Yes, ma'am," Tammy said, pecking at her console industriously. "There you are. And, by the way, if it misses the round won't go anywhere career ending."

"I'd expect nothing less," Katie said. "Fire when ready."

Tammy pushed a button with a dramatic gesture. The boat shivered slightly. "There."

"Great. Guess we just wait now. How long?"

"Nineteen minutes and thirty-seven seconds. Approximately."

"Might be an idea to make the occasional blustering demand they heave to. Don't want them wondering what we're up to."

Even with the distraction of Tammy's imitations of a frustrated and officious Space Force officer, the minutes and seconds went by with excruciating slowness.

Finally, after almost twenty minutes, Tammy exclaimed, "I'll be! We hit them. In the engines. Outgassing. They've lost acceleration. We're going to catch them."

Katie grinned. It was all she could do not to whoop in triumph. "Great. Good work, Tammy. But let's not relax until we've got them alongside and in custody on Mars Station. It's going to be tricky to rendezvous and a long tow back. Also, it's not likely, but they could be armed."

Tammy grinned back at her. "Right, wouldn't do to count our chicks before they hatch."

Katie nodded. "Indeed. That'd be most unprofessional."

Ship's boats travel a lot slower than their railgun rounds. It was well over an hour before they started to approach the apparently dead in space smuggler.

Katie was still feeling high, but increasingly worried that the smuggler still hadn't replied to their periodic hails.

She didn't think one small caliber railgun round could have killed the ship's entire crew. And if that wasn't the case, it suggested the smuggler still thought they could get away somehow.

Katie was dearly tempted to put a few more railgun rounds through the still unidentified civilian ship just to make sure of it.

Only that would be what they call "career limiting" and immoral too. Even criminals have rights, and SFHQ's guidelines were clear: the use of force had to be proportional and clearly justified. Pumping a few extra railgun rounds into a unidentified civilian ship that hadn't done anything other than attempt to evade inspection didn't count.

Even wary out of puzzlement at the damaged ship's behavior, Katie and Tammy were surprised and slow to react when the supposedly unarmed civilian fired on them.

It sprayed a full salvo of thousands of rounds from a Gatling gun at them. Gatling guns were mainly anti-missile weapons, but they'd do fine against a lightly armored boat that happened to get too close too.

Fortunately, the hostile ship, smuggler or whatever, fired a little too soon. Katie wasn't so slow that she didn't manage to evade most of the gunfire. At least two loud bangs indicated that she hadn't completely succeeded.

Katie didn't get time to ask Tammy for a damage assessment. The "unarmed" civilian immediately launched a follow up salvo of small missiles. Katie became rather busy jerking the boat around in a high gee run almost directly away from their opponent. Small as they were, if any of those missiles hit, they could spoil Katie and Tammy's whole day.

Tammy, Katie noticed, with a quick sidewards glance, was busying herself trying to make the best use of the little boat's rather minimal ECM and anti-missile packages. Katie elected not to distract the woman with directions and to concentrate on flying.

It was another stern chase, only in the opposite direction and much more frenetic.

It only lasted a very long quarter hour.

But by the time they'd run the fuel of the missiles seeking them dry, Katie was sticky with sweat. So tired it hurt too. It'd been a long fifteen or so minutes. Still, it was nice to be alive and the boat still seemed to be intact and working.

"Damage?" Katie asked Tammy.

Tammy tried to sound calm, but her voice shook slightly. "Not bad. Couple of punctures through the cargo space it looks like. Losing atmosphere from it, but I've sealed it off, and it doesn't look like anything important in propulsion or life support has been damaged."

Katie nodded. "Good. Thank you. And our unfriendly target?"

"Oh," Tammy replied. "They're getting away. Guess they got their engines fixed."

"If they were ever damaged in the first place," Katie grumped, thinking she'd been snookered.

"Well, they've got good acceleration, but it's short of what it was before. So, I guess we did take a piece out of them. Woke them up, they're making constant small changes in vector and acceleration now."

Katie hated to give up. "So, no more easy pot shots. Any

chance of getting back into effective weapons range?"

Tammy snorted. "No. Not even if you wanted to." The clear implication being that no one sane would want to after one near death experience already. "Between their own acceleration and ours directly away from them outrunning their missiles, there's no chance of making up the delta vee."

"Guess that's that."

"Guess so."

"Alright, we're aborting this patrol and taking the boat back to the *Humber*. We need to check out and repair the damage."

"Yes, ma'am," Tammy said with genuine enthusiasm. "Hey, cheer up. I'm sure we gave them a scare and maybe we'll have better luck next time."

"Sure, you never know."

***

Katie was fuming.

She'd had a lucky break. She'd made one, not to be modest. And it'd all gone for naught.

Katie could admit that to herself now. Now that she was alone back in her cabin.

Right after returning with a couple of sets of new holes through the ship's boat. She'd needed to put the best face possible on it for the benefit of the crew and the captain.

They'd all seemed rather impressed and excited by the outcome rather than depressed. The captain had commented in the privacy of his cabin on her proclivity for damaging Space Force property, but in a jocular tone. His negativity had seemed more habitual than heartfelt.

"Keep this up, XO, and maybe they'll have to recall us early to repair everything," he'd said. The prospect seemed to cheer him.

They had managed to demonstrate that smugglers did exist. Only Katie thought that'd been pretty obvious anyway.

That they'd been armed had been a surprise. One that was bound to get the attention of the pooh-bahs back on Earth. Katie only wished she believed they'd get around to doing something about it before the next century. But, yeah, she had to admit it was something.

And likely too, in the future, smugglers would be a little

more careful when swanning about in Martian space.

Again something, but not entirely a positive something. It meant Katie probably wasn't going to catch them by surprise again. And even with the advantage of surprise and a sub-optimal response by the opposing captain, she'd not managed to stop them.

Wasn't likely going to be a next time. If there was, it wasn't likely to go even as well. Ouch.

So what to do?

Well, the boat would be patched up and ready to go in another day, two at most, and the captain had greenlighted further random patrols. Katie expected this was mostly because, like Katie, he didn't think another encounter with smugglers was likely now that they'd been warned. If they hadn't had snitches keeping an eye on the boat's movements before, they'd have them now.

Still, the optics would look good. Their bosses back on Earth would be pleased that a Space Force presence in Martian space was being exerted. If the captain said that politically that was useful, Katie had to believe him. She found politics counterintuitive and unpleasant. Didn't mean they weren't important.

So, if her job was at least partly to only play scarecrow, she could do that. Would do that.

She'd like to do more, though. Again, what?

Katie could think of two things.

One, getting the *Humber* herself out on patrol as scheduled. The corvette might be only a very small warship, but she was more than a match for any armed merchantman. That was mainly in the hands of the engineer. The patrol being effective was in the ops officer's hands. She needed to support them and continue to let them concentrate on their technical jobs.

There were definitely problems with the internal administration of the ship, but she'd have to bypass them to some extent and handle those herself.

Second, as there were definitely smugglers, likely more than one group, and because logically they had to have some presence on Mars Station, there had to be some way of finding them. Finding them and rooting them out.

There, she had goals.

All she needed now were actual plans, and to execute them. Try to avoid getting killed or maimed in the process.

Just details, really.

Sometimes Katie amused herself.

***

Pat was feeling disappointment and regret.

Disappointment that the local smugglers hadn't been competent enough to properly mousetrap Kincaid and kill her.

And regret it because meant he'd probably have to handle the job himself. He hadn't wanted to be the one to kill Kincaid.

Pat mightn't be beyond skimming a little cream off for himself. Pat certainly didn't approve of everything about how the Space Force operated.

But he was a Space Force career NCO and proud of it. He also believed in its mission.

The disrespect most Martians showed the Force grated on him.

If Kincaid had managed to get herself and a couple of other Space Force members killed in combat with an armed smuggler, it would have served two good purposes.

It would have kept Kincaid from complicating his life, and his retirement specifically, for one.

It would have also provoked a strong response from SFHQ back on Earth. SFHQ couldn't have let something like that pass. Even if they wanted to, and they wouldn't have, the public wouldn't have tolerated it.

Kincaid would have done the cause of imposing Space Force control over Martian space immense good simply by getting herself heroically killed in the line of duty.

Who says heroes aren't useful?

Kincaid had the guts and the ideals to be a hero. Only she seemed to move too fast and too unpredictably for the villains. They were failing to give her the heroic death she deserved.

Too fast and too unpredictably for most villains anyhow. Not for Pat, he suspected.

It was beginning to look like they were going to find out.

As much as Pat was coming to respect Kincaid, it was

beginning to look like he was the one that'd have to end her.

Pat regretted that.

But a man does what he has to.

***

Rob was in danger.

In danger of relaxing.

There was no way it was going to be safe to do that until he was off of the *Humber* and back on Earth.

Only his messmates weren't acting so cold anymore, and that was a good feeling.

Rob, in his real life, had done well. He was a successful and respected businessman back on Earth. Only there was no way an ex-Martian tunnel rat was ever going to entirely fit in with small businessmen or even tradesmen who'd lived their entire lives on Earth. He'd never felt like he could be entirely himself with them. There were some attitudes and habits a tunnel rat had that were bound to discomfort any respectable person who'd never left the Mother Planet.

It felt like it was safer to let his guard down and just be himself with these fellow Space Force enlisted people.

They were all sitting around their mess's central table, enjoying a few beers and shooting the shit. Odds were there was no one present who had any agenda other than relaxing a little after work.

It was tempting to give into the feeling. Only it'd be a mistake. Rob didn't fit in here anymore, either.

That was a little depressing.

On the other hand, his messmates did seem to have warmed up to Rob some. Somebody had primed them to think the worst of both him and Kincaid before they'd even appeared on board.

Now that Rob had proved himself a hard worker and no complainer, and it was obvious someone was gunning for him, the crew of the *Humber* seemed inclined to give him a second chance.

This was even more true of Kincaid.

Kincaid and her little battle with the armed smuggler ship were the talk of the table.

Spacers, in general, admired a can-do attitude and an

ability to get things done. Space Force spacers in particular admired guts. Having the guts to face up to trouble and being tough enough to handle it are different things. Spacers admired a willingness to try.

Kincaid had shown herself to have guts and a can-do attitude. She'd also shown she was tough and made things happen. So color the enlisted hands on the *Humber* provisionally impressed.

"Girl," one man began to say.

"Woman," one of his female mates corrected.

"The lady," the grizzled Leading Spacer continued. Rob figured Mike Maddox had made PO and been broken more than once in a long career. "The lady," Mike said, "is not one for quitting. Not one to back down. You've got to give her that."

His foil, an Able Spacer by the name of Tisha Gonzales, snorted. "You're surprised?"

"Guessing we all heard the stories," Mike said. "Only figured they'd been spiced with a liberal helping of star dust."

Tisha took a swig of her beer and banged its container down on the table harder than she needed to. "Young Belter girl who looks like she could be your kid sister goes to the Academy and makes it through. Nothing made up about that."

"Figure she's a lot better looking than Mike's kid sister," Tom Vanderhoop, the mess card put in. His sally got limited grunts from his messmates. One doesn't rightly think of one's XO as anyone's kid sister.

Tisha looked disgusted. "Anyone who watches the news knows the facts. It was on the Space Force channel when she graduated. They made a big deal of it and how it proved anyone with talent could become a Space Force officer."

That did get some snickers. It was funnier than most of Tom's attempts.

"And then there was Vesta and Ganymede. That *girl* has seen more action than the rest of the Space Force officer corps put together." Tisha looked around the table, daring anyone to debate her facts.

"Peace, Tish," Mike said. "No one's arguing the facts. Only you've got to admit it was hard to believe they weren't exaggerated. And even if they weren't, hard to believe anybody could do anything with the mess we've got here."

A few warning grunts from their audience greeted that. There were things it was safer not to talk about too explicitly with too many people around.

"Well, yeah, but I'm damned proud somebody had the guts to show those Martian crooks nobody can push the Space Force around. Not without getting pushback," Tisha answered.

"Gives a body hope," Mike conceded. "Makes our rather prolonged stay, shall we say, out here like maybe it was worth something."

"Get to it, Mike," Tisha snapped. "What's your 'but'?"

"But, so far, besides showing fight, all she's done is get herself shot at."

"A couple of times. And, almost blown up, almost electrocuted, and, almost poisoned too. Pretty sure almost killed by a freak accident in the Boat Bay to boot," Tom Vanderhoop supplied. "Really popular, our XO."

"Well, here's to the XO's good health," Mike said, raising his beer container high. "Long may she live, God help her."

"Because God knows she's going to need the help," Tom said.

And wasn't that the truth, Rob had to think. It was great that the crew was warming to him and Kincaid.

Mightn't keep them alive, though.

11: Katie Does E-mail

Working through her e-mail backlog wasn't cheering Katie up.

It needed to be done. Only as far as Katie could tell, it wasn't doing anything to advance her cause. All it was doing was taking up time and keeping things from getting worse.

It seemed like the story of her life right now.

Her altogether too short life if her luck didn't hold, and she was beginning to wonder how it could.

She'd started the day early, fighting for her life and Tammy's too, in the wee hours. At least they'd left the flight engineer, PO Kroftchek, behind. That was one life that hadn't been endangered.

It'd been the last in a sequence of near-death experiences. And what did she have to show for it?

Not much, really.

It could be that the next attempt on her life would succeed and what would she have to show for her time on the *Humber*?

A slightly less congested in-box for the next poor soul condemned to be her XO, that's what.

Not that Katie was bitter about her predicament. Well, she was trying not to be.

Katie pushed her chair back and, leaning forward, rested her head on the edge of her desk. She closed her eyes. She tried to clear her head. She attempted to settle her heart.

She devoted many long heartbeats to the effort.

Let's be calm. Let's be rational. Let's take inventory.

The *Humber* was a cleaner ship for her presence. If nothing else, the whole crew had been reminded that the Space Force had standards, and they had to meet them. Not the sort of thing you wanted on your gravestone or which you dreamed of future historians writing about once you passed on. Still, it was an important part of an XO's job. Part of keeping ships capable of deploying for long periods in space was proper housekeeping. Otherwise, life support started to go wonky in funky ways. The scientists that studied it had fancier words with a mixture of Greek and Latin roots for it, but that's what it was. Life support going funky and a hell's brew developing that was the devil to fix once it'd got established.

"*Life finds a way,*" they liked to say. True that, but not always a good thing.

So she'd done part of her job and that was a good thing. Something she could take a solid, if limited, pride in.

Probably not why someone, likely multiple someones, was trying to kill her.

The world no longer made complete sense to Katie, but she was pretty sure that was the case.

Also, she was pretty sure SFHQ had stuck her out here around Mars as bait for the bad guys.

If she managed to survive the attention, she was going to have to make a point of learning just who at SFHQ had been responsible for that. Didn't seem friendly. Seemed to Katie someone supposedly on the same side as she was didn't really wish her well. You might not be interested in politics, but politics is interested in you. True of war too. True of too many things Katie would rather ignore. Fine, she needed to keep that in mind, but it wasn't really pertinent to her immediate problems.

Main and most immediate issue was that people were trying to kill her. As a consolation prize, they might accept hurting her so badly that she was hospitalized. Hospitalized back in Earth space, most likely. Gee, at least that'd be less final if likely more painful.

In any case, it'd interfere with her getting her job done, and with her career progress generally. Didn't want that.

Katie needed to figure out who was targeting her. She needed to identify them all. She had to seek them out, and she needed to take care of them before they took care of her.

The best defense is a good offense.

Besides, Katie was ever so tired of playing sitting duck.

So, yes, the ship needed to be kept clean and shipshape. And, yes, the boat patrols had to be kept up. They had to continue to show the flag. But Katie's main goal had to be finding her enemies and taking the fight to them.

Great. She had a clear top-priority goal.

Katie had to think making staying alive her top priority shouldn't have involved so much intellectual effort. Still, better late than never. So, where to go from here?

She had no idea.

Katie sat and stared at her terminal's screen with its derisive messages regarding her overflowing e-mail in-box and all she got was a big whopping blank.

At first, she hadn't even been sure all the near escapes from death and injury had really involved deliberate attacks on her specifically.

Someone else could have been the target of the explosion at the passenger terminal. The boobytrapped gear could have been intended for another target or no specific target at all, just the ship and its mission in general. Even the gunfight on-station could have been aimed primarily at "Saul". She had to admit the poisoning of her supper was kind of personal, but she still had no idea who'd done it.

In fact, she only had, at best, circumstantial evidence for who was behind any of the attacks.

Nothing solid, but worse, the thin evidence she had all suggested multiple different enemies were behind the attacks.

If there was nothing else Katie had learned from her stint playing engineer, it was that it was sometimes hard to track down the cause of a single problem, but that when you had multiple intertwined problems, it was almost impossible.

The first step in solving multiple problems was somehow separating them out. Isolating your separate faults from each other and solving them one by one.

Yet another fine prescription that Katie had absolutely no idea how to execute on.

Katie resisted the urge to start banging her head on her desk. Was it possible to commit suicide that way? She almost hoped so.

She was tired and getting nowhere.

There was work that needed doing, but right now, she wasn't up to it.

Katie didn't think she'd be able to get to sleep, but she needed to try.

Maybe it'd all look better in the morning if she managed to get some rest.

She doubted it.

But she was tired.

Katie dragged herself to her rack.

Fell asleep.

Had anything but restful dreams.

***

"Somebody, somewhere was complicit."

Katie had started off tiredly, going through the motions of informing the local marine commandant about the recent action she'd fought against a smuggler. She found she was becoming increasingly emotional about what she was telling von Luck.

It hadn't occurred to her before, but at least someone in each of Martian space's overall traffic control and control for the specific region that ship had lifted from must have known what was going on.

Katie had sent every traffic control center, police and important administrative office on Mars and Mars Station full records of the action and of everything she knew about the smuggler ship. She'd requested help in identifying the ship and who might own it. And it was only then that the fact that some of the authorities she was asking for help must have been on it had occurred to her. Ouch. How to be naïve and clueless, Katie.

Captain Heinrich von Luck was bearing the brunt of her

growing frustration. Katie had decided she needed to brief him and Brigit Kharkov in person. Brigit hadn't arrived yet, so Katie was venting in the meantime.

They were meeting in a nice "outdoor" patio of an upscale cafe on Mars Station. It was Friday afternoon and normally they'd have all gone off for a session of sparring in an hour or two. Katie wasn't sure that would happen today.

Katie had actually managed to get some good sleep this morning after a late night. It'd made some difference. Katie was still tired, but not the stumbling about in a fog tired she'd been before.

Katie was thinking she'd messed up getting into such bad shape. She needed to be more careful about getting enough rest to remain alert in the future. Katie was still young, but not getting younger and managing her time and health was only going to become more important as she became older.

Be that as it may, she wasn't as tired as before. She was thinking better now.

Most of the first part of the day had been getting the report on the action done and distributed. There'd been unavoidable administrative duties, too. It was only now, talking to von Luck, that some of the context for Katie's space battle was becoming clear to her.

It wasn't making her happy.

Katie continued her tirade at the calmly listening marine. "Only reason we caught them at all was they were fat, happy, and dumb and not expecting any trouble."

Von Luck nodded solemnly. "Yes, not a good sign."

"Worse, once we'd tagged them, they didn't think; 'The gig's up, we need to surrender'. No, they thought; 'Oh, here's a chance to teach the pesky Space Force to mind its own business.' Absolutely outrageous!" Katie wound down and glared at von Luck like it was his fault. It wasn't, but he was here, and she didn't know where the damned smugglers were.

"What's outrageous?" a voice came. Brigit had arrived.

Katie composed herself and tried to answer in level, rational tones. "The nerve of that smuggler ship. The fact that it shows they're used to getting away with their illegal activities. It shows there's people in authority around here who haven't been doing their jobs."

Brigit sighed as she sat down. "Most of us try, I think."

"You and Heinrich, maybe, but it's pretty damned obvious there are people in traffic control, and likely elsewhere, who're in bed with the crooks."

Brigit shrugged as she waved a waiter over. She made Katie wait while she ordered coffee before answering. "Well, that's good news, isn't it?"

"I don't know. It makes me mad. How?"

"You're mad, outraged, and you mean to do something about it. Only, you're not sure what. Right?"

"I'll figure something out if it kills me."

Von Luck frowned at that and Katie remembered that it just might. At this very moment in time, she couldn't give a damn. Katie meant what she'd said literally.

Brigit smiled. "Hopefully not, but at least now you have some leads. We probably can't get at the people on the surface. However, traffic control up here, with my help and Heinrich's, them you can give a thorough shaking down. I'll be surprised if something doesn't fall out."

"You'll get pushback though," von Luck said. "You'll go from being a problem to being an existential threat. Stir this pot and you'd better start keeping a marine bodyguard with you twenty-four seven."

"These people need to be taught a lesson. All of them," Katie answered.

Brigit nodded.

Von Luck did so too. Slowly and without enthusiasm. "Enemy gets a vote too," he said. "Just be ready for it. This may need to be done, but it's not a safe thing and not a sure one either. You've already put them on notice. With their attacks on you and what you've revealed, there's no way SFHQ is going to continue to ignore the situation. I think they were going to turn their attention this way anyhow. You've sped the process up. You could just tough out the rest of your tour here and you'll have done your job. You don't need to push the bad guys into a corner and make them desperate. Desperate men used to violence. They're going to strike back. Are you sure you want to do this?"

"Yes," Katie answered. "I'm going to nail these bastards if

it's the last thing I do."

***

If Pat hadn't already planned to start his retirement shortly, he might have been worried.

Kincaid was certainly making a big splash in the local pond and the ripples were spreading out widely.

"Bunch of holes stuck through a Space Force vessel," the Medic was saying. "Can't see even those lard butts back in SFHQ ignoring that."

They were enjoying "Happy Hour", the traditional late Friday afternoon boozefest. The hour tended to last into the evening and sometimes the next morning. It was also not so much "*happy*" as a chance to dump a week's resentments and frustration on one's mates and anyone else willing to listen. And if nobody wanted to listen, which was entirely possible, at least there was socially approved anesthetic available to dull the pain.

Pat also found it a useful time to gauge the mood of the ship's company. He always attended and always listened more than he talked. "True that," he replied to the medic's observations. True, but not entirely the full picture.

Pat had never believed that SFHQ was going to ignore Mars forever.

When you're a species with two and a half planets and a few space stations, you can't afford to ignore your second planet. The deliberately stupefied masses on Earth mightn't be aware of the fact, but Pat figured even her politicians knew better. He had no doubt the people at SFHQ whose job it was did. Only they had limited resources. Limited attention too. Both had been focused on Vesta and Callisto for the last few years. Before that, the smuggling trade to the Star Rats operating through Ceres had needed addressing.

Pat was kicking himself that he hadn't thought to take Kincaid's involvement there as an omen. He had, without really thinking about it, dismissed her as just a young girl at the time and her involvement as purely incidental.

A big mistake. He should have known better than to judge a package by its wrapping. No, as unlikely as it might seem, Kincaid was someone who made things happen.

That she, of all people, had been sent here was sure confirmation SFHQ had been paying attention. They were trying to smoke people out before turning up in full force. When they did, Kincaid, and the people who'd been holding the line these last few years, would get blamed for all the problems, and SFHQ and its favorites would take all the credit for fixing them.

"So Bosun, what're you thinking?" Sally, SPO Forsyth, his lead weapons tech, asked. Sally was someone Pat could count on to support him out of more than fear. He'd been careful to leave no traces that would implicate her in any of his shady schemes. She should be able to weather the coming storm fine. In any case, he'd hinted that when she left the Space Force, he'd likely be able to find her work. It was an implicit promise he had every intention of keeping. Here and now, the main thing was that if Sally thought maybe he should explain himself, he probably should.

"Thinking SFHQ might be full of butt covering political weasels, but it's not like they're all stupid either." Some hastily suppressed snickering greeted this judgment on their lords and masters. Quickly followed by a quiet anticipation of the next shoe about to drop.

"I figure they were always going to get around to taking care of these fine independent people here on Mars, but had other fish to fry for a bit. Figure they're about to act and sent Kincaid out to prepare the way and take the blame for everything that goes wrong."

"Ouch," Sally said. "Figure Kincaid's being set up as a scapegoat?"

"Yep, ugly, isn't it?" Pat meant that. He was also impressed. Load Kincaid up with all the blame for everything wrong and kick her out the airlock. All tidy and you get to start with a clean slate. It was brilliant, if evilly cynical.

"She can't be as smart as they say if she's falling for that," the medic said.

"She's smart," Pat said. "She's just young and idealistic. She's always lucked out before, too. She doesn't really believe the revolver she's playing Russian Roulette with has bullets in it because she's never got hurt pulling the trigger before."

"That's not stupid?" someone muttered.

"That's being young, invincible, and thinking you'll live forever, winning every battle you fight," Pat said. "People don't start out as cynical old rats scurrying around avoiding trouble like us old geezers."

"Speak for yourself," Sally joked.

"Anyhow, you ought to be glad Kincaid's here," Pat said.

"You think?" the medic asked. Man was getting a bit bold, but it wasn't like Pat needed to put up with it much longer.

"Yep, if she's the scapegoat, SFHQ is free to bury the rest of our dirty laundry out here. Nobody's going to feel a need to audit our books for the last few years too carefully."

"Here's to Lieutenant Kincaid, our XO," Sally said, raising a beer container.

"Here!" Pat declaimed with the others. He raised his beer, too.

Considering he might have to be the one to end her and her career, it was the least he could do. Being young and naïve might be understandable.

Didn't change the fact it could be fatal, too.

**

Life abounds in irony.

Rob wasn't a connoisseur of the fact. He preferred to have things straightforward and honest. Ironically, for a spy, Rob didn't like murky little mirror house games. He preferred to be straightforward and constructive in his dealings with people. He made it a primary value in his electrical business.

So, he wasn't amused that a general improvement in his circumstances was making it harder to do his job. His peers were beginning to warm to him. Even Chief Caligari was beginning to cut him more slack. And that meant he had less undisturbed time to sneak off. Less time unobserved to snoop around and write reports to his bosses back on Earth. It was ironic, and Rob wasn't amused by it.

It was late Saturday night. The *Humber*'s crew, having spent Friday night blowing off steam on board ship, were now ashore on the station, doing the same there.

Rob had wandered off from the crowd that was drinking itself silly in one of the establishments that catered to people like the *Humber*'s crew. Unattached young or early middle-aged sorts without immediate family around. Spacers, dock workers, miners, minor tradespeople still working for other people, and even the odd security type. At one point, Rob had found himself buying a round for some marines. They knew him from escorting him back to the ship from his various encounters with bad guys and their knifes and bombs. The marines didn't seem to hold it against Rob, and Rob certainly wanted to keep it that way.

Anyhow, Rob had wandered off from one of those establishments. From one with durable furniture and cheap booze to a twenty-four-hour noodle shop that wasn't significantly more upscale.

But where he could have a degree of privacy in the sense of being ignored by the people around him.

He'd quickly make his report, scoff his noodles, and leave the chip at a dead drop on his way back to join his shipmates.

Just another day in the life of a modern-day James Bond. Rob wondered where the glamour and girls were. World had gone downhill since the good old days. Could be that, despite his efforts to fake drinking more than he really was, that Rob had had too much. For better or worse, he didn't have much to report.

Yes, there were problems here in Mars space and on the *Humber*. Rob believed he had positively identified at least three different groups of bad guys. He thought it was more likely there were four. He wouldn't be surprised if there were more. Somebody needed to come in with a big broom.

That somebody couldn't be Rob. In fact, it didn't even look like there was much more in the way of useful intelligence he could hope to gather.

At this point, if this had been a normal mission, Rob would have asked for permission to bail. He'd never done that before, but he'd never been in such deadly danger with his cover essentially blown with regard to multiple sets of hostiles.

Only this wasn't a normal mission. In addition to gathering intelligence and keeping himself alive, Rob was supposed to be guarding Kincaid's back.

Ironically — Rob really didn't like irony — Kincaid was probably the one person in the entire Solar System that more people were out to get than Rob.

Rob had reached the conclusion that he had only two primary sets of enemies. One, a ring of crooks within the *Humber*'s crew appeared to be mostly concerned about protecting their own backsides. The second, a local criminal element, he figured, had tried to have him killed several times. As Kincaid had shown, there was a group in local space that had invested very heavily in smuggling. Supposedly, everyone had to pay tariffs on all goods transported on spacecraft. It was how the Space Force was funded.

Quite evidently someone with at least one armed spaceship, and almost certainly more, hadn't been paying tariffs and didn't intend to start. Apparently they didn't think the Space Force was up to reasserting its nominal control of Martian space. Or any space beyond near Earth space, in fact.

Very short sighted of them. The local crooks had got used to the Space Force being missing in action. Only the people in charge on Earth were painfully aware that contact with the galactic community was coming. Also that, said community wasn't on current evidence a group of committed altruists. Humanity, and to Rob's bosses, that meant them, had to appear to control its own home system at a minimum, or the sharks would appear. Appear and tear a divided humanity apart.

So Rob had two main groups determined to thwart his mission, only one of which was outright determined to kill him.

Kincaid had at least three groups determined to kill her. The local Martian smugglers and the "Star Rat" ones she'd already annoyed on Ceres and at Vesta and Callisto to start with. And of course, the ship's own criminal ring, whom she was a much more immediate threat to than Rob. Rob might rat them out to SFHQ backaround Earth, but Kincaid was right here with the authority to, in theory, spoil a crook's whole day.

Rob quickly outlined all that in formal, if unusually succinct, bureaucratese in his report.

As for what actions he planned to take, he didn't have much.

The crew was softening on Kincaid, and hostile exceptions should stand out more. Rob would keep an eye out for them.

The "Star Rats" smugglers Rob didn't know much about, but it was apparent they were system-wide. Which meant a presence in Earth space. Rob knew SFHQ was already working on that case. He suggested they redouble their efforts.

Finally, the local crooks who were smuggling. Who even had their own armed ships. They were a bigger deal than Rob had expected. A surprise to SFHQ itself, he suspected. He could put out feelers in the local community about them.

Rob could also try to anticipate any further attempts they tried to make on Kincaid. As small and discreet attacks on her had already failed, some escalation, harder to stop, but also easier to detect, seemed likely.

He informed SFHQ that in the absence of contrary orders, he'd drop cover and take on the job of organizing Kincaid's personal security properly. He gave them a couple of weeks. Longer than he'd really have liked to, but Earth was a long way off when one was passing messages via secure couriers. There was no fast way of communicating without blowing his cover. Electronic channels not being safe.

Rob also gave his opinion that SFHQ should prepare to extract both him and Kincaid early. It might be that they faced a soft mission failure in that the *Humber* might be too compromised to be able to do its primary job of patrolling local space.

That would be bad.

In the meantime, Rob would do what he could.

Right now, that meant dropping off his report and getting back to some serious drinking.

A hard life, but someone had to do it.

12: Katie Never Quits

"It never rains, but it pours," Katie told the assembled officers of the *Humber*. They were all present except for the captain. The captain had already given his marching orders first thing that morning. The *Humber* was due to start a month-long patrol to the nearer Belt in a week. Exactly. If there were any problems, he wanted to hear about them pronto and he wanted a plan for solving them.

Everything else was secondary. The boat patrols, the investigations the planetary and station authorities were making into the smugglers, how clean the ship was, all secondary to the goal of the *Humber* departing on its patrol as scheduled.

Which, in Katie's mind, was unfortunate because immediately after getting out of her meeting with the captain, she had received a message from Brigit Kharkov that she'd like a meeting with Katie. One that would include von Luck and Police Chief Kabukicho, as well as Katie and Brigit. In a high security on-station Police conference room, this Monday afternoon. Just hours from now. Katie wasn't going to get time for a long lunch.

Katie could think of only one reason for such a meeting. They had a lead on who the smugglers were and they wanted to work on plans to move on their on-station accomplices. Likely they wanted both a boat standing by to prevent escapes and the *Humber*'s marines to help in any raid. The smugglers had already shown they were heavily armed and willing to use those arms. Brigit and von Luck would want all the force they could muster available.

For once, Katie was glad they were so shorthanded. There were only five of them around the wardroom table. Lieutenant Rous, the engineer, for one was obviously impatient to get the meeting over and back to his engines.

"Sorry to take you away from making sure we're ready, Kevin," Katie apologized to him. "But it's critical we're all on the same page for the next week. We've been so heads down with so many balls in the air that I'm afraid co-ordination has suffered."

"That's fine, XO," the engineer answered. "We all work for you and the captain in the end. This isn't going to take long anyhow, is it?"

"No, it won't," Katie said. "And you've got the most important task. The engines have to be ready. If I understand right, they're ready right now and we could sail this morning. That there's only some tuning and checking to do. Is that right?"

"They're working," the engineer said, "but it's been five years since their last visit to a dockyard and they need a lot of TLC. We'll launch, I'm sure. We want to finish our patrol without problems, then I think we need to do all the checking and fine tuning we can. At least with just a ship's crew. We don't have the equipment a dockyard has. It makes it all harder, longer, and trickier."

"Understood, Engineer. Just a few more minutes, so you know what the rest of us are up to and I'll let you get back to that."

The engineer nodded. "Yes, ma'am."

"So, the captain was clear sailing on time was his top priority. First thing next Monday morning, a week from now, and he wants the *Humber* on its way. Sounds like the engineer has that in hand, but all the rest of you have to make sure your people and departments are ready, too."

Katie's fellow officers just nodded at this.

"Tammy, I'm afraid you're temporarily our supply officer. Food, bum wipe, candy, beer, spare parts, air and water, whatever we need for a month, make sure we have more than enough. Brian's Ops plan for the deployment was pretty detailed, so you can use that as a checklist. By the way, great plan, Brian."

"Thank you, ma'am," Lieutenant Brian Broomfield said. He couldn't help smiling at this praise for his baby. He'd worked on little else the entire few weeks Katie had been on board.

"It's been a long time since the *Humber* has undocked, so we've got to make sure the ship's gear, especially the sensors and comms, and the personnel who'll be operating it are all up to it. That's your main job now, Brian. I want you to spend the next week running drills. We need to test both our gear and our people. Keep them busy, but don't run them ragged. You can offer them Friday off and a long weekend before sailing if they perform well."

"Yes, ma'am. They'll like that," the operations officer responded.

"Finally, Tom much the same for you as Brian. Not as much you can do alongside and we don't have the time to do any exercises on the firing range, even if we had a proper firing range."

"Yes, ma'am," Lieutenant Tom Rompkey the weapons officer replied. "Weapons might work, but like with the engineer's machinery, it's been years since they've been properly checked out and zeroed in. Through no fault of their own, all my people are rusty, too. Normally, I wouldn't worry too much. We take pride in doing well in competitions, but we almost never fire anything in real anger. Only after your run-in with that smuggler I'm concerned."

Katie was trying to keep this low key and friendly. She puffed out her cheeks and blew out a breath. "Do your best. That's all anyone can ask," she said. "I'm afraid there's more for you and Tammy, though."

"You want to keep up the boat patrols?" Tom asked.

"More than that," Katie answered. "Horrible timing, but I think the Station Police have some leads on the smugglers here on Mars Station."

"Captain told me directly he wanted a marine guard on you full time," Brian, the operations officer, said. He smiled. "Apparently he doesn't have complete trust in your sense of self preservation."

"I don't know for sure what's up," Katie said. "I don't know what the Station Police have, let alone what they plan, yet. We've got a meeting scheduled first thing this afternoon. I'm guessing, though, that they'll want to raid the premises of some suspects. Also, that they won't want me along because my leaving the ship might tip off the bad guys. Given the levels of violence those bad guys have been willing to resort to, I do think they'll want all our marines."

"Have to juggle some schedules to allow that, ma'am," Brian answered. "And there's the matter of your safety."

"Quietly stand the marines down pending further orders, with the exception of a guard for me," Katie said. "Come the time, I'll stay safe on the ship for the few hours the raid takes. I can do without the guard for however long it takes. There's been some sabotage on board and that's worrisome, but I don't think any of the crew is going to make an armed attack on me, do you?"

"No, ma'am. We might have a bad apple or two, but I'm sure most of the crew is good and can be trusted. I'm sure you're safe on the *Humber*."

"So, no problem, right, Brian?"

"No problem, ma'am," the ops officer answered, not seeming entirely happy

"You've got a point about the few bad apples," Katie said. A point she should have addressed right at the meeting's start and had forgotten. Better late than never. "We need to be concerned about OpSec. A few careless words in the hearing of the wrong person and we could tip off the bad guys as to what's happening. So, no discussing any of this anywhere else, not even between yourselves if you can help it. Clear?"

A series of nods. A few quiet "Clear, ma'ams."

"It's worse for you, Tom and Tammy, than it is for Brian,"

Katie said. "You're right. I'd like you to keep on doing boat patrols. Not only are they important themselves, but whenever that raid that's likely coming happens, I want you two out on patrol somewhere near Mars Station. I want it to look like a coincidence. We don't want any of the smugglers getting away, but we don't want to tip them off either."

Tom and Tammy both nodded. They tried to look professional, but Katie could tell they were feeling stressed. Not only was Katie asking them to pursue two different sets of priorities, she wasn't giving them much solid detail about what was required, either.

"I know it's vague so far," Katie said to address the unspoken concerns, "but I wanted to give everyone as much warning as possible. And to let everyone know what everyone else was up to. I'll pass on further detail to each of you as soon as I get the info myself."

The weapons officer and co-pilot both nodded again. "Yes, ma'am," they answered in a ragged chorus. They seemed a little placated.

"Okay, well, I promised the engineer this wouldn't go on too long," Katie said. "You all have plenty to do. Good luck, but I'm sure you don't need it. We're going to do this."

"Yes, ma'am," her officers each said as they rose to go start their week's work. They all looked pensive. They all had a lot to juggle.

Shouldn't be more than they could handle, though, Katie thought.

Shouldn't be too much.

Not if everything went as it should.

**

Monday night, and it was proving at least as exciting as Saturday night had been. The joys of being an SIS agent.

Rob was tasked with keeping Kincaid safe. He was pretty sure she wouldn't be very happy with how he was going about doing that.

She would doubtless be incensed to discover he had a backdoor into the *Humber*'s internal net and therefore to all her communications via that net.

This little on-station recce he was doing because of what

he'd learned by monitoring those communications wouldn't make her any happier.

Too damn bad. The young woman had too little in the way of a sense of self preservation and it was Rob's job to make up the difference. Rob had no doubt that her marine guard wouldn't be enough when push came to shove.

Neither Kincaid nor her on-station contacts were complete idiots or totally naïve. They hadn't been totally oblivious to questions of OpSec, Operational Security. They were keeping most of their communications face to face in locations they could be sure weren't bugged.

Only they were in a hurry and getting sloppy.

Their unusual meeting this afternoon had been a big hint to anyone paying attention that something was afoot. Rob figured it was pretty obvious that it had to do with information gained as a result of Kincaid's run in with that smuggler ship. And given the haste with which the meeting had been called pretty obvious too that they planned to act on that information.

A raid on suspect premises being by far the top candidate for such action.

All very obvious not just to Rob, but he figured the targets, the local smugglers, themselves.

He figured the station manager, impatient and militarily Inexperienced, was insisting on action.

And that was an issue.

Any raid on the local smugglers was like as not walking into an ambush.

In a sane world, Kincaid wouldn't be anywhere near that raid, but she had a talent for being near the action, and Rob wasn't willing to bet on it.

So here he was, late Monday night, sneaking around Mars Station once more. The rather disreputable part that Kharkov's communication had accidentally revealed as being the likely smuggler's HQ.

Ideally, he'd detect any trap without tripping it. If he did trip it or alert the smugglers inadvertently, at least Kincaid wouldn't be in the line of fire.

In any case, there'd be more information for his bosses back at SFHQ to chew on.

The guards were good. He didn't notice them until far too late.

It was good training that permitted that much. He'd stopped and waited, watching the wide corridor behind him, because it was what his trainers had taught him. It slowed everything down to a crawl and cut into what was already going to be inadequate sleep, but those trainers had been emphatic. The key to stealth was patience. You wanted to get in undetected and out alive, then you took your time.

Hugging a wall behind a piece of moving equipment, Rob watched the shadows behind him and saw one move. Move where no one ought to be. No one had legitimate business down here this time of night.

So, at some point, he'd acquired tails. Guards he'd missed and were now following him. No doubt there were others ahead of him. He was in a trap even if it'd yet to snap shut.

Rob was going to have to fight his way out.

He let his followers get closer. Only two of them. That was good. One moved. Rob fired at them. At the center of mass like he was trained. He moved quickly; ducking and rolling. So the flurry of fire from the second follower missed him.

Rob paused to fire back briefly, full auto in the direction that fire had come from.

Re-loading a magazine as he ran, he fled the shouts and gunfire from behind him.

It was a hard run, but he'd planned out an escape route beforehand.

He gave his pursuers, the smugglers presumably, the slip.

Even better, he got back to his berth without any questions being asked.

The guard on the ship's access seemed to accept his story about having a girl ashore.

For once, Rob appreciated the lax discipline and corruption that had taken hold on the *Humber*.

The guard should stay bribed.

No one, the smugglers, the police, or Kincaid, would know it'd been him.

In an ideal world, Kincaid and the police would cancel their raid on the alerted smugglers.

In an ideal world.

***

Pat wondered what it was about life that events could never manage to happen in nicely ordered, easy to handle ways. No, for some reason whatever Deity had created the universe had felt it necessary to build in long stretches of nothing happening interspersed with multiple things all blowing up at once. Why? For the pure amusement of it, as far as Pat could tell. Pat, for one, refused to acknowledge the existence of, let alone worship, such a Being.

Which would disappoint his poor old, sainted mother who'd become steadfastly religious at the end. Only his mother, God bless her soul, had been a sentimental drunk. She'd fallen almost completely apart after his Dad's death.

She managed to make sure he was clean and properly dressed and to send him off to school every day. Managed to hold down cleaning jobs somehow, and managed to go to mass regularly. Which was something he guessed, but it'd all been on auto-pilot. She'd hardly been conscious most of the time. For the remainder, she'd just lain about blubbering.

His mom had been, like his Dad, an example of what not to be to Pat.

So, Pat didn't lie about, and he didn't blubber on because life was hard and unfair.

Not like his pet communicator, Petty Officer Adnan Awad, who he had currently cornered in the Comms Shack and was laying the law down to.

"Adnan, buds," Pat was saying. "We're sitting pretty. Take this old bucket on a lazy tour of local space and then cash in. We're all done and living the life of Reilly for the rest of our days." Pat punctuated this assertion with a big goofy grin he knew most people found reassuring.

"New XO is stirring things up, Bosun," Awad said.

"Sound and fury signifying nothing, Adnan. She's got nothing. She's running about trying things, so she looks busy. Also makes her a moving target."

Awad frowned. "Somebody really doesn't like her, do they? Look, Bosun, I know we've had to look out for ourselves, but I'm not on board with offing officers." The man made an effort to sit up straighter, like he'd suddenly developed a backbone.

Pat decided not to look amused at this. Instead, he mustered the blandly baffled but basically unconcerned expression he'd mastered at the ripe old age of eight. He'd have thought that as he grew out of childhood and presumed innocence that it would have become less useful. Not so, though. "No, of course not, Adnan. Only the XO, she's been on the shit list of some seriously bad people since before she left Ceres. Ratting out a criminal conspiracy will do that, you know?"

Awad's eyes widened as he digested the sting in the tail of what the bosun had said. Sadly, he likely thought Pat had put it there accidentally. There were days Pat felt underappreciated. "Yeah, and I guess her record makes all the other crooks nervous, too."

"No doubt of it," Pat agreed. "Anyhow, the point is the XO has got a lot on her plate. A lot is happening in the next week. Doing a deep audit of the ship's books to make sure all her NCOs were always following the regs to the letter is not high on her list of things to do. I repeat, not high on her list of things to do. Kapeech?"

"Sure, Bosun, sure, but I don't understand why I have to go out on a limb to keep monitoring the station authority and marine channels then?"

"No extra risk to it, Adnan," Pat answered. "And it never hurts to keep an eye on things." No need to remind the communicator that they had friends who'd misappropriated supplies as well as funds and that supplies needed to be fenced to be turned into funds. Fenced by individuals who might be swept up in a general round up of crooks and rat on everyone.

"Guess not," Awad said skeptically.

"For sure not," Pat asserted with a broad grin. "Just another couple of days and we're in the clear. Sure, they're up to something, but the XO isn't going to spring it just before the ship has to leave. Captain would have a fit. And there goes a promising career, right? Nope, Kincaid's not doing anything over the next weekend and she's not going to let her friends on-station do anything either."

"So, anything going to happen it's in the next three days?"

"Yep, they do have something planned, but given the reports of fights down in the warehouse district, and how worried they have to be about leaks, I'm guessing they're pulling the trigger as soon as possible. Tomorrow, or the day after, Wednesday at the latest I'd guess."

"And then my poor sore stomach gets a rest?" Awad asked hopefully.

"Yep, your digestion will improve and you'll sleep like a babe!" Pat said with a toothy, reassuring grin. Really, maybe he should have gone into selling medicine. On the other hand, retail was constant hard work. Better to be making a bit out of everybody else's hard work. Pat hoped what he was telling Awad was true, too.

He really didn't need any more fusses right now.

Only he was going to have to tip off his associates on-station. He could hope they had the sense to just use the warning to pack up and skedaddle, but there was altogether too great of a chance they'd try to protect what they had and couldn't move. That they'd try to give the authorities a bloody nose.

That could be a mess that would attract a lot of attention. It could delay the *Humber*'s patrol, bringing the ship more adverse scrutiny than it was already under. Not what Pat wanted.

The other side of the coin was that given the young woman's taste for risk, it might take care of Kincaid. Get her invalided back to Earth or killed. Girl was a wild card. Pat would feel better once she was out of the game and in the discard pile.

What he didn't want to do was take direct action himself. Needs must, though.

He'd do what he had to if it came to that.

"Don't worry, Adnan," Pat said as he turned to leave. "It'll all work out."

Pat would see to that.

***

Katie had just fallen into a solid sleep when she was woken by a piercing burble. A high priority, needs immediate attention, message. Katie half expected it to be a video call. Urgent calls usually were.

Not this time. It was from von Luck. Supposedly, her communications with the station-based marine were more secure than those with the station authorities. So instead of contacting her directly, they'd decided to use von Luck as an intermediary.

One of those precautions they'd set up earlier today during Katie's afternoon meeting with them.

They'd also agreed to keep such communications down to a minimum and to stick to face-to-face communications except in emergency.

So what was the emergency?

Katie hoped the hell he wasn't asking for yet another meeting first thing tomorrow morning. She had already scheduled a regular inspection for the morning. The last one before the ship departed on patrol. There was no way she could miss that and not alert the whole ship that something was seriously wrong.

It turned out to be worse than that.

Von Luck — between the lines, Katie read that as Brigit Kharkov — wanted an immediate meeting in person. On the station. In the Police HQ. They asked she bring all her marines along.

What the hell?

Katie knew her increasingly short temper wasn't a good thing. All the same, she was tempted to tell von Luck to take a hike. Only nothing she'd seen of the man suggested he was an alarmist, given to overreacting, or inclined to making frivolous requests. He was the stereotypical solid, dependable marine officer. If he was asking her to do this, it had to be important.

Katie frowned and tersely replied she'd be there as soon as possible. She paused to think. She'd likely need five or ten minutes to roust the marines and then another fifteen minutes to get them moving. A further fifteen to twenty minutes for the trip. Allow forty minutes to an hour, she wrote before hitting the send button. It might have been marginally quicker to have used the internal comms system, but the terse vagueness of von Luck's missive suggested it was best not to trust any comms system.

Katie would take the time to roust her marines in person.

Wasting no motion, Katie pulled on a uniform ship suit and exited her cabin.
She was on her way.

13: Katie Commits

Katie was proud of herself. It mightn't be a big accomplishment in the wider scheme of things, but on checking the time she saw it'd only taken her thirty-seven minutes to make it to Mars' Station Police HQ with all of the *Humber*'s marines in tow.

Of course, a lot of that was down to the marines themselves. Katie was proud of them, too.

What Katie found arriving at the Police HQ was less gratifying. It turned out the place was locked down.

It wasn't immediately obvious entering the main reception area out front. It was quiet, but Katie, checking her comms, found they didn't work. Also, there wasn't the heavy two-way foot traffic she'd come to expect. All the traffic was one way. The receiving sergeant was directing police officers into the back rooms, but no one was coming out. Katie didn't think it was just the late hour.

Once Katie and her accompanying marines entered those back rooms themselves, they found a scene of controlled chaos.

Knots of constables were spilling out of conference and briefing rooms. Something big was afoot. You could cut the tension in the air with a knife.

It wasn't any calmer when Katie reached the conference

room that contained von Luck, Brigit Kharkov, and a very tired-looking Police Chief Kabukicho. They looked up as she arrived and seemed relieved. That was nice.

"What's up?" Katie asked. No point beating around the bush.

"Somebody gave our suspected smugglers a premature poke," the police chief replied. "Stirred them up. We're trying to do damage control."

"Too many actors in this little drama," Brigit commented bitterly. "And somebody leaked our intelligence."

Von Luck studiously inspected a far corner of the room. Katie could almost hear him thinking; "Not my circus, not my monkeys."

"I discussed it with absolutely nobody. Not even Captain Smith. Haven't had the time, but will have to bring him into the loop, eventually. You think our comms are compromised?"

Brigit sighed. "At this point, I'm almost certain. Sorry, but this was the best shot we've had for years. It may have just misfired."

"We've shut down all communications in and out of Police HQ," von Luck said. "We're letting officers in, but not out. At this point it may be too late, but I'm sure of my marines, and there won't be any more leaks from here."

"I feel confident of my people," Police Chief Kabukicho said, "but we have a lot of civilian support and traffic through the HQ so I can't be certain of our infrastructure."

"You think we have a leak on the *Humber*?" Katie asked.

"They'd have to be pretty incompetent crooks not to have at least one plant," Brigit answered. "And they've probably bugged the *Humber*'s comms. They've had years to do it."

"Okay, I'll take care of it," Katie said. "What's going on? What do you mean 'prematurely poked'? What do you plan to do? What do you need me to do?"

"Another gunfight. A little over an hour ago. Down in the warehouse district near the address of interest to us. Responding officers found two bodies of known suspects," von Luck said. "We think someone intercepted our intelligence and decided to take a look. Only they were detected and ambushed. Fought their way out, but alerted our targets in the process.

Don't know who. Like Brigit said, there are too many parties meddling in this mess."

"So, waiting on further intelligence and launching a raid later this week isn't going to work anymore?" Katie asked.

"Not likely," the police chief answered. "We're mounting one immediately as soon as we can gather the bodies. We're trying to plug any leaks that might warn the suspects of what's coming. They know we're on to them. We believe that they won't expect us to act so fast. We hope that they're going to be trying to evacuate, not waiting for us in an ambush."

"Sounds like we're going to have an exciting night," Katie said, trying to be upbeat about what was, in fact, an awful mess.

"Some of us, yes," von Luck answered, "but not you. As the head of security for the Space Force on Mars Station, I'm forbidding you from going along on this raid. Also, I'm sorry, but I need your marines."

Katie was shocked by this sudden dictate. "You can have my marines, of course, but I can be useful too."

"Sorry, Katie, but we've got a bad record of protecting XOs off of the *Humber* on Mars Station. I don't think SFHQ would forgive us if we lost or damaged another one of them," Brigit said apologetically.

Von Luck gave her a hard, if sympathetic, look. "Professionally, it's the right thing to do. You're too valuable in your primary role as the *Humber*'s XO to be risking in gunfights with on-station crooks. This raid has a lot of potential to go sideways. It's all too likely people are going to get hurt. We can't take the chance you might be one of them."

"So, I just go back to the ship and wait it out?" Katie asked. "What about putting the boat out to prevent any of the bad guys from escaping?"

Brigit and von Luck both looked uneasy about Katie's questions. Like they had something to say they'd rather not. Police Chief Kabukicho just looked very bland.

Brigit looked at von Luck and her police chief and evidently decided to bite the bullet. "Our top priority here is your safety. Even more important than the raid succeeding and capturing the suspected smugglers."

"Which means," von Luck said, "that unless we can be sure it's safe to let you return to the *Humber* we'd like you to stay here. Taking on armed smugglers in another dogfight without the advantage of surprise is completely out of the question."

"You're kidding," Katie said. "You may have jurisdiction on-station, but local space operations are up to me and the captain. Me, since the captain likes to delegate."

"And to be picky, you have no way to get back to the *Humber* without transiting a station I'm morally certain isn't safe for you," von Luck answered. "That said, we're all reasonable people here. We're all on the same side. If you can assure me, you'll be safe on the *Humber* and you won't personally pilot the boat to prevent an escape, we could use you there."

"With comms blacked out, you need me to return to the ship to get the boat launched?"

"Ideally, if you would. Only, please, don't pilot it yourself. Also, Brigit is right, your safety is our top priority and we're certain the smugglers have accomplices on board the *Humber*. We think there's a good chance they're going to be gunning for you. Since we're stripping you of your normal marine protection, you're going to be vulnerable. Only there's another problem and you're the only one that can handle it."

"And you need me back on the *Humber* to do so? You not only think there's a plant on the *Humber*, you think they have access to its comms. You want me to lock down the *Humber* for you before they can tip off their buddies on-station."

Brigit sighed. "But we also want to keep you safe."

"And it might be too late anyhow," von Luck said. "We might be risking you for nothing."

Katie wondered what it meant that Brigit and von Luck seemed more concerned for her safety than she was. "Okay," she said, "here's a plan. You spare some of your less combat-ready officers to escort me straight back to the *Humber*. I order a lockdown immediately. Hope the captain doesn't mind too much. Roust Lieutenants Rompkey and Wentzell and order them out on patrol around the station in person. No comms. All face to face. Then I go down to the combat bridge, lock myself safely in, and cut all comms on and off the ship from there. Also, I do have backup I can call upon on board. Backup I can depend upon to watch my back. Will that do?"

Brigit took a deep breath and looked at von Luck. "I think it should, don't you?"

Von Luck grimaced. An unusual expression on his face. "I don't like it. It's probably the best of a bad set of options." He looked at Katie. "You're giving me your honest assurance that you'll be safe on the *Humber*. I know it's a hard thing to accept not being safe on one's own ship, but you need to be realistic. Also, I'm curious about this mysterious backup of yours. I can restrain that if I have to."

"Like Brigit said, too many actors in this drama," Katie said. "The plant has either already acted or they're still off guard, and I'm sure most of the crew is reliable. Given that and given that I'll be safe in the combat bridge, and given that there's only a very narrow window for whoever the plant is to intercept me, I think my safety is pretty well assured."

"Okay, time's wasting. We'll go with your plan, Lieutenant Kincaid," von Luck answered.

"Collins, Ishkhand," the police chief barked. "You're on escort duty. Get Lieutenant Kincaid here back to her ship."

"Yes, sir," Collins and Ishkhand, stepping forward, chorused. They were an older stout woman and a large, but very fresh faced, young man.

"Right. Let's get going," Katie said, spinning on her heel and striding off.

The police constables followed.

***

Katie wasn't in a good mood.

She had a surplus of reasons for that.

Take your pick. Being told her own crew couldn't be trusted was pretty high on the list. That she should go hide in the corner and stay safe was way up there, too. Having a marine captain feel it was necessary to dictate that to her and not trust her to act like a reasonable adult was not good. It hurt, too, to have to send Tom and Tammy out to face a danger she wasn't allowed to share. She knew her marines less well and so their going in harm's way without her was fractionally less galling. Fractionally.

And personal peeves aside, there was the general overall stinking situation.

They'd had precious few leads on who the local smugglers were. People who thought it was fine not just to smuggle the odd thing but to do so by the armed shipload. And willing to engage the Space Force in a fight in order to keep doing so. That wasn't just galling, it was alarming. She'd never have dreamed it'd gotten so bad.

And now their only good lead on the bastards had been compromised. Von Luck might have been sincere about not knowing who could have done so, but Katie had a sneaking suspicion Hood the SIS agent might have been involved. The crap hadn't even hit the fan and SFHQ was already involved and messing the thing up even more. Katie felt guilty she'd sat there and kept that information from von Luck, who'd never been anything but honest and helpful to her. It was by the book, but Katie wasn't happy about it.

She was also feeling guilty about how her anger was quite obviously intimidating her police escorts. Collins, the older woman, Ishkhand the young guy, if she remembered correctly.

"Sorry, Constables, none of this is your fault," she said as they came in sight of the *Humber*'s docking port. "I assure you, none of my unhappiness is with you two. I'm afraid that I do have more for you to do. I need you to stand guard here at the docking port to the *Humber*. Don't let anyone on or off, and log everyone that shows up. Wish we had the resources to detain them, too. Handcuff and secure anyone that gives you a hard time and assume they're dangerous. Otherwise just let them go."

"Yes, ma'am," Collins, the senior of the two, answered.

Katie repeated the orders to the guard the *Humber* had posted on the inside of its docking port. Made it clear to him by using his name, Able Spacer Johnson, that she knew who she was talking to. She also told him to confiscate all personal comms devices. Every member of the crew had a "phone box" to keep personal comms devices in when the ship was under a communications blackout, so there was no problem of logistics there, at least.

She also made it clear to the Able Spacer that it was his career, and a probable stay in the crowbar hotel, if he passed on the news of her arrival back on board to anyone other than the captain.

With that done, she went off to spoil Tom and Tammy's morning, too.

At least they were going to get to swan about in the boat.

***

Katie didn't bother going back to her own cabin. If von Luck's fears had anything to them, it was counter indicated and there was no reason to take the extra time in any case. What Katie needed to do was get Tom, LTSG Rompkey the Weapons Officer, and Tammy, LTJG Wentzell holding the Co-pilot slot, up and out on near station space patrol pronto.

Then, as quickly as possible, get down to the combat bridge and lock down the ship's communications. Also, in deference to von Luck's and Brigit's concerns, she'd be safe there. The place was designed to be defensible. Theoretically, terrorist or pirate attackers might board the ship and try to take control. It'd never happened in the hundreds of years of Space Force history, but it was a theoretical possibility that the *Humber*'s designers had allowed for.

Convenient right now.

Katie figured now might be the time to call on Hood's help, supposedly available in an emergency. Well, this was an emergency, wasn't it? And Katie also had some questions she'd like to get him alone to ask. She didn't like the game SFHQ and SIS, in particular, seemed to be playing here. At the very least, they didn't have to leave her completely in the dark. That was downright rude.

So, on her way up in the lift to the officer's portion of the gravity ring, Katie took out her issue phone and typed in the code she'd been given. Only a couple of weeks before, but it seemed like ages.

To the "Merry Men of Sherwood", she addressed her message. These guys weren't anywhere as amusing as they seemed to think they were. "Emergency. Personal protection required. Req @ combat bridge ASAP," she wrote.

There, that ought to do. And she was out of the lift, and on her way.

Katie wasted no time. She didn't knock, explain, or wait for questions.

She barged into the cabins of her pilots using her executive overrides, shook them awake, and barked her orders. "Emergency. Get to the boat and launch pronto. Emergency protocols. I need a near station patrol to stop possible fugitives. Possibly armed. Likely from docks 17 to 25 inclusive. Move. Move. Don't stop to piss or anything. I want that boat out there by 0320 at the latest. Got that?"

Both Tom and Tammy, in turn, gave identical bleary nods. And confused automatic "Yes, ma'am"s.

Katie would have liked to take the time to shepherd them on their ways, but she didn't have it. She had to stay inside the bad guys' reaction loop. Being a few seconds faster than the other guys could make all the difference. At the very least, she wanted comms shut down before the boat launched or anyone saw Tom and Tammy rushing down to it.

They didn't want potential fugitives knowing what was waiting for them.

So Katie left her befuddled pilots behind to cope and rushed back to the lifts.

She needed to get to the spindle and the combat bridge located there.

As fast as humanly possible.

***

Katie made it down to the combat bridge in record time.

She would have gotten out and pushed the lift down to make it go faster if that had been physically possible.

Despite the wonky gravity in the spindle because of the *Humber* being docked, she made it up and into the combat bridge in a fast scramble that closely approximated what she could have done in true full zero gee.

Even better, Katie made it to the combat bridge without any incident. Without seeing a single other human being, in fact.

Once there, she paused for breath and made her way over to the comms station. She'd been trained on it just like she'd been trained on every other bridge position, but it'd been a while. She was rusty.

Also, locking a ship's communications down, completely down, was not a normal evolution she'd practiced much. Hell, let's be honest, she'd never done it before. Katie might have watched someone else demonstrate the procedure once before some years ago. She wasn't sure. Katie couldn't remember even that much, let alone how to do it.

Fortunately, the station's software had a self-explanatory menu system for less frequent functions. She popped up the "*Administrative Communications Routines*" menu. It had an "*Emergency Measures*" option. Great, she was batting five hundred here to use the American idiom. The Americans, bless them, were a can-do sort of people and had all sorts of idioms to describe getting on with the job. She was proud to count them among her ancestors.

What she encountered next wasn't so pleasing.

A large, garish warning dialog with an excessively long message popped up. Apparently there was no just hitting an "*OK*" button without reading that message and getting on with it. The "*Continue*" button was grayed out and unresponsive. There were open edit boxes above it. Empty except for a blinking cursor in the leftmost one.

So, Katie gritted her teeth and read the damned notice. Stripped of its pompous stilted language, the message asserted that emergency measures were only to be used in the rarest of circumstances and after due consideration of the consequences by qualified and authorized officers who could provide the right identification codes. See below.

With determined patience Katie entered her rank, both her two main names, her date of birth, the date of her commission, her service number, her position on the ship, her command password, and, last but not least, she chose the nature of the emergency action from a menu of options. "*Prevent All External Communications*" rather than "*Prevent Unauthorized Communications*", that seemed too vague and subject to interpretation. She'd hoped she'd gotten it right.

An explanatory dialog popped up. How helpful. It went into excruciating detail on what blocking all external communications meant. It also outlined the dire consequences of doing so. Especially to one's career and even freedom if you were mistaken about the choice.

Katie hit the "*I Have Read the Warning And Understand It*" button. It was a very wide button, Katie observed. She guessed it needed to be. She fantasied about visiting whatever software shop had produced the program and giving them a piece of her mind.

For a split second, she didn't have the time to do more. Not right now.

A dialog, asking if she was sure, appeared. Grinning without humor, Katie assured it she was.

And, finally, what she'd wanted happened.

A message appeared. "*All external communications, both to and from the* Humber, *have been blocked*," it read. *Halle,* bloody, *lujah!*

Katie sighed in relief.

"What's up?" came a deep male voice before she even finished exhaling.

The bosun stood, filling the aft hatchway into the combat bridge.

In her haste, she'd forgotten to close and secure it.

14: Katie Fights

Katie had a bad feeling.

She punched the logout button before turning and facing the bosun, who filled the hatchway into and out of the combat bridge.

Katie still had things she wanted to do. She didn't have time to play games. She wasn't sure she had much choice.

The bosun wasn't someone she trusted. Katie wasn't sure that distrust was fair. Still, she didn't plan on being locked in the combat bridge with him.

"Bosun," Katie said in as strong a voice as she could muster. "Good to see you." A blatant lie. "I need you to gather some trustworthy crew members and lock the *Humber* down solid. Everybody to stay either in their racks or their messes. Nobody allowed on or off the ship. No communications on or off her, either. This is time critical. You need to go now. Quickly."

The bosun returned her a big shit-eating, highly amused grin. Bigger than even his usual, ever so annoying, smiling smirk.

"Think you're pushing on a string, little lady," the man said.

"It's just you and me here. You even tell the captain you were shutting his ship down?"

"Every second counts. There's no time. Go now. We've got at least one plant working for local crooks on board. We have to keep him from warning his buddies that we're moving on them."

The bosun chuckled at that. "Well, you're not totally wrong, girl."

Katie wondered at the continued emphasis on her gender and youth. A surreal thought in the circumstances, but maybe her subconscious was trying to tell her something. Then it occurred to her. It was blindingly obvious once it had. The man was trying to intimidate her. Maybe she was broken somehow, but if the bosun had known Katie better, he'd have realized she simply couldn't be intimidated the way most people could. Maybe someday Katie would meet someone who scared her so badly she felt forced to buckle under to what they wanted. That day hadn't yet arrived. "I repeat; time is short, seconds count, Bosun. Explain and make it quick. Then go follow your orders. Or I swear, bosun or not, I'll have you up in front of the captain. Not a good way to end your career. Do I make myself clear?"

"Oh, you're being clear enough," the bosun answered, his amusement manifest but now tinged with a certain impatience. "You're bluffing. You don't know what's going on for sure and you're trying to bluff your way through it." He shook his head in mock sadness. "Not very professional. Not very professional at all. I'm disappointed in you, Lieutenant."

"Not as disappointed as I'm in you, Chief. Consider yourself under arrest. You're to go to your cabin and remain there until I have time to deal with you." Now Katie really was bluffing. "Go now."

The bosun laughed. It sounded altogether too relaxed and genuine for Katie's taste. The man was obviously convinced he was in charge here and things were going his way. Katie wasn't sure what his way might be, but it certainly didn't seem to involve following Katie's orders. The bosun shook his head. "Little girl, there are so many things you don't know and you don't understand. You're right, we don't have the time. Let's start with the fact we're alone here. I'm in your only way out, and I'm twice your size and weight. Just as a starter. You logged out when I turned up, didn't you? Inconvenient that. A few things I would have liked to do using your permissions without having to beat your codes out of you. Only right now, in this very moment, it means you can't call for help. Not before I can reach you."

"You're one of the bad guys?" Katie blurted out. Ouch, dumb thing to say. She'd have been better off keeping her mouth shut, only the longer she kept the bosun talking, while trying to figure out a way out of the predicament he'd so accurately described, the better.

The bosun snorted. You could have cut his derision up into little cubes and served it for dessert. "Such a simple-minded young thing you are. Everything black and white, right and wrong, bad guys and good guys, real world's not so simple. I've served the Space Force for longer than you've been alive. Served them and myself too. Like most everyone else on this tub. We all got our little schemes and a lot of us have various friends and associates ashore we do business with. And you have to come in full of ignorance and self-righteous moral pretensions and screw it all up."

"Yep, you're one of the bad guys." It was stupid. But simple-minded defiance was all Katie had right now.

"Enough blather," the bosun answered. "Let's cut to the chase. We can do this the hard way or the easy way. Easy way, you do what I tell you to and when we're done, I tie you up and go on my way. Hard way, I have to show you who's boss, and you get banged up, hurt, and damaged, maybe permanently. Rather not be bothered."

"I won't be threatened."

That earned a short, disgusted snort from the bosun. "And no doubt you think I won't get away with this. You need to consume a better class of entertainment," the man said, stepping forward. Katie shrank back despite herself. The bosun turned around. "You should have shut this hatch and secured the space first thing. But, hey, better late than never," he said as he locked them in together. Katie could override that lock, but it'd take time she wouldn't have to enter her codes.

Also, she'd have to get through the bosun first.

Katie looked around the combat bridge frantically for something she could use as a weapon against the bosun. Anything that might offset not just his greater weight and larger size, but his greater strength and longer reach, too. Testosterone did have its uses.

All she could see that wasn't harmless and locked down was a first aid kit. There weren't even any handy fire extinguishers around. The bridge had been carefully designed to contain nothing that could burn. Katie grabbed the kit, and pulling it open, rummaged through it. Bandages and small blunt-tipped scissors weren't going to help much.

The bosun, watching her, laughed derisively. "Nothing in there to help you. Not much you can do with tiny little scissors with blunt tips. You're starting to annoy me, girl." He moved towards her.

Katie whipped out a can of instant "spray on" bandage. Good for those wounds hard to dress with regular bandages. But costly and space consuming. Also, they'd been warned to watch where they pointed the nozzle. Arm extended, she sprayed the bosun right in the face with the sticky quick-setting substance, not necessarily something you wanted to get in your eyes.

The bosun got an arm up to partly cover his face, but not quick enough. He screamed and bellowed. And charged forward blindly. Yep, seemed like instant bandage in the eyes hurt. Good.

Katie dodged his blind blundering charge and sprang past the bosun, making it to the hatch out. While he blundered about behind her trying to find out where she'd gone she had time to get her codes in. Seemed like forever, but finally the hatch lock released with a "beep" and a "thunk". Katie spun the wheel to release the mechanical dogs and pushed the hatch hard. It opened. Her way free was clear.

And a huge, hard paw wrapped itself around one of her ankles. "Gotcha, witch."

Katie twisted around and tried to kick the bosun in the face with her free foot.

He dodged. She only managed a glancing blow to one side

of his face. Still hurt, it seemed. Bellowing with rage and filled with adrenaline fueled strength, the bosun swung her around bodily. He flung her around in a full one-eighty arc and at the command consoles on the bridge's forward side.

They weren't soft and Katie hit them hard. Stunned and in pain, she was barely able to force herself to turn over and look at her assailant.

He looked worse for the wear, too. His face was a mess. A red, bruised, scraped mess. One eye was swollen shut. Both of them streamed tears. Man wasn't smiling now. He was showing his teeth, but he wasn't smiling. Despite the pain and the horrible position she was in, Katie did smile. No way the bosun was getting away scot free now with some cock and bull story. She'd marked him.

"You're going to regret not doing this the easy way," the bosun ground out. He started for her.

Katie tried to get up to face him as best she could. Her aching body wouldn't do what it was told to.

The bosun smiled. Genuinely and nastily.

A voice came from close behind him. "Stop right there, or I'll blow you away."

Rob Hood had finally turned up.

The bosun spun around with horrible, decisive swiftness, grabbing the gun pointed at him with one hand as he did so. Good Lord, the man was dangerous in a fight. The weapon went off, its frangible projectiles splattering off a display less than a meter to Katie's left.

"Let's see how you do without your little toy," the bosun gleefully growled as he grabbed Rob around the throat with his other hand. He lifted Hood, not a small man, clear of the deck. Impressive even in a quarter gee.

Katie was having none of it. Finding her feet, she leapt at the bosun's back. She got a choke hold around his neck.

The bosun thrashed about, trying to throw Katie clear so he could breathe. He dropped Hood while doing so.

Katie's grip slipped too, though. Then she lost it entirely. Falling to the deck in a heap, she was vulnerable. It was all she could do to gain her feet and face the bosun again.

She managed it in time to see Hood distract the bosun again with a hard fist to the man's battered face.

Growling, the bosun grabbed Hood bodily again, and lifting him free of his feet, threw him at Katie.

Katie and Hood went down in a heap, and Katie figured they were done for now. The bosun was too big, too strong, and, most of all, too fast for even the two of them together to handle.

The bosun surprised her yet again.

He fled the combat bridge through the now open and clear hatch.

Katie hobbled over and secured it behind him.

Had they won or lost?

She didn't know.

***

Katie had time to think now. To process her emotions.

She felt gutted.

Empty, but cautiously optimistic. At least technically optimistic. On a little reflection, the facts seemed to support that. She was alive, if somewhat battered. The same was true of Rob Hood, who was currently watching her with a wary curiosity. They were locked in the combat bridge together, waiting for the dust to settle. Unlike with the bosun, Katie felt perfectly comfortable with Hood, even though she hardly knew the man.

Katie had done everything she could from the combat bridge. Which was quite a bit, really. The ship's Communications, external and internal, were now completely shut down except for communications that went through Katie. The ship's boat was out and on patrol.

The bosun had escaped for the time being, but his malign influence had been neutralized. Nobody could gainsay the fact the ship was locked down hard on Katie's orders now. She'd messaged the captain about it, woken him up, and he'd confirmed them. The captain had done so after listening to Katie's report and without any fuss or questions.

And there was no spinning a fight between the bosun and Katie that had left them both visibly hurt into anything acceptable. Not even if Katie hadn't broadcast the fact he'd attacked her.

The man's career was over. As was his influence over any

crew member who wanted a future in the Space Force.

The bosun and anyone that could be proven to be one of his cohorts were facing hard time.

That was all to the good.

What wasn't good was that it'd been so bad in the first place. There was no putting lipstick on that pig.

Katie didn't want to lend any credence to the bosun's assertion that it wasn't really his fault. That it'd just been business as usual, only under unusually unfortunate circumstances. She didn't buy that. Not wholesale.

Only she didn't think a mess as profound as the one on the *Humber*, and in Mars space generally, could be put down to a single bad apple. Or even to a few bad apples. No, the bosun might have been making excuses, but that didn't change the fact that there was obviously something systemically wrong.

Katie sighed.

"A right mess, wasn't it?" Rob Hood said.

"Believe me, nothing except a battle lost can be half so melancholy as a battle won," Katie answered. She wondered if he'd ask about the quote.

"Fewer dead horses, a lot fewer dead overall, and us wounded don't have to worry about the scavengers doing for us in the night," the man replied.

Katie fought to conceal her surprise.

Not too successfully. Rob Hood smiled at her in amusement.

"Yeah, I guess we've made some progress in the last few hundred years," Katie said. An inane answer, perhaps, given the existence of nuclear weapons and the potential for someone to artificially recreate the asteroid impact that had ended the Age of Dinosaurs. But she'd needed to say something. "I'm sorry. I grew up reading old books on pre-modern military history, but I've gotten used to people's eyes glazing over when I reference them. It's not a popular interest."

"Sadly," Rob said, still smiling. "In case you're wondering how an ex-Martian tunnel rat learned enough to recognize the quote. Well, I got a good educational foundation before my family's fortunes went sideways. Then, after joining up, I had time to wonder just how the world had got so weird. None of the official or more recent histories were helpful. It's almost like history has been on hold the last few centuries. So, I started reading everything I could about the times before. People I work for now, they have what you might call a long-term strategic outlook. They encouraged it."

"Wow, that's almost a relief," Katie answered. "There have been times I thought maybe me and my grandmother were the only ones who cared. The only ones that see that things aren't going to stay as nice as they are."

"Not all that nice for all of us right now," Rob said. But his words held no sting. He didn't seem to hold a grudge. "Here's a thing. When we're telling the captain and the rest what happened, let's not mention I work for the SIS."

"Or that you have a backdoor into the ship's systems I used to message you."

"Precisely. I couldn't sleep and was catching up on some maintenance work when I saw you and the bosun go by."

"Lucky that. Okay."

***

Rob had resented the extra complication of having to look out for Lieutenant Katie Kincaid.

A desperate battle with the bosun who'd proved altogether too proficient a brawler shouldn't have softened his feelings. Rob would have wondered where the man had learned to fight like that. Only he knew. They were both graduates of the Martian Tunnels school of fighting where you learned how to win or you died trying.

Sitting here in the combat bridge with the young woman, he was finding it hard to hold on to his anger. Having fought on the same side of a desperate fight might have been part of it.

That she seemed like a reasonable human being, despite what everything in her record indicated, was also certainly part of it.

That she seemed like regular people, and one who treated him like another regular person, shouldn't have surprised him given her upbringing in the Belt. Only he was all too used to the unthinking condescension of Earth born Space Force officers and couldn't help appreciating the difference.

That they had a shared interest in pre-modern history was just the cherry on top of the sundae.

Yeah, given their circumstances, Rob was warming altogether too much to the young woman.

"Good," he replied to her agreement not to blow his cover. "It's too bad my cover means we won't be able to talk about it more. Kind of too tired right now to work up too much enthusiasm for history." He grinned at his superior officer. "You know what they say about adventure?"

"Bad things happening to other people far away," Kincaid answered.

"Yep, reality seems more like a lot of hard boring work with brief intervals of sheer terror to break up the monotony."

"I've noticed that."

"Way of the world," Rob said. "Anyhow, even if SFHQ doesn't have the station authorities manufacture some reason, they need to hold me for questioning so that I miss patrol next week. I won't be around much longer than that."

"I saw your orders," Kincaid said. "You're posted here until the tour is over. You're supposed to be part of the crew that takes the *Humber* back to Earth."

"Only my cover is already looking thin," Rob said. "They're going to want to extract me as quickly as possible before it's completely blown. You're losing the bosun for sure, and I think maybe a few other key people, and the *Humber* was short hands already."

"SFHQ will use that as an excuse to send us a draft of replacements?"

"Yes, just like they already should have. I'd be willing to bet on it. They didn't want to acknowledge the problem before. Now they've got no choice."

"I hope this doesn't mean we're going to need to delay the patrol. The captain will be furious."

"Pretty sure there are temporary emergency measures you can take as long as everyone knows they're temporary," Rob replied. "Crew that's left is going to want to be showing themselves in the best light. That'll tide you over for a while if you can promise them relief is coming."

"So, you don't think the rot is too widespread?"

"Bosun wasn't stupid, or over inclined to sharing," Rob answered. "From what I've been able to determine, he only subverted a few key people. And not all of them voluntarily. Rest of the crew may have turned a blind eye, but pretty sure they weren't happy about it. You pretend it didn't happen and they'll be glad to play along."

Kincaid grimaced. This news didn't entirely please her. She was young. Idealistic too. Her rise up the career ranks had been too fast for all of that to have worn off. "Okay, I guess that's good."

"So, any questions?" Rob asked. "This might be the last time we can talk frankly. Once SFHQ gets me clear, our paths will probably never cross again."

Kincaid grinned at him. Was he imagining a malicious glint in her eye? "Oh, not with the Space Force the way it is most likely," she said. "But you know Mr. Hood, if that's really your name, someday they're going to figure out FTL."

"Eventually, I suppose," Rob said, wondering where she was going with this.

"And then, all of a sudden, the Space Force is going to be way too small. It's going to need all the qualified spacers it can find. Everybody semi-qualified will be conscripted and promoted to ranks they never expected to reach. You wait and see. I think our paths will cross again. I think you're likely to have a commission. You'll be one of those despised snots yourself."

"Yes, ma'am," Rob replied.

He'd believe that when he saw it.

***

Pat was surprised by how calm he was.

He'd been angry. Not surprised, given a choice, it was clear Kincaid would do things the hard way every time. Girl might be only medium-sized at best and young, but she was a fighter. Had enough heart for a giant of a man.

Pat had badly underestimated her.

That was on him.

Now his future in tatters, on the lam, and lying on a stretcher pretending to be semi-comatose, unable to move or speak, he found he was, at worst, annoyed. Mildly disappointed rather than bitterly so. Surprising. Maybe he'd never really wanted to be a retired spacer and gentleman homesteader on Mars after all.

He'd miss his girl, but given how eager she'd been to take the opportunity to escape to Earth and her family there, maybe she'd never really been his. That hurt, but it was what it was and there was nothing to be done for it.

"Our orders from your XO are that nobody's to leave the ship," the gruff voice of an older woman was saying.

Pat couldn't see her. Couldn't see anything for the thick bandages covering his face.

"If she wasn't busy, or the comms were up, she'd tell you herself that this is a medical emergency," the medic said with confident impatience. Pat was glad to have him along. He was a good man. Sticky fingers, but practical, and knew how to get things done.

"What happened?" the woman, some sort of official, a police sergeant Pat would guess, asked. She sounded skeptical and a trace uncertain all at once. Pat could sympathize. As soon as you got a little responsibility, the world seemed determined to throw important decisions at you that you weren't qualified to make, and if you were, you weren't given enough information to be sure. Explained why character, and especially determination, were more important than just brains or book learning.

"The XO woke a bunch of us up from a sound sleep and this ox gets up and trips over his own feet," the medic related with finely acted disgust. "Falls flat on his face. Literally. Hurts sure, but not so bad. Only some yob gets the idea of spraying his face with instant bandage."

"Ouch," a younger male voice commented. By its depth, a large young man. The older woman's partner?

"Sergeant, you know sometimes I think anyone could do most of my job, but then some idiot does something like that," the medic continued.

Someone sighed heavily. "I know what you mean," the older female voice said. "Common sense isn't so common."

"Isn't that the truth," the medic agreed. "Anyhow, seems

like a bunch of instant bandage in the eyes really hurts. Bob, here. He's a brainless lunk."

Pat didn't mind being called a brainless lunk. He appreciated the medic not only spinning a fine story, but having the presence of mind not to use Pat's real name.

The medic rambled on. " I don't know how he managed to pass his stoker exams. Anyway, Bob goes nuts. Starts flailing and stumbling about. Manages to not hurt any of his mates. Not seriously, but he beats himself up even more. Still in a tizzy when I get there and pump him full of sedatives. Could be I used more than I should have. Want to get him to the hospital to check that. Need to get there anyway to make sure he didn't get any of that instant bandage stuff in his lungs. Look, Sergeant, this is urgent. If we don't get Bob checked out as soon as possible, it probably won't kill him, but he could be disabled for the rest of his life. A big strong man unable to do much because he can't breathe properly. I don't want that on my conscience."

"Okay, carry on, but I want to hear from you as soon as you reach the hospital. If I don't do so within the hour, somebody is going to come looking for you and they won't be happy. Understood?"

"Understood. Loud and clear, Sergeant. Thank you."

And then their little parade was on its way again. In addition to the medic, he had Wally, the supply guy, and Awad, the comms guy, acting as stretcher bearers. The bought and paid for flunky of his who'd been guarding the docking port was along, too. Pat wasn't sure what the medic had him doing, so that he didn't stick out. Probably carrying a bunch of medical stuff.

Pretty soon, they'd branch off from the path to the hospital and make their way to the on-station apartment Pat rented under another name. Pat had civvies they could change into there. He had alternate identification for them, too. For the medic, Awad, and Pat himself, it was even pretty convincing and would stand up to more than a cursory inspection.

Past that point, Pat needed to think about.

It wasn't clear how long it'd be before their hidey-hole was found. Could be as little as a few hours. Pat figured that was unlikely. He figured they had a few days at least. If Kincaid went off on patrol and the station police had other priorities, they might get as much as a month and a bit. But that was the best they could hope for. So they needed to move on as fast as possible.

Pat would reach out to his usual associates on-station, but he wasn't sure what they'd be able to do given that they seemed to have their own problems.

Worst come to worst, they'd split up and try to take crew or passenger positions on a variety of ways out, counting on the fact the police might be spread too thin to cover all the possibilities.

Pat's battered appearance, which had been so useful in getting them off the *Humber*, would become a liability at that point.

He was trying to think of solutions to that problem when, all of a sudden, they came to a stop.

"Easy now, we just want to talk," a man's voice came at this point. A professional, competent voice, but not a reassuring or very polite one.

Pat could now hear the slight movements of people all around them. Just out of arm's reach, it seemed. He guessed someone was making it known they were surrounded.

"This is a medical emergency. It's urgent," the Medic blustered.

"You're on the run and in need of new employment. We know who you are," the voice stated dismissively. "Fortunately for you, we have need of trained spacers."

Pat reached an arm out to where he thought the Medic was, touching him to gain his attention. He felt the man turn towards him. Pat made an okay sign with his hand.

"Good. That's settled," the voice said. "Let's go."

15: Katie Cleans Up

Katie still didn't have it all figured out, and she knew the ship and her crew still had their problems. But things were definitely looking up now. It was Thursday afternoon, and she'd just completed an informal walkthrough of the *Humber*, talking to the crew members she encountered as she did so.

She was going to have the pleasure of giving the crew Friday off. They'd get their long weekend before departing on their near month-long deployment out to the near Belt.

Katie hummed to herself as she prepared the broadcast message for the crew.

She'd managed to get the crew's respect. They'd proven themselves as willing to work hard for her and the new bosun as they had for the old one. That was good. She'd been worried that with Chief O'Conal gone, and the fear he'd apparently instilled gone too, that the crew might slack off. So far, it hadn't happened that way.

Good, but she was looking forward to showing she wasn't just someone who wasn't to be messed with. Katie wanted to be seen as more than someone who was a fighter, tough, and a demanding taskmaster. She wanted to demonstrate she was someone who would take good care of her crew, too. Katie was looking forward to showing them she wanted the *Humber* to be a happy ship, not just one that did its job.

And, so for all her nervousness over the many things that could go wrong and prevent the ship launching for its patrol come Monday morning, Katie was happy to be giving most of the crew the weekend off.

Katie wouldn't be taking the whole time off herself. One of the many things she'd be doing would be going around and assuring the unlucky souls who were drawing "harbor watch" when their mates were ashore with family or carousing with friends was that they weren't forgotten and would be remembered come the end of the patrol.

Technically, their immediate NCOs were responsible for seeing to that sort of consideration. By the book, Katie would be micromanaging far too far down the chain of command. She didn't intend to make a habit of it in the future, but she did intend to make sure she established a standard for how she wanted things done. The crew was unsettled by losing its old bosun and his immediate cronies. The lead comms tech had been replaced. A cross trained station marine was acting as medic. A problem but an opportunity too. It meant the crew was open to a new way of doing things. The old way was obviously past.

Katie still needed to check in with Tammy Wentzell about the supply situation, too. The lead supply tech had confessed to fiddling the books for the bosun, but confined to the ship was enthusiastically working overtime in apparent hopes of lenient treatment. Informally, during hastily grabbed meals in the wardroom, Tammy had indicated that she thought they'd managed to get everything they'd need. Katie needed to double check and make it formal.

Thinking of formal, Katie still had a huge back log of e-mail to handle. Looked like asking the captain for a reprieve might not be avoidable. She'd try to make a dent in it, though. Despite complications.

Captain von Luck, acting as the local SFHQ security authority, had indicated that she should avoid deleting any records that might be of interest to the investigation of the

Humber that was doubtless going to occur. He'd also indicated with a wry smile that they'd not likely be in any mood to air more dirty laundry. It was going to be a bury the embarrassing Bodies, not exhume them, sort of formal investigation.

Von Luck had been more apologetic about the unfortunate necessity of detaining Leading Spacer Hood on station for questioning. The *Humber* would be short an electrician for its patrol. And after it, too. It'd turned out Hood's posting had been a horrible clerical error. He should have never been sent out to Mars. They were sending him back home as soon as von Luck was finished with him. Second class, not third class this time. Probably on the same ship as Alice Younghusband would be taking. Alice had just missed the previous departure and Katie didn't think von Luck would be detaining Hood for very long.

SFHQ had sent Katie a message asking her to apologize profusely to the man. Katie had gone through the motions. She sensed Hood had been just as amused as she had been. Katie did like the man for all the difference in their backgrounds. Shared secrets? Shared danger? Katie didn't know, but she regretted she'd likely not be seeing more of him anytime soon. But that was the Space Force, threw people together and then pulled them apart. Also, given the difference in their ranks and that he was technically in her chain of command, any personal relationship, however innocent, was suspect.

SFHQ was also demanding all sorts of paperwork, demonstrating that they were properly preparing for their patrol. SFHQ wanted things done either by the book, or if not, they wanted to know why. They wanted reports filed and forms filled out. And not just from Katie. But also from the captain and both Ops Officer Broomfield and Weapons Officer Rompkey. It was keeping them all busy.

Katie sighed. So her world wasn't perfect, even if she'd survived and was doing her job. Lars had recently sent a message saying he'd been dating other girls, and one in particular was looking interesting. Katie had swallowed a degree of jealousy, and replied with friendly good wishes. Assured him he'd always have a place in her affections and she considered him a good friend.

So, Katie's life wasn't perfect, but it wasn't bad.

Katie was looking forward to the coming patrol. It'd be good to be doing her real job. Not chasing crooks, or dodging bullets.

Katie just hoped she could manage to relax a little this weekend.

A body could only take so much drama and stress.

Katie was crew too.

She had a duty to take care of herself.

To be happy if she could.

***

Pat was still smiling. He'd kept smiling throughout the events of the last couple of days despite a sense it annoyed some of his captors. His new employers, too, as it happened.

And, if that wasn't amusing, what was?

They hadn't wasted any time making their offer.

It wasn't a bad one given Pat's currently rather limited options. They'd disappear him for a few years, give him secret but interesting and useful employment, and then return him to the wider world both rich and rehabilitated.

Not exactly the same as being a Martian homesteader, but that was off the table now. Even if Pat had a way down to the surface, the Martians, as much as they resented Earth and the Space Force, weren't likely to welcome the attention Pat's presence would bring them. They might protect him, they might not. They'd certainly not be pleased with him.

Pat had made sure that their captors, strike that, *new associates*, had made offers to his followers off of the *Humber*. They'd said they always had places for trained spacers, comms techs and medics in particular, and that even Johnson would be useful muscle.

Pat had also made it clear to his followers that this was a deal they couldn't refuse. They'd not been entirely happy, even less so when it was clear Pat was going to get priority processing. All the same, they'd acquiesced. Pat had hopes of seeing them at his new place of employment in the not too distant future. He felt confident they'd speak well of how he'd looked after them.

It was work, but team building was important.

In a few years, Pat looked forward to being even more

important than he'd been as the bosun on the *Humber*. His career in the Space Force had been capped. Worse, the *Humber*'s sorry fate was only typical of a largely moribund organization. There might be a few eager beavers back in SFHQ and the odd bright spark like Kincaid, but the Force overall was staffed with time serving dead wood. It wasn't a place for anyone ambitious who wasn't already one of the ruling elite.

It wasn't prone to innovation. It'd been barely doing its job in circumstances largely unchanged for generations. It wasn't likely to be able to cope with real change.

Pat's new bosses presented themselves as the solution to that problem.

"Some of our activities aren't exactly legal, but we're not crooks," their representative had asserted. "We're hard headed idealists concerned for humanity's future. To that end we've cut deals with similarly concerned groups among the Kannawik, the Star Rats, as the vulgar like to call them. We want the Solar System to be able to defend itself and chart its own course once galactic contact is made."

Pat had nodded enthusiastically throughout the pitch. Hell, it might even all be true. In any event, it didn't hurt to seem newly enlightened and on board.

And, so mere hours after leaving the *Humber*, Pat had found himself on another ship. It'd been a little uncomfortable being smuggled aboard in a cargo container, but no worse than faking being comatose. Where he was bound for, he had no idea. Only that it was going to be a secret base and he was supposed to organize its crew and get it up and running. "They're all qualified, and have good reason to co-operate, but most of them can be a little difficult at times, too," his recruiter had said. "We think you know how to handle those sorts of people. We'll back you fully."

Pat figured he did. He said as much.

"Good," the recruiter had said. "You'll be isolated and there'll be no leave for a few years. When it's all done, though, you'll all be handsomely paid, and if you performed well, get a position within a powerful organization. You'll be a hero and one of the new elite running things here in the Solar System."

Well, maybe.

Time would tell.

Pat would cope with whatever happened.

And keep smiling throughout.

***

The marine facilities on Mars Station were overbuilt for the small detachment actually deployed there. It was a sure sign that the best plans of men and mice often go astray.

Rob didn't mind for once. It meant he got a whole rather nice cabin to himself.

The story was that it was in partial apology for both the clerical error that had got him sent to Mars, and for the subsequent suspicious grillings he'd received once there.

In fact, of course, SFHQ, working through von Luck, was eager to isolate him from his former shipmates. And, for that matter, from anyone else who might want to confirm their suspicions about what had gone down on the *Humber*.

It was a transparent effort, unlikely to completely convince the locals. Only SFHQ was mainly concerned about the impression among Space Force members and the political classes back on Earth. The first had powerful reasons to believe whatever story they were given. The second were likely still not paying much attention to what was happening elsewhere in the system.

There'd been multiple actors working at cross purposes. It had created quite the muddle. Nobody was likely to get a clear picture of what had really happened.

Something that the folks back at SFHQ might be happy about, but which Rob himself found rather unsatisfactory.

And not just because he had a report to write and would likely be facing a debriefing once back at Goddard Station. Rob was curious on his own behalf.

That there'd been, at least, three different groups stirring the pot on the *Humber* was pretty much confirmed now. That engineer that had turned up dead, Johanson, seemed to have been coerced by the bosun into laying traps for both Rob and Kincaid. And, been killed rather surprisingly by the bosun, directly or indirectly. Probably not a planned thing, but a falling out between desperate crooks.

Rob didn't really know and didn't really care. A major problem affecting the *Humber* at one time, the bosun's lot had now been largely rooted out. A local criminal group, and one now missing its kingpin. A not trivial success that.

There was the purely local smuggler group that had had the audacity to defy the Space Force in the person of Kincaid on the *Humber*'s boat. It was also, at least temporarily, no longer a problem. Their whole operation on Mars Station had just been rolled up.

Their plant on the *Humber*, one of the cooks, had turned himself in, pleading for protection for his family and friends. He was singing like a songbird. He'd confessed to several of the traps laid for Kincaid, saying he'd had no choice.

The last group was the one they'd already known had it out for Kincaid. Just how badly, and how strong and pervasive they'd proven to be had been unpleasant surprises. The so-called "Star Rat smugglers" were likely the ones behind the initial attacks that had greeted both Kincaid and Rob. The ones that had greeted them immediately upon their arrival on Mars Station.

It was obvious to Rob they had agents back in Earth space and deep pockets both. He suspected they had some long-range plan other than just making money from smuggling, too. Rob had little doubt the SIS's analysts back on Goddard would reach similar conclusions. Just what they could do about it was unclear. Rob was glad it wasn't likely to be his problem.

The Star Rat smugglers were proving to be disconcertingly effective planners.

The first sure sign they'd had a plant on the *Humber* was when one of Rob's fellow electricians had disappeared. He'd let himself out on an EVA during the ship's lockdown and never returned.

When the ship's crew and the station police realized this, they'd launched a search for him. They'd failed to find a body or any other trace of where'd he'd gone.

Rob figured this explained some of the more sophisticated attacks on him. Likely some of those on Kincaid, too.

It was a bloody miracle either of them had survived.

Those Star Rat smugglers were going to be a continuing headache for the Space Force. As were the various Mars factions who'd been a little less hands-on. Not Rob's problem, though. His cover might have survived well enough to deceive a disinterested public, but it was pretty much blown with all the serious actors.

Rob's time as a spy and with the Space Force was effectively over.

Rob had a lot of respect for Lieutenant Kincaid and her intelligence. He still figured she was likely wrong in anticipating dramatic changes in the near future. The Solar System had settled into a stable state a couple of centuries ago. Rob didn't really think that was going to change in his lifetime. People were more or less content with things as they were. Rob didn't think aliens eager to change that were going to appear on humanity's doorstep any time soon.

Kincaid was intelligent, but she was also young, and rather over imaginative. Eager for adventure and to make a difference. Age would mellow her.

It'd certainly mellowed Rob.

He was looking forward to being a simple small businessman back on Earth and being done with all the spy stuff.

He'd had enough excitement for one lifetime.

***

As usual, the captain's working cabin was dim with only a pool of light around the desk he was sitting at. Sitting at and bent over working on his big data display. Not drinking. Not just staring off into the distance at disappointing prospects.

It was a change. A good change.

They were due to depart on patrol in just a few hours. It was the early hours of the morning. They'd had a lot of work to do to get the *Humber* ready for her deployment. Katie had given most of the crew a long weekend off, but she'd burned the midnight oil herself. Mostly checking all was ready. That and preparing reports to the distant, but determined to micromanage, SFHQ on those checks.

Katie had managed, though. She was here to report that. Katie waited for the captain to acknowledge her. He seemed quite absorbed in what he was working on.

It was a minute or two at most. The captain looked up and grinned. He had an alert twinkle in his eye. It was the same life-beaten face she'd gotten used to over the last month, but he seemed a different man. "Made a point of digging deep and thinking about what I found, XO," he said.

"Yes, sir."

"It's been too long since I've done that. No reflection on you, Katie. Quite the contrary. I'd invite you to sit, relax, and have a drink, but we both know that's not a good idea."

"I appreciate the thought, sir. I trust everything is in order. Is there anything you want done before we depart this morning?"

"Well, I need to thank you for the good work you've done here. You've done a splendid job of getting everything ready for the patrol. That's excellent, but we both know you've done much more than that."

"Sir? I truly regret what happened with Bosun O'Conal. I did my best and I think the crew is getting sorted out, but there's no putting any lipstick on the pig. It was a mess, and it's going to take a while for everyone to get over it."

"Yes, but the crew has started to do that."

"Yes, sir. I believe they have."

"I haven't been as completely oblivious as I might have seemed at times, Katie. They think the world of you. Some of the younger hands seem to almost worship you. Keep this up and nobody will remember anything other than that there was some sort of problem and you fixed it."

"Hope that's true, sir."

"I've every faith you'll make it true, XO. You didn't create the problem. Sadly, I could sense it, but couldn't figure out what it was. It's my ship. It was my responsibility to work it out and fix and I didn't. Before you arrived, I wasn't getting the help with that that I should have. You saw there was a problem, figured out what it was, and despite the difficulty and risk to your own safety that it involved, you fixed it. I'm impressed. You can feel proud. You can be certain that whatever else happens that my evaluations of you for SFHQ are going to be glowing."

"Sir. Thank you, sir."

The captain smiled a crooked amused smile at her. "You're embarrassed by the praise. You shouldn't be, it's deserved. You're going places, we both know that. Personally, I think that's a good thing. I think you're going to be good for the Space Force, whatever the future holds. Only, not only is that going to mean high praise that creates unrealistic expectations for you, it means unfair criticisms and even ugly calumnies, too. You're going to have to learn to take both in your stride."

Katie was tired. She wanted to sigh. The captain was giving her good advice, and she appreciated it, only right now she wanted to rest. "Never stops, does it, sir?"

The captain nodded. "Command demands everything you have and a bit more. If you're not careful, it'll suck you dry." He stared bleakly into the distance for a few seconds. Katie realized that was exactly what had happened to him. He'd been serious about his responsibilities but unable to meet them, and trying had worn him almost away. She realized she was looking at, at least, one person she'd saved. The captain looked at her. "If you're lucky, you'll have good help in carrying the burden. In any case, for everyone's sake, you need to pace yourself, however much you may regret not being able to do more. Understood?"

"Yes, sir. Understood."

"Imagine it's a waste of time telling you to go get a solid eight hours of sleep. You don't want to miss our departure."

"No, sir, and the optics wouldn't be good."

"True. So go get a couple of hours of sleep. I'll allow you a little time to make sure all is well after we're on our way, but then I want you to stand down to get some rest. I can take care of our ship for a while as you do so. Clear?"

"Yes, sir. Clear."

"It's a marathon, not a sprint, Katie."

"Yes, sir."

"Dismissed, Katie. Off with you."

Katie left. Still tired, but strangely cheered, and ready to face the future.

River Class Corvette Fact Sheet

Introduction:

Corvettes along with scout-couriers have been the mainstay of the Space Force since its inception. Unlike scout ships, the corvettes are capable of being deployed for months at a time and are much more flexible.

They are essentially the smallest ships capable of being deployed for extended periods and being crewed in a fashion similar to that of a ship in an oceanic navy. As such, they're considered an essential element in building a deep space naval capability.

They're also the smallest ship able to maintain combat superiority over an armed merchantman.

The River class ships are the latest class of corvettes and were originally designed and built in the late 23rd century. Even the newest of them are becoming somewhat long in the tooth.

Class includes:

Name	Hull
Euphrates	K451
Elbe	K452
Tiber	K453
Humber	K454
Elbro	K455
Weser	K456
Indus	K457
Nile	K458
Congo	K459
Mekong	K460
Murray	K461
Susquehanna	K462
Pearl	K463
Don	K464
Yukon	K465

Manning:

Ship's Total Crew (55 to 70) (8 to 12 officers) (47 to 58 enlisted men)

Fifty-five crew is adequately manned, seventy is fully manned. Additional berths are available for one officer and eight enlisted supplementary personnel, usually trainees of one sort or another.

Layout:

The shape of a River class corvette is basically a 71 meter long, mostly 10 meter diameter main spindle with the shape of a cylinder with an octagonal cross section. There are bulges for the gravity ring mounting and boat bay of 4 and 6 meters, respectively. The gravity ring mounting bulge is symmetric. The boat bay protrudes more to the port and starboard than it does "up" and "down".

Also appended are a sensor array on its forward end, and on its stern end, the propulsion systems and main engines.

The appendages give the ship an overall length of 78 meters.

A set of detachable external propellant tanks are arranged around the very rear of the main spindle around the engineering spaces and ahead of the engines.

Spindle section lengths are:

Sensor array	3 m	3 m
Combat Bridge	4 m	7 m
Forward Guns	4 m	11 m
Forward Missiles	4 m	15 m
Gravity Ring Mounting & Storage	12 m	27 m
Storage	4 m	31 m
Boat Bay	24 m	55 m
Aft Missiles	4 m	59 m
Aft Guns	4 m	63 m
Armor, shielding, hatch	1 m	64 m
Main Engineering Control (Engine Room)	3 m	67 m
Auxiliary Machinery Space	3 m	70 m
Inboard Propulsion Space	4 m	74 m
Engines	4 m	78 m

Gravity Ring:

The provision of gravity is essential for the long-term health of crew on sustained deployments. To this end, the class mounts a large gravity ring on its spindle, within which the crew spends most of its time. Generally, the spindle is only manned by skeleton watches. The exceptions are for maintenance and during battle stations. At full battle readiness, the gravity ring is despun and locked down.

All the crew's normal living activities and regular cruising watches are performed from within the gravity ring. Their exposure to zero gravity is logged and limited by regulations. Exercise programs are mandatory.

The gravity ring has a 24 meter radius. The ring has a cross section of 8 meters wide and 6 meters high.

From the inside, the gravity ring has the form of a long corridor that runs for some 152 meters and has "spokes" with lifts, damage control stations, and escape pods at 38 meter intervals. To each side of the corridor are the ship's living quarters, eating and recreation areas, and a variety of work spaces.

Using the cruising bridge as our starting point and working clockwise around the ring when looking aft at its forward wall, the interior space of the gravity ring is divided as follows:

Cruising bridge
Captain's cabin
Other officers' cabins
Wardroom
Admin offices
Galley
Damage control and escape pod stations, lifts (first quarter spoke)
NCOs' mess
NCO living quarters
Hands' mess
Hands' living quarters
Canteen
Laundry
Medical Bay and Infirmary
Damage control and escape pod stations, lifts (second quarter spoke)
Remote Engineering Control Room (opposite bridge on ring)
Engineering Workshop
Tool crib and parts storage.
Marine barracks
Armory
Gym
Damage control and escape pod stations, lifts (third quarter spoke)
Remote Weapons Control
Weapons Workshop
Ready storage for victuals.
Ready room
Damage control, escape Pods, and lifts. (fourth quarter spoke)
And back around to the Cruising bridge.

If you enjoyed this novel, please leave a review.

To be notified of future releases visit my website at
https://www.napoleonsims.com/publishing

Manufactured by Amazon.ca
Acheson, AB